Ruthless Sky

5/17/24

Glenn,

Ruthless Sky
A NOVEL

Hope our next 'mission' goes as well as the one this week!

Kin

D. K. Broadwell

Cozmic Cajun Press

Copyright © 2023 by D. K. Broadwell

All rights reserved. No part of this book may be reproduced in any form, except as applied to brief quotations incorporated into critical articles or reviews.

This is a work of fiction. Names, characters, businesses, places, events and incidents are either the products of the author's imagination or used in a fictitious manner. Any resemblance to actual persons, living or dead, or actual events is purely coincidental.

Published by: Cozmic Cajun Press

Cover Design: cheriefox.com
Interior Design: Creative Publishing Book Design

ISBN Paperback: 979-8-9890680-0-5
ISBN eBook: 979-8-9890680-1-2

If NASA acronyms have offended,
Think but this, and all is mended.
There's a glossary at the back,
To aid you till you get the knack.

Prologue

28 January 1986
Kennedy Space Center, Pad 39B
Space shuttle Challenger, *Mission STS-51L*

On this date, the space shuttle *Challenger* launched into a clear, windy, and frigid sky. Within seventy-three seconds the shuttle broke up and the crew perished, but this disaster was not inevitable. There were many opportunities to break the chain of events leading to *Challenger's* loss. The story that follows is an alternate history: *Challenger* and Mission 51L were launched successfully, and NASA continued to plan ever more formidable and risky space shuttle missions. Mission STS-92A of the shuttle *Intrepid* was one of the most ambitious.

PART ONE

22 September 1989
Space shuttle Intrepid, *Mission STS-92A*
T+5, Five hours after launch
Hour three of unscheduled spacewalk (extravehicular activity)

Cat Riley arched her back and stole a moment to gaze at the bright Pacific racing four hundred miles below her. *Earth looks like a landless water ball from here,* she thought, letting the planet's blue wash over her. Outside in the vacuum of space, Hayes Bartlett struggled with *Intrepid*'s balky cargo. He was perched on the end of the space shuttle's robotic arm, which Cat was controlling from the aft cockpit.

Their payload was bigger than a school bus: the *Odysseus* solar probe stacked on its Centaur G rocket. The whole assembly in its launch cradle was stuck halfway up, and the probe could be neither launched nor stowed until it was freed up.

Hayes had been working to get it loose for hours. Seeing him stop to flex his fingers, Cat knew his hands were cramping in the stiff gloves of his space suit. But he wasn't going to complain about it; astronauts rarely mention such matters. Jack Badger, Hayes's partner on this spacewalk, also noticed the pause.

"Hayes," Cat said on the intercom, "would you like a reposition? Your angle to the stuck cradle looks a little awkward from here."

"This jammed bolt is not coming loose without a power tool," Hayes said. "We need to saw it off. Jack needs to give me a hand. He's been napping."

Jack, tethered nearby Hayes in *Intrepid*'s payload bay, replied in his best Chuck Yeager drawl, "A poor workman blames his tools. What do you say, Houston?"

"*Intrepid*, Houston," replied fellow astronaut Liz Trujillo over the radio from the Mission Control Center at the Johnson Space Center. "Payload Ops doesn't think your toolkit hacksaw can access the bolt as is. But we want you to try anyway."

Moments later, Hayes said, "Mission control is right. Can't get the hacksaw behind the bolt head to cut it. The blade needs to come off the handle."

"We're with you on that," Liz answered. "You can use the wire cable you have. It's the right gauge for you to make a little two-man crosscut saw. You can be Paul Bunyan; Jack can be Babe."

"Do we get to sing the lumberjack song from Monty Python?" asked Jack as he dug out the wire cutters from the tool kit on his suit.

"Permission denied." The authoritative voice of *Intrepid*'s commander, Terry Rogers, joined the conversation. He was floating next to Cat in the cockpit, and he was scowling. "This EVA is wasting time," he said to Cat. "No mission is going to hell on my watch."

NASA forgot to issue Terry a sense of humor for this mission, thought Cat. But the pressure was building. This was taking too long. Only two orbits remained until too much of the rocket's liquid hydrogen fuel would have boiled off to launch. *Maybe it will inspire Hayes to fix this mess quicker if I finally promise to go on a date with him after the mission. That would sound great on the open comm channel.* She allowed herself a half smile.

Before anyone else could speak, the locking pliers Hayes had clamped to the rocket cradle popped off like a home run baseball. Cat saw it ricochet off the Centaur rocket body and careen out of sight over the lip of the payload bay.

Shit. Bad. Leaking rocket? Hole in radiators? How did that happen? Cat knew the shell of the Centaur's tank was so thin you could put your finger through it if the tank were unpressurized.

"Pliers overboard," Hayes said on the communications loop. "The vise grip flew off the cradle. Bounced off the Centaur and went starboard. I don't see anything spewing from the upper stage case. Permission to check the coolant radiators and payload bay door. And someone check the contract for that tool."

"Yeah, the arm's wrist cam caught that little excursion," Liz said. "Let's have Cat take you over the side for a look-see. If any coolant is leaking from the radiator panels, stop immediately."

Dominick Petrocelli, the shuttle's pilot and fifth crew member, came online with, "Radiator valves and temps still nominal, Houston." The payload bay doors were lined with coolant radiators that kept the heat-generating parts of the shuttle from getting toasted. Covered with silvery Teflon tape, the two fragile panels on each wing were curved to nestle in the payload bay doors. When lifted away from the doors to dissipate more heat, they gave the shuttle dragonfly's wings.

Loss of a coolant loop might abort the mission, but we can't go anywhere with Odysseus stuck halfway up. We can't shut the payload bay doors. This was getting scary. Jack and Hayes extended the robot arm so Cat could move him out of the payload bay. She began to lose direct sight of him, but cameras on the arm joints displayed where Hayes was going.

"Houston, EV1," Hayes said, using his identifying call sign. "The radiators look intact. The vise grip is stuck on the outside lip of the payload bay door, and it's an easy grab. Can you see it, Cat?"

"Affirmative. Waiting for the go-ahead to move you closer." She nudged him a few feet farther toward the right wing while awaiting official permission.

"*Intrepid*, Houston. Cat, you're go on taking EV1 in for tool retrieval."

"Roger, Houston," Cat answered. "EV1, let me know when you're in position."

Recovering the pliers was easy by EVA standards. As he reclaimed it, Hayes said, "I've got the wayward tool. It didn't do any damage." Liz congratulated him. "Cat," he said, "can you see the wing on the wrist cam? There's something . . ."

"I'll take you in for a better view of the wing."

"Cat, put me just beyond the edge of the payload bay door . . . Closer . . . Stop."

On the wrist cam screen, Cat stared at a gap where a large chunk of *Intrepid*'s wing was missing from its front edge. She knew everyone, including the engineers in Houston, could see it. The leading edge of the wing looked like a great white space shark had taken a bite out of it.

Intrepid is doomed. We're as good as dead.

Astronaut Group Twelve selection week, 1987
Johnson Space Center, TX

Cat clenched her jaw in pain as she lay staring at the ceiling of her dank motel room. The rattling AC unit wasted its energy making noise instead of cool air. She imagined picking up the phone and saying, "Hi, NASA. Dr. Catherine Riley here. I've got wicked menstrual cramps, so would it be okay for me to postpone my astronaut tryout? And I barely slept last night."

Cat took a deep breath, exhaling slowly to relax. Like the other finalists in this round of astronaut selection, she had come to the Johnson Space Center for a week of interviews and medical tests. A lucky fifteen would be selected as astronaut candidates—"AsCan" rookies. After a successful year as an AsCan, you were a fully qualified astronaut.

Cat cranked up her heating pad and pressed it below her navel. She could faintly imagine Alan's touch there. Alan could massage her aching tummy and magically make it better. As she focused on his memory, she felt the familiar ache in her chest growing. She tried to push it away, translating the painful void into medical jargon—retrosternal dysphoria—to no avail.

Enough of this. Cat sat up and looked at herself in the mirror across the room. "You need to be on your best game today, sister." The phone rang and Cat recognized the voice of her cousin June on the other end of the line.

"Hey, Junie. Good to hear from you. I could use a friendly voice. How you doin'?"

"I'm fine, although sometimes I think the little darlings I teach are going to get the better of me. How are you on your big day?"

"Tell the truth, my soul and mind are 100 percent, but my bod is not cooperating right now," Cat said.

"You'll rise up, girl. You always do," June said. "I tracked you down to wish you luck during the astronaut tests. Your office snitched on your whereabouts. We all know you got the right stuff."

"Everybody keeps saying that, and I hope it's true. What I've got is a dream to leave our little planet for the wild black yonder. And I've got fear; the prospect of failure is scary."

"I know, sweetie," said June. "And I know you miss Alan and his faith in you. He would have been so proud."

"I was just thinking about him. I miss him so. I was starting to lean on him like a partner and now he's gone—with not even enough time together for chinks to show in his shining armor." Cat's eyes began to moisten. "I better change the subject before I tear up. I don't want raccoon eyes for my NASA physical today."

"Poor baby," June said. "One day you'll find a good one, like I got. There's a guy for you, too, but he'll have to be as special as Alan and as special as you. You'll know him because he won't let you get rid of him. Don't give up hope."

"Meeting Alan was a miracle. When I get out of the OR, it's all I can do to drag myself home and sleep. If I'm picked to be a shuttle mission specialist, the love department may as well shut down." She sighed. "Who knows which overachievers NASA wants this time around? I think, why not me? But it's a long shot. I know I can do this job, but does NASA? If you get this far and aren't picked, NASA sometimes offers you another job here at the Johnson Space Center, like a farm-team baseball league. If they do that, I'll dazzle them. The next time around they'll select me to be a big-league astronaut. I'm not giving up. I want to be up there in orbit with the best of the best."

"I know you're going to get in," June said. "After you're an astronaut, please promise me one thing. Will you take me and my class to a shuttle launch?"

Cat laughed. "You got it, cuz. Thanks for calling. Talking to you is like a warm hug. My lab tests are today, and I can't take even a Tylenol. NASA checks for every known drug and chemical, including OTC painkillers. And alcohol. I want my pee to be squeaky clean. But I gotta go—it's showtime." After hanging up, she spoke again to the mirror. "Buck up, girl. Let's work up a little charm." She grabbed her satchel and left for the Flight Medicine Clinic.

♦

The doc performing her exam introduced himself as Dr. Matt Wallace, one of the flight surgeons who provided medical support for space shuttle operations. He was a tall, lanky figure who still wore his light brown hair in a long 1970s style and sported a moustache. After taking her medical history, he was happy to answer her questions and seemed to expect she would also be forthcoming. The interview turned into banter, and Cat wondered, *Is this part of the interview? Am I supposed to be chatty?*

"So, tell me about your name," Wallace asked, as he shuffled papers around on his desk.

"I was named Catherine Riona Riley as an Irish–Cajun French compromise. My Cajun mother wanted to pronounce my name the French way, 'Cat-uh-*reen*,' but of course that never worked out in Texas. Riona means 'queen,' an Irish form of my Cajun aunt's name. Irish Dad wanted that. Of course, nobody says 'Ree-on-ah' correctly either, so I'm just Cat." *My name is about the only thing Mom and Dad ever compromised on.*

"You're a urologist at Baylor. Interesting specialty for a woman." Wallace waited for Cat to answer.

Another man thinking about me looking at penises. Women have bladders, too, fella. Trying hard to be cheery, she said, "Yep. I do clinical urology but also research the micromanipulation of cells. I have a patent on a microsurgical tool, and I'm guessing that helped me get a second look in the towering pile of astronaut applicants."

They talked about her research. Wallace said he was impressed. Cat laughed. "Do you think the selection board will be impressed, too?"

"Several of the current female astronauts are physicians, much to the annoyance of male docs who wanted those doctor slots. But the board's inner workings are opaque, even to me. Any given year they're looking for a mix of ethnicity, talent, race, and, for all I know, what congressional district you live in." Patty, the clinic nurse, knocked on the door to signal it was time for the physical part of the exam if they were to stay on schedule.

When the exam was finished and the nurse had left, Cat sat down at a table opposite Wallace. Pointing at his watch, she said, "I have a very expensive wristwatch, but I'll trade you."

Wallace chuckled. He was wearing a nondescript quartz sports watch, except for one feature. It had "NASA" printed on the dial, and it was only issued to astronauts, flight surgeons, and pilots that worked for the space program. "You're not the first nor the last to work her butt off for a cheap NASA-issue watch," Wallace said. "I've had an F-16 fighter jock wearing a massive Breitling chronograph on his wrist make the same offer."

Picking up Cat's chart, Wallace said, "I don't see any showstoppers in your medical exam or history. You seem well-qualified, and the fact that you're beautiful and charming will not be a disadvantage."

Oh, no, I don't like where this is going. This is getting unprofessional, Cat thought. Wallace got an odd look on his face and looked down, as if he were debating. Cat got a familiar feeling. *Shit, he's going to ask me out.* She had been there too many times, in medical school and during her residency.

Cat wasn't very old before she realized she had *something*. In parochial school, the boys wanted to be around her. In the third grade, boys who thought girls were icky would follow her around, pull her hair, and want to sit next to her and steal her lunch. It was a mixed blessing then, and still was. Medicine was an old boys' club, even now. She'd hoped the NASA culture would be different.

Cat had inherited a graceful Parisian model figure from her mom. Piercing light blue eyes and long dark hair came from her Celtic dad. She never failed to make an impression. As a friend once remarked, "After a party, no one ever asked, 'Which one was she?'"

Cat liked men; she often liked their attention, but it was a burden or a bore most of the time. Men were caught up in her beauty and missed the person. She enjoyed sex but got pissed off because so many men felt entitled to it.

Peering up and down Cat's body, Wallace said, "The review board is all men, you know. You're clearly a very capable young woman but using *all* your assets would probably be in your best interest."

Cat gazed directly into Wallace's eyes and clenched her fists under the table. She said, "It's always a pleasure to meet a fellow doc who is a true feminist," then forced a smile. Accepting the jab, Wallace laughed. Cat thought the best tactic now was fake jollity and hope it would stop. She was accustomed to being harassed, but she felt her cheeks starting to flush. She seldom had good options in such situations. *I need to get out of here now before I lose it and damage my chances.*

Her next stop was the lab, where she had blood drawn and donated her urine. Soon after, she took two pain pills and went for a drink.

It wasn't far down NASA Road 1 from her motel to The Outpost, a well-known watering hole for astronauts and NASA engineers. The wooden building leaned slightly, looking like the WWII leftover it was.

She stepped inside and whiffed musty wood and stale beer, the calling card of Texas roadhouses. Cat smiled at the space memorabilia and pictures on the bar's walls, longing to be a part of it all. She'd wanted to go to space even before *Star Trek*. Before James T. Kirk, the Mercury through Apollo astronauts were her heroes. She still had the newspaper clippings from John Glenn's sky-breaking three-orbit flight under her bed. Most of her friends couldn't understand her ache to go to space. She'd flutter her eyelids and tell them in her best syrupy southern drawl, "Some souls are born with stars in their eyes." But it was more than that—a pebble in her shoe, an itch that did not fade. And Cat told no one her secret: things would be better if she proved herself the best.

She sat down at the bar; she had dressed in jeans to hide her legs. The usual happened anyway: she ordered her gin and tonic with lime, and in under two minutes a man was at her elbow, striking up a conversation. She averted her gaze and tried to enjoy sniffing her lime wedge, but eventually she turned to see a giant Mach 25 jacket patch and a NASA worm logo; he was an astronaut who had already flown a shuttle mission. He wasn't bad looking, but he was no James T. Kirk.

"Good evening, ma'am. Mind if I join you? I saw you looking around, and I would be happy to give you a tour of these hallowed walls. Terry Rogers is the name."

Cat was used to such attention, but this was different. "Terry Rogers? I'm honored. You were commander of the shuttle mission that repaired Starsat One, weren't you?" She remembered from her reading about the current astronauts that he was married, but he wasn't wearing a wedding ring.

Terry puffed up and sat on the next stool. They made small talk, and she told him she was a physician. Hoping for a graceful exit, Cat did not volunteer she was an astronaut finalist.

"Are you hungry?" Terry asked. "May I take you out to dinner? I know where we can get some great steaks."

Cat hid her frustration and worked up her best five-hundred-watt smile. "Terry, you should know I am one of the applicants here for astronaut selection week, and our going out is probably not a good idea. I would love to hear more about you and your work, but that will have to wait until after I get selected."

Terry's face went from jolly to dark in an instant. "You could've told me that, earlier, Cat." As he turned to leave the bar, he added, "Good luck to you."

She wondered if he had much to do with the selection process. She hoped not. She really hoped not. *Damn. All I wanted was a drink.*

Office of Dr. Dacey, pediatrician
October 1959

"You've been a very good girl, today, Catherine. What color lollipop would you like?" The receptionist at Cat's doctor held a basket of bright suckers toward her as she and her mother were checking out.

"It's Cat-uh-reen. I want a black one," answered seven-year-old Cat.

In a most condescending voice the receptionist said, "I'm sorry, Catherine, we don't have any black ones. Which other one would you like?"

"None, thank you." She pulled her mother's hand to go.

"Cat!" Closing the office door behind them, her mother grabbed Cat's shoulders and looked directly into her face. "Why were you so rude? You know they don't have black lollipops."

Cat looked up with her big blue eyes and a serious expression. "Yes, Mom. But I want what I want."

March 1988, eighteen months before Intrepid *launch, STS-92A Flight Medicine Clinic, Building 8*
Johnson Space Center
Houston, TX

Dr. Matt Wallace entered the Flight Medicine Clinic and saw Nurse Patty in the hallway holding a chart. "Good morning. Who's on first?" he asked.

"Jack Badger, who arrived early—in a hurry. They're always in a hurry." Handing him Badger's folder, she added, "Room two. He's all yours."

Matt flipped through the thin chart of Lt. Col. Jack Badger, USAF—not much to it, and the astronauts liked it that way. They didn't like coming to the clinic and didn't like meds. A month ago, he had finally convinced a reluctant Jack to start medication for his high blood pressure. The public expected astronauts to be perfect human specimens, but as they aged, they developed the same problems as anyone else. NASA had far too much invested in veteran astronauts to ground them for minor medical issues. As a black male, Jack had a higher risk of high blood pressure than the population average.

"What can I help you with today, Colonel?" Matt asked as he entered the exam room.

"Hey, Doc. I've had a dry, hacky cough for a couple of weeks. It's not getting worse, but it won't go away."

"None of the astronaut physicians had a diagnosis?" Nobody consulted the docs in the clinic until they had checked with at least two of the astronauts who were also MDs.

Jack wrinkled his nose. "Nah, everybody said to come see you. It's bothering me at night, too."

Matt took more history, did a brief exam, and offered a quick diagnosis. "I did this. Your blood pressure med is effective, but some patients develop a cough like yours. Stop the medication and your cough will clear up. We'll find another blood pressure drug for you later."

"I knew you guys were trying to poison me." Jack laughed.

"Never—the government says you're too valuable. Speaking of which, are you up for a mission yet?" Matt always considered carefully before asking this question. Who got a shuttle flight and when established an astronaut's rank in the unspoken hierarchy of the Astronaut Office. Astronauts who were bypassed could wait years for a flight.

"Yes, I was recently assigned to STS-92A for backup EVAs. We'll launch the solar exploration probe *Odysseus*—hopefully in the summer of '89. We call it the 'Solar Polar' since the probe goes out of the solar system ecliptic over the sun's poles. It's counterintuitive, but to launch into a solar orbit like that takes a tremendous amount of energy."

"The '2' in STS-92A means a Vandenberg Air Force Base launch, right?" Matt said. "NASA's alphanumeric system for naming shuttle missions using the fiscal year is too confusing. It should just be called STS-40-something."

"I agree. It's classic NASA overcomplication," Jack said. "But we all know why it was changed—before we got to STS-13."

"I'm always embarrassed by NASA's superstition after Apollo 13," Matt said. "We're supposed to be a scientific organization." Signing his note and closing the chart, he asked, "Who's your commander?"

"Terry Rogers. It's a crew of five because of weight limits on the polar orbit launch. There aren't any EVAs scheduled, but Hayes Bartlett and I will be ready if something goes wrong."

♦ *Ruthless Sky* ♦

Jack was finished dressing and apparently had more important things to do than chatting with his flight surgeon. "Thanks, Doc. See you in two weeks, or sooner if I'm not better. I'm headed for training in the WETF, and a coughing fit isn't a good idea in a space suit."

Matt wasn't concerned about Jack's leaving for NASA's giant swimming pool for weightless space suit training. But he pondered Jack's bad luck. His commander was egotistical and inflexible, a classic my-way-or-the-highway military man. *More than the mission manifest, it's the commander who determines whether it's a prime mission or not.* Patty had told him Rogers had been secretly voted by the astronaut corps as the person "most likely to be sent EVA without a space suit."

It was time for the flight medicine chief to announce the crew surgeons for several upcoming flights, including Jack's STS-92A. Despite the commander, the first Vandy launch would be very cool. Matt swiveled his squeaky Apollo-era chair to look at the NASA feel-good poster behind his desk, a shuttle clearing the launchpad titled "Going to Work in Space" like it was routine. It wasn't routine. It was obvious the original fourteen or more shuttle launches per year NASA had planned were a bureaucrat's fantasy. Even bringing *Intrepid* into the fleet as a fifth shuttle wasn't going to change that. *And the first launch out of Vandenberg is bound to be a dicey business.*

Launch day, 1989
STS-92A
EVA hour four

Hayes trained his work light on the newly discovered wing rupture while the NASA engineers decided what to do next. He heard Terry call for attention on the local-only EVA intercom loop. *Can't wait to hear what he has to say about this.*

"Listen up. Our mission is to launch this billion dollar, very important solar probe. That's job one and needs to be our focus. We must launch *Odysseus* within the next couple of hours, or it's junk. Hayes and Jack, you need to redouble your efforts. We've got to let Houston work our other little problem while we take care of ours."

Hayes thought, *Yeah, plutonium-powered space junk stuck in our payload bay. He's right about our other little problem. Houston is surely scrambling. One thing at a time.* Panic had been trained out of him long ago, replaced by a reflex to master any situation. Addressing Cat, Hayes said, "As soon as mission control has enough video of this wing breach, crank me back down to our naughty satellite."

Everybody got on with their jobs. That was who they were, what they were. Jack had finished rigging the hacksaw blade; he and Hayes each wrapped a padded end of the cable around a glove and started sawing on the cradle's balky bolt after Jack braced himself as best he could in the payload bay. They made good progress until Jack's line on the blade snapped, and he flew out of the cargo bay restrained only by his tether.

"Cat!" Hayes called. "Jack, I'll grab you." Cat moved Hayes over to the nearly taut tether, which he grabbed to reel his partner in.

"That was fun," Jack said. "Hayes, you should try it."

"I should have cut the line and been done with you, Badger. You're nothing but trouble."

They rethreaded the blade and were soon back at it. The blade was getting dull, but they didn't have time to change it. When the jammed bolt head was finally off, Hayes hammered the shaft out of the hinge. The cradle was free to move again.

"How much time's left?" he asked. After hours of work in his pressurized suit, his hands were at their limit. He had come close to turning the work over to Jack, but his pride pushed him on.

"The drop-dead time is in one hour, ten minutes," Dominick answered. "Payload Ops needs the rest of the launch window to crank 'er up and check 'er out. And we need to back *Intrepid* out of the firing zone."

"Here goes," Cat said. "Powering up the cradle now." Hayes tensed and then went limp with relief as he watched the Centaur upper stage cradle rise perpendicular to the payload bay, ready for launch. He heard Terry's voice before the rocket reached full verticality.

"I know what you're thinking. No time to look at the wing. EVA team, ingress now."

Liz at mission control answered, "Congratulations, *Intrepid*. We weren't worried."

So pleased with your confidence, mission control, Hayes thought. *Now please fix the hole in our wing.*

Besides the hole, *Intrepid* had other problems—one of the shuttle's main communication systems wasn't working. Despite her efforts to hide it, another level of tension seeped from Liz's voice as she said, "Dom, we're getting Ku-band data fine, but the S-band system is not coming through at all. Can you cycle and check that system?"

"We noticed, Houston," Dom answered. "I'll get on it as soon as *Odysseus* is on its way."

Hayes and Jack made their way back into *Intrepid*'s airlock and shut the outer hatch. They worked their depress/repress checklists as the shuttle airlock pressurized. When they finally doffed their helmets and gloves, the airlock was filled with what Hayes called "the smell of space"—an acrid, pungent odor reminiscent of welding fumes. They moved into the middeck to finish removing their space suits. Hayes was more than ready to get out of his.

He removed his pants quickly and worked his way out of the upper torso of his suit, leaving just the tight-fitting ventilation suit that circulated cooling water to keep him from overheating inside his space suit. Hayes noticed that Jack was having trouble with his suit's pants. Jack was grimacing as he worked to get them off. Normally, another crew member would be helping them, but everyone on the flight deck was busy with the *Odysseus* countdown.

"What's up, Jack? You stuck?"

"My right knee is killing me. Can't flex it too well. Give me a hand."

"You whack it when you went sailing off?" Hayes asked, as he helped Jack out of the lower torso section.

"No, it was hurting before that. I think it's the bends. I had trouble with my oxygen prebreathe when my nose clip came off, and Terry told us to suit up and go out damn quick . . . as soon as the launch cradle jammed. I guess the airlock prebreathe protocol wasn't enough."

"Damn. You probably should stay in the suit. Let's talk to Dr. Cat." *Another fucking problem,* he thought. *Will anything ever go right on this mission?*

Cat came "down" from the flight deck, where she had been video-surveying the orbiter wing with the robotic arm's cameras.

"Jack's right. Looks like decompression sickness. It should be better now—you're back at 10.2 psi cabin pressure, but I'm concerned that other symptoms might develop. For now, go back to the airlock, get in your suit and repressurize to the full 4 psi. We'll tell Houston we need a med conference with the crew surgeon. I'm sure they'll want to bring the orbiter atmosphere back up to 14.7 psi. Nobody's going to be doing any more EVAs while you're in this condition."

The commander's voice broke in. "Cat, please stow the RMS," he said, referring to her Remote Manipulator System robotic arm. "Payload Ops says *Odysseus* is alive and ready. We need to maneuver away."

"Hayes, you help Jack. I gotta go," Cat said, as she went back to her station.

Odysseus had a successful spring-assisted deployment out of its cradle in the payload bay, and Terry and Dom moved *Intrepid* a safe distance away with a short firing of the ship's maneuvering rockets. They rolled the shuttle into a state where they couldn't see the rocket to protect the windows. As the orbiter and the space probe approached the North Pole, the Centaur G ignited with a flare rivaling the sun, and it was gone.

After a prolonged rocket burn and probe separation, the ground controllers were satisfied with *Odysseus*'s performance. Normally, everyone would have been ecstatic; the first research probe launch from a space shuttle in a polar orbit was a milestone.

Ash in our mouths, thought Hayes.

Launch day, STS-92A
Mission Control Center
Flight Control Room comm loop

NASA flight director (FLIGHT): "The crew has requested a private medical conference, so *Intrepid* will be offline while somebody talks to the surgeon. Listen up, people. The whole world now knows of *Intrepid's* wing problem, thanks to our live EVA telecast. We can't be distracted by media drama while we're working this anomaly. Public affairs, your folks need to tamp down the fires. Nobody talks to anybody about this outside of MCC. Marshall Payload Ops and the Jet Propulsion Lab have the Centaur G and *Odysseus* firmly in hand. Our priority is now the crew. I want everybody to task their people in the support rooms to come up with crew activity plans to help them get home. What info do we need? What fixes get them back? I want these items at the beginning of my shift tomorrow. Do it and do it well."

Launch day, STS-92A
T+6
Johnson Space Center
Houston, TX

The Johnson Space Center has a special vibe during a shuttle mission. *We're flying* is foremost in every mind. Matt could feel it as he drove through the gates—the guard was more serious, there was less traffic, and few pedestrians. As crew surgeon for 92-A, he had spent the last week at Vandenberg with the crew of *Intrepid* as they prepared for launch. As soon as *Intrepid* had reached orbit safely, he had jumped in a T-38 jet with astronaut Doug Lewis and headed back to Ellington Field in Houston.

Matt stopped by the Flight Medicine Clinic to change out of his flight suit before going to the Mission Control Center, where his colleague, Dr. Lloyd Patel, was on duty. Lloyd was the deputy crew surgeon for STS-92A and had been at the SURGEON console in mission control since launch.

Dr. Helen Swansen, his boss at flight medicine, met him as he entered the clinic's back door. A statuesque Scandinavian beauty with platinum blond hair worn in a bun, today her eyes were red with bags under them. She had a tightly balled up piece of paper that she was tossing between her hands. Matt had seen her do this once before when a serious medical issue had developed on an earlier shuttle mission. Something was wrong. Really wrong.

Helen kicked a chair toward him. "Heard you had landed," she said. "Hope you enjoyed your flight. We're all in a sad pile of caca right now. I just got a brief from Lloyd. Sit down."

Matt grabbed the chair but didn't sit. "I tried a phone check-in at our fuel stop in El Paso, but all the lines were busy. What's up, besides the mayhem at the Vandy Space Launch Complex after the explosion?"

"Sit down, please. The crew could not get the *Odysseus* launch cradle up and ready, and almost immediately went to an unscheduled EVA. Jack and Hayes had to saw on the damn cradle to unjam the rocket, but that's the least of it. While chasing a wayward tool, Hayes spotted a hole in the orbiter's right wing leading edge—a breach several inches across. That's the most heat critical part of the shuttle. Matt, they can't get home like that."

Matt sat down, rubbing his face with his hands. "God Almighty, Helen," he said, "There's no procedure for an in-orbit repair like that. How are they going to fix it?"

"Don't know, but I'm feeling sick about it. You can bet the space program is back on TV. No more thirty-second blurbs. Continuous coverage of this catastrophe, despite having no facts to go on. As for the Slick Six launchpad at Vandenberg, looks like the steam system they put in for hydrogen suppression didn't work correctly. One of the two exhaust ducts under the pad blew up immediately after lift-off. *Intrepid* was clearing the tower as the explosion occurred, but the gantry is wrecked. They couldn't launch another shuttle from there, even if one was ready."

"I was there when the gantry blew, but I didn't think the orbiter took much damage. The crew said they were really jerked around, but I thought they were okay after that. Got any more good news?"

"My engineer friend out there says he thinks there wasn't enough water in the acoustic sound suppression system either. There were horrendous sound pressure echoes. You know they never really tested that system?"

"I saw no glass left unbroken."

"Matt, you've been up all day and half the night. Go crash somewhere and get some sleep or at least rest. Don't turn on the TV."

"You look stressed out yourself. You need a new ball of paper," Matt said pointing to her hands. "That one is pretty tore up. And I know how close you and Jack have become. I know that makes the situation worse for you."

"I'm fine. We all have our jobs to do. Yours is to take care of your crew. I'm sending two of the flight surgeons out to check on Terry's and Dom's families. They have an astronaut support person there much of the time, but Flight Medicine needs to see if there's anything we can do to help."

"Yeah, like an antianxiety prescription. I could use one too," Matt said. "I'll get out to see the families as soon as I can." Gathering himself up, he turned at the door and added, "Take care, Helen." Matt headed directly to Building 30, Mission Control Center. *Or is it mission-out-of-control?*

Biomedical Support Room
Mission Control Center
Launch day, later

Matt found his deputy crew surgeon on an MCC floor populated with "back rooms" providing tech support for the engineers managing the consoles upstairs in the Flight Control Room. Each FCR console had responsibility for one of the shuttle systems, and flight surgeons had their biomedical support team here in a room where the Houston communications tech would direct the private medical conference. On a special comm loop, only the comm tech and the flight surgeons could hear what the *Intrepid* crew said.

"Lloyd, Lloyd, Lloyd," Matt said, as he collapsed in a chair. "I was still cataloging all that went wrong on this flight when I reached the Ficker, and they said you were on your way here for a PMC." Matt, like everyone else, pronounced FCR as "ficker."

"I was as surprised as you," Lloyd answered. "With the media frenzy over the wing problem, a crew medical issue is more chum in the water. Hayes and Jack just finished a brutal EVA. Sounds like Jack accidentally broke the oxygen prebreathe protocol but went out anyway. I'm thinking decompression sickness unless he got injured during his EVA."

The communications technician came on the line. "Listen, Docs, you may not know we are having communications issues with the shuttle. There is intermittent coverage with our tracking and data relay satellite, and we get blackouts. You've got another few minutes to wait for a window to talk to *Intrepid*. I'll give you a heads-up."

"You look beat, man," Lloyd said to Matt. "Were you in launch control when Slick Six blew?"

"Yeah, and it became obvious how close LC is to the pad. The blast shutters were down, so I didn't see it, but I felt it and there was glass everywhere when I left the building. The Lompoc Hills reflect the launch noise—much louder than at Kennedy. Helen says maybe the sound suppression system was subpar too. You've seen how much more compact the Vandy site is compared to Kennedy. If a solid rocket booster exploded there, it would kill everybody."

"That place is bad juju. Did you know the Chumash Indians put a curse on the land where they built Vandenberg? The Feds stole it from them. Might even be a cemetery there."

Matt leaned back in his chair. "Lloyd, I thought your parents were Indians from India, not Native Americans. What do you know about Indian curses?"

"You're such a racist, Matt."

"Signal acquisition in sixty seconds, Docs."

"It's your shift, Lloyd," Matt said, "but tell Jack that I'm here, too." He motioned to the biomedical engineer to start the audio tape and begin a log of the conference.

"*Intrepid*, this is SURGEON," Lloyd said. "How can I help you?"

"SURGEON, *Intrepid*," Terry Rogers said. "We've got a problem. Jack Badger's been having pain in his knee since the end of his EVA. He's in the airlock hung on the wall with his EMU pressurized, per Cat's suggestion. He's on the loop. Go ahead, Jack."

"Hi, Doc. Sorry for the bother. I've had bad pain in my right knee since about forty-five minutes before the end of our EVA. I probably wouldn't have mentioned it if I didn't know we were going out again. It feels a lot better now."

"That's good to hear, Jack. You're smart to let us know. This is Lloyd and Matt is here, too, back from the launch. Jack, do you have any feelings like pins and needles anywhere or feel any arm or leg weakness? Have you been able to pee?"

"Negative on any other symptoms, Doc. Cat told me to drink lots of water, and I'm happy to report the plumbing is working, too—maybe too well. In fact, I would love to get out of the EMU. My maximum absorbency garment is maxed out if you get my drift."

The docs understood. Jack's space suit diaper was overloaded. "Dr. Riley, do you have anything else to add?" Lloyd said.

"No, Lloyd," Cat said, "but I didn't get a chance to examine him before I stuffed him back into the EMU . . . other than I didn't see any skin rash. Consistent with DCS, no evidence of any spinal hits."

"No fair, making diagnoses. I'll be expendable. Okay, Jack, it's most likely a mild case of the bends. We're going to ask the commander to bring the shuttle cabin back up to standard one atmosphere pressure, and we'll ask you stay in your suit at 4.2 psi for a little longer. Drink all the water you have, and then drink a liter of water per hour times four when you're out of the suit. Sorry about your overloaded MAG. If you get a rash, you can use the steroid cream from the med kit. We'll transmit a schedule for your rehabilitation to the onboard computer. We'll schedule another conference in sixteen hours."

"When can he go back out with me to look at the wing?" Hayes said.

"Bartlett, stay off the loop!" Terry said. "Give us a second, Doc.

"Roger."

After half a minute of silence, the Houston communications technician broke in. "SURGEON, Comm Tech on private air-to-ground. Are you finished?"

"No, we are waiting for them to come back," Lloyd said.

"Oh, roger, all right."

After another forty seconds, Terry spoke. "SURGEON, *Intrepid*."

"Go ahead, *Intrepid.*"

"We'd like a wild-ass guess on an answer to Bartlett's question about when Badger is good to go, assuming he feels fine. But I have a question, too. We're getting the mushroom treatment here." Lloyd and Matt looked at each other knowingly. *In the dark and having shit tossed on you.* Matt pointed at himself to indicate he would answer Rogers. Terry said, "We've had a hell of a day, but I want to know what happened at Slick Six during launch. They told us there was a hydrogen explosion in the main engine exhaust duct at launch. It was a rough ride. We got torqued all to hell. What happened? Is that what damaged the panel on the front of the wing?"

"Commander, Matt Wallace here. I can't answer your last question about the breach. I don't think Mission Ops can either, at this point. I can tell you that Slick Six is not usable for another shuttle launch. As for Jack getting back in the EVA saddle, I'm going consult our navy decompression treatment experts. We will send that info up to your computer, ASAP. We won't clear him for least forty-eight hours. The navy will probably advise seventy-two hours, but I know Jack and Hayes need to get back out there.

"Signal loss in about one minute, sorry," said the communications tech.

After a ten-second pause, Dom Petrocelli said, "Matt, call my wife. Tell her I love her."

"You can call her yourself, as soon as you get back to California. Comm Tech, we're done with the PMC."

"Thanks. That's good because they're gone. I-I mean, their relay is gone for now."

Several Weeks after Launch Day
Space Shuttle Intrepid, *Mission STS-92A*

"I like to dance," said the girl astronaut.

The boy astronaut asked, "Is that possible in zero-g?"

"I'd like to try."

Flight Day Two, STS-92A
Johnson Space Center
Headquarters, Bldg. 1

The director of the Johnson Space Center greeted the deputy director of operations for the Space Transportation System. "Good morning, Bob. Hell of a fix we're in, but we're going to find a way out of it, aren't we? Have a seat. I know your boss is up to his ass in alligators. Talk to me. What happened?"

"Sir, so much has gone wrong on this mission, it boggles the mind. Here are the best pictures we have so far of the fractured panel twelve on the right wing of the orbiter. We initially thought the damage to the wing happened when the Slick Six explosion occurred at lift-off. Here are the pictures of the gantry at Vandenberg now—not pretty. Most of the explosion went out the pad exhaust duct, and that's not what damaged the wing.

"To make matters worse, we're having trouble communicating with *Intrepid*. Their S-band communications system is down. That's significant because the S-band system doesn't depend on an antenna pointing towards NASA's communications relay satellite. *Intrepid* had nearly cleared the tower before the blast, but the reflected energy off the mountains may have damaged the S-band antenna system on the skin of the orbiter. Probably shook up the payload, too, causing the Centaur launch cradle problem. We're very lucky that the *Odysseus* payload had a good launch, but the crew is in a bad way."

"So, the explosion degraded their communication system and the cargo. Did the blast damage the wing?"

"No, that's another problem. This morning, the Launch Video Working Group reports a large piece of insulating foam broke off the external tank and struck the right wing about ninety seconds after launch. It's blurry, but you can see it here in these stills. We've seen foam shed from the external tank before, damaging thermal protection tiles during other launches, but nothing like this. This piece is from the same place on the external tank where foam separated on STS-7, 61-B, and 71-D. This hasn't previously been regarded as a safety-of-flight issue by the Shuttle Projects Office. They tell me it's 'in family,' you know, to be expected. Sounds like BS to me now that I say it."

"A piece of foam can knock a hole in the leading edge of the orbiter?" the director said. "Isn't that the toughest part?"

"No one thought this could happen. It is foam, but it's very hard and brittle because of the supercold liquid oxygen in the external tank. When the foam chunk broke off, it slowed down rapidly compared to the accelerating shuttle, but it still impacted at five or six hundred miles per hour."

"How are we going to get them back?"

"I will be getting back to you on that later."

"We don't have a clue, do we?"

"No, sir, not yet. Even if we could get a rescue orbiter ready—and we can't—the Vandenberg launch site is out of commission."

"Bob, you know Congress is on the fence about future funding for Space Station *Freedom*. We're on the cusp of needing real money if we're going to bend metal and move forward on this program. If there is a shuttle tragedy now, that will be it. They'll cancel the space station and the future of NASA's space program. We must find a way out of this. We must save the crew."

"No one knows that as well as I, Director. Those are my friends up there."

Flight Day Two
The White House
Washington, DC

The phone next to President George H. W. Bush's bed rang at 3:00 a.m. He fumbled for the handset and heard the national security duty officer.

"Mr. President? This is Kaufman, sir. We just got a fax on the hotline from the Soviets, sir. Mr. Gorbachev would like to speak with you. Can you come to the situation room for us to set up a call?"

"Gracious, yes!" answered Bush, now wide awake. "They haven't used the hotline since the Beirut barracks bombing. Dang it, don't they know what time it is? What the hell is up, Mark?"

"I don't know, Mr. President. We don't know of any global developments that would warrant a call."

"Well, give me fifteen to get dressed and splash some water on my face. You can start the wheels turning for a call. Who else needs to be on it?"

"We don't have any idea, sir, none at all. I'll notify Mr. Scowcroft, if you wish, sir."

"Please do that, Mark. The national security advisor needs to be in on this."

◆

President Bush's translator sat next to him, as they waited for the call from Gorbachev to be put through. "He will have a translator as well, sir," he said, "so as soon as I have translated for you, go ahead and answer him directly."

"Good morning, Mr. President," Gorbachev said.

"Good morning, Mr. Chairman. What is concerning you this morning?"

"I know it is early there. I hear you are having a serious problem with one of your spacecraft currently in orbit. An orbit, I might add, that takes it over the Soviet Union several times a day. However, I am not calling about that. I'm calling to offer to help you with your problem."

"That is very . . . generous of you, Mr. Chairman, but the engineers at NASA have a good grip on the situation. But since you are making a hotline call, what did you have in mind?"

"We both know when problems happen, it is important for the man at the top to have the best information possible, Mr. President. My experts are telling me your shuttle crew is doomed without a rescue. The Soviet people would like to offer them a chance. We offer them our . . ." Bush's translator hesitated. "Blizzard. Our cosmonauts will rendezvous with your vessel and bring the crew home."

The American translator shrugged, as President Bush looked around the table for help. No one spoke. At this point, Gorbachev's translator broke in and began speaking in English. "Mr. Chairman is referring to our spacecraft *Buran*, which flew last year. It was being prepared for another flight as your shuttle was launched." Bush nodded with a vague recollection of a Soviet space shuttle–like vehicle that had flown shortly after he was elected president in November. The most senior NSC staffer of those who had been roused to attend the call was shaking his head with a confused look on his face.

Bush had little to go on as he answered Gorbachev. "Mr. Chairman, your offer is most intriguing to us. But of course, as we Americans say, the devil is in the details. I'll speak to our NASA leaders about this as the situation unfolds with our shuttle mission. We're speaking frankly here, Mr. Chairman, so I'll ask you: Why are you so willing to come to our aid at what is doubtless a risk to your own people?"

"We have a saying in Russian, 'the devil is not as scary as they draw him.' I did not expect you to give me an answer now. The ambassador of the Soviet Union there in Washington can arrange for our people to talk about this more with your space agency. We ask for nothing in return for our help, Mr. President, except that it not be kept secret. The world must know of our generosity."

"I understand, Mr. Chairman. Thank you for your call and *do svidaniya*."

"You are welcome, Mr. President, and good-bye."

President Bush looked around the room. "Jesus!" he said, addressing no one in particular. "Can they really do what Gorby is offering—save *Intrepid*? I'm awake—get the NASA administrator up. We need to find out if this is Russian BS or not and what NASA is doing about the situation. Somebody, please get me some more coffee. Where's Scowcroft?"

Early 1984
Fort Rucker, AL

Captain Stephen Hayes Bartlett, US Army, caught fire on the day he watched Neil Armstrong step on the moon. Like millions of Americans, he was captivated by the spectacle on his family's grainy black and white TV. West Point, helicopter pilot training, navy test pilot school, and a masters in aeronautical engineering were his path to becoming astronaut-worthy. This year, he had made the first cut—the army had submitted his name as part of the military's slate of candidates for the upcoming selection of the astronaut group for 1984. Tall, with close-cropped blond hair and light gray eyes, everyone said he looked like an astronaut, so he thought he may as well be one.

As dawn was breaking, Hayes arrived at his off-base apartment. He had spent another night in a Black Hawk helicopter, flying above the Alabama countryside while wearing night vision goggles. The army had sent him to Fort Rucker to help tweak the night vision goggle training program and to improve system ergonomics. It was hard work, but Hayes never tired of the surreal landscape that glided below him while flying at night. He could see everything below, and everything below heard his UH-60 helicopter. Like a mythological creature with magical powers, he saw the deer fleeing his noise in the pitch dark. It was exhilarating to fly at the treetops with cat vision, but the intense focus was exhausting.

As he crawled into bed, the woman next to him stirred. Lt. Janet Cooper, RN, propped herself up on an elbow and looked at him one-eyed. "You got a message on your machine from the base commander, hon," she said. "You were long gone. He said to call him at 0700."

Suddenly wide awake, Hayes sat up on the side of the bed. "The base commander called me at home? What's that about? Did he say anything about us shacking up, um . . . fraternizing?"

"No, he only said to call him. His wife probably wants to invite the appealing Captain Bartlett to dinner." Putting her arms around his neck, she whispered into his ear, "As long as I'm awake, hon . . ." Her warmth pulled him under the covers.

♦

Hayes sat across from a beaming Major General William Stockman. "I am very pleased and proud to tell you of your selection as a finalist for NASA's astronaut program. You'll be going to Houston in a month for the next step in the process." Standing up, he extended a congratulatory hand.

"General, I don't know what to say, except . . . I've been working toward this my whole life. I will continue to give it my best."

"See that you do, Captain. You are the only army they took this year as a finalist. NASA always seems to favor those jet jockeys from the air force, marines and navy. Since all your academy class is close to promotion, we can advance you to major before you go to Houston. We need to impress them, eh?

Your assignment is now to wrap up your work here and take some time off. Talk to my adjutant on the way out to work out the details."

"Thank you, sir. My circadian rhythms are out of sync with all this night flying."

"You've done a great job here at Rucker. One more thing—get that nurse out of your apartment. Looks bad. Keep it zipped, son. NASA is very prudish." He clapped him on the back. With a nod, he said, "I did hear her attitude at the clinic has improved. Dismissed."

An elated Hayes went back to his apartment and found Janet had left to work her shift. He lay on the bed. Though he was exhausted, he stared at the ceiling for an hour. He knew that as a rotary wing pilot, he would never pilot the shuttle, but he would be very happy as a mission specialist. His goal was to wear a space suit and be *in* space, like Neil Armstrong and all the great spacewalkers. *I'm going to Houston!* He let himself say it aloud. "I'm going to Houston, and I'm going to be a goddamn astronaut."

◆

When Janet got off duty, he met her at the door. "Janet," he said, but she interrupted him.

"Old news, hon." She grabbed his hands. "Congratulations. I know you are going all the way with this."

"Dinner's on me. I don't have to fly tonight. We, uh, need to talk about some stuff."

"Way ahead of you on that, too. I'll be packing up my few things. My shriveled-up old bag of a boss wanted to lower the boom on me for being naughty, but you're the golden boy of our dear General Stockman, and I'm covered by your halo. It's a 'boys will be boys' army, after all."

At dinner, Hayes made small talk and struggled to bring up the future of their relationship. Unlike writing a critique of helicopter systems, such topics did not come easily to him. His palms were getting clammy. Before he could mention it, Janet preempted him once again.

"The time has come to talk about us, hotshot. I do really care for you even though you're often a self-absorbed doofus. I'll miss you. I'll also be missing the army, soon. My hitch is up in a couple of months, and I'm going back to Buffalo to marry the boy next door. It's a done deal."

• Ruthless Sky •

"I thought maybe you had fallen madly in love with me and wanted to be with me."

"Now, that truly would be foolish, wouldn't it? You're married to the stars, or at least to reaching for the stars. "

"How long have you been engaged?" Hayes asked.

"Never mind. Are you opposed to girls having fun, too?" Janet laughed, and he smiled slowly. He was off the hook, romantically. He hadn't wanted to go through another dramatic breakup. He considered the possibility that he'd been used, but he didn't give a damn. He recalled "Use Me," a Bill Withers tune from a dozen years ago. *Yeah, you can use me up.*

Flight Day Two
Intrepid

The Beatles' "A Hard Day's Night" came through the tinny speakers on the shuttle. Designed for warnings and alarms, the shuttle's speakers were pressed into service each wake-up cycle to play a tune selected by mission control, with help from astronauts and their families.

"Damn right about that," muttered Hayes, as he slipped out of his sleeping bag. "*Intrepid*, Houston. That was for you, Cat." Everyone knew that Beatlemania was Cat's other major affliction after her NASA job.

"Thanks, CAPCOM, and good morning to you," replied Cat, using the name cherished since Project Mercury for the astronaut in mission control who talked to the space crew. "You can't go wrong starting the day with John, Paul, George, and Ringo."

Although on many shuttle flights the crew would work and sleep in shifts, allowing round-the-clock attention to the tasks on their mission manifest, after their exertions yesterday, mission control instructed everyone to take a long sleep cycle. As she woke up, Cat was more aware of her body's adaptations to zero-g. *My head feels full, but I'm getting used to it.* Everyone's face looked puffy from the fluid shifts in weightlessness. Her brain wanted an "up" and a "down" that her body was not supplying.

She saw Jack was a little slow out of his bag this morning. "How's that knee? Still on injured reserve?" she asked.

"Feels fine now that the flight docs finally released me to cabin pressure. That's my story, and I'm not going to change it," Jack said, demonstrating a vigorous zero-g bicycling motion. "My irritation from wearing an overloaded MAG is better, too."

Terry was wide awake and looking at the new crew activity plan that Houston had devised for them. No commander since Jim Lovell on Apollo 13 had been handed this kind of situation. Holding the floating snake of the printout, Terry said, "While the printer is spitting out everybody's timeline, I'll give you an overview. Prime objective today is to get the launch cradle stowed away, and Cat will use her dexterity with the RMS to backup Payload Ops. Since someone sawed a hinge off the cradle, they're concerned it won't fold up correctly." He looked at Jack and Hayes.

"It was already broken," said Hayes. "We fixed it."

Cat was looking at the schedule Dominick had handed her from the reams of paper flowing from the printer. "I need to talk to Payload Ops. How's the comm system doing today?"

Dominick shuffled the floating sheets. "According to the engineers, the communication system is still giving them fits. They sent some good times to talk."

Cat could see that he wasn't feeling well. She pulled him aside. "Are you still puking?" she asked. "Would you like another shot for nausea?"

Dom waved her off. "Thanks, but I'm feeling better today. Working on the S-band comm failure yesterday, Houston had me moving my head all around, flipping switches and swapping between the decks. Too much for my newly weightless body."

"You'll adapt quickly," Cat said. *Thank God that space motion sickness hasn't laid me low, too,* she thought. *It's the only luck I've had.* She took the list from him. "I have questions for Houston at our next comm window," she said.

Terry read through the printout and told Jack, "It looks like no EVA for you until first thing flight day four. They're being too conservative with you. You look fine to me. Houston doesn't believe we're going to learn much of value, and I hope to prove them wrong. I'm as impatient as you for more information about the wing damage.

"Two more items. We are going to an eighteen-hour lithium hydroxide canister change-out schedule, instead of every twelve. This extends the time we can stay in orbit. Medical doesn't think there will be any health impact. Everyone will keep a close eye on the CO2 levels. Our reserve of the other main consumables, hydrogen and oxygen, aren't as limiting."

The LiOH canisters that absorbed the carbon dioxide expired by the crew were about the size of a one-gallon coffee thermos and had to be changed out by the crew frequently. Cat thought, *We don't know what will run out first—our oxygen, the fuel cells that give us water and electricity, or the canisters that clean our human exhaust.* None of those scenarios was a pleasant end.

"The other item, which I take issue with, is they've cancelled our scheduled TV session for today. Shuttle TV ratings are usually low, but we're now front-page news. We would acquit ourselves well, but they don't see it that way."

"That's cowardly on the part of NASA," Hayes said. "We've all got to face what's happening up here. Plus, we did a hell of a job getting *Odysseus* launched yesterday."

"NASA wants want more information before we show up on TV," Terry said. "For now, public affairs is saying, 'The crew is too busy—maybe tomorrow.' I disagree as well, but we'll have to wait. In the meantime, we need to execute the supplementary experimental objectives assigned to this mission. Don't you have a sterile water for injection device to put through its paces, Hayes?"

"Aye, aye, mon capitaine," Hayes said. "That's on my timeline for today and I'm on it."

Dominick left for the flight deck, saying, "I know what's on my line—back to the radio snafu."

As his crew scattered to their corners of the spacecraft, Terry said, "For God's sake, everybody, eat something."

"I'm not hungry," said Dom over the intercom.

"Me neither," Cat said. She watched Jack and Terry float by the printer while more paper churned out. It was whining under the load. They would soon need to reload it again.

March 1988
18 months until launch
Astronaut offices, Bldg. 4
Johnson Space Center

"Before I crank up the slideshow, let me make this official," said Terry Rogers at the head of the conference room table. "Look around and meet your crewmates on STS-92A. We're going to be the first polar orbit mission from Vandenberg's Space Launch Complex and will launch the first space probe to use the Centaur G upper stage. You should all feel honored for this selection, and I know we're going to have a perfect mission. It's my job as your commander to ensure it."

The four astronauts did as they were instructed, burbling congratulations to each other across the table. They could exhale. It was real. They were going flying on *Intrepid*.

Cat's felt giddy and grabbed her knees hard to calm herself. This was her dream, but her commander had made a pass at her. Elation was doing battle with uneasiness about the weirdness of how NASA operated.

She looked around the table at the rest of the crew—three rookies like herself, and a veteran of one mission, Hayes Bartlett. *This is a special group*, she thought. *Don't know Hayes well, but he pulled off an EVA coup with a satellite rescue only last year.* Here he was assigned to another mission. She liked Dominick, who had worked with Jack Badger on an assignment at Marshall Space Flight Center for several months. She'd heard Jack had a knack for analyzing problems. Their commander had a reputation as a hard ass.

Terry said, "I wanted our first briefing to be only us. There will be more interest than usual in our unique mission. The embarrassing delays and challenges have finally been overcome for a Vandenberg launch. Prepare yourselves for many requests from the appearances office for dog and pony shows over the next year. I know it's a distraction for us, but public relations are part of the job." Looking pointedly at Hayes, he added, "Some of us hot dogs even like the attention."

The first briefing for the crew of STS-92A covered their training timeline, mission manifest and launch windows. At the end of the meeting, Terry stopped Cat as she was leaving; he closed the door after the others had departed.

"Cat, I want you to know that I went to bat with the Astronaut Office for you for this mission. I've been watching your work with the Canadarm all through your training, and you're going to be a first-rate addition to the team. You're top notch with that robotic arm, and you really shined on your special assignment at Edwards AFB."

"Thanks, Terry. I appreciate your confidence in me for a mission with this many new wrinkles." She turned to leave, but Terry held up a hand. He looked uncharacteristically ill at ease.

"I want to apologize for the evening we met at The Outpost. I was out of line. My wife and I had been having some . . . issues at the time. We're much better now. You'll find out, if you haven't already, that being an astronaut is not very conducive to a healthy marriage or social life."

"You're right about the social life, Terry. Currently, it's on hold. Apology accepted. I know it took a lot to offer it. It was very awkward for me too."

"You're right. It wasn't easy to dredge this up, but I want the best for this mission, and that's why you're here. But I needed to clear this up."

"I'm on this trip 100 percent, Terry—heart and soul," said Cat. She felt the gauze of distress draped over her assignment rip away as she left the conference room. Now she could relish her assignment—the notion of her bright and high future was making her giddy.

She walked down the hall and was surprised to see Hayes loitering near the room. He was idly looking at the pictures on the wall, while squeezing a ball in each hand. Spacewalkers exercised this way to strengthen their hands against the stiff and unwieldy space suit gloves. Cat said, "I see you have the tennis ball burden of all the EVA astronauts."

"Congratulations on being picked for this mission. You're already the teacher's pet. You're the first one in your selection class to get a trip. Are you available for lunch to discuss our good fortune?"

"Do you eat while holding the tennis balls, Hayes? That would be gross."

"No, I use a knife and fork. What do you say?"

Hayes reminded her of a cute puppy dog. "Sorry, Hayes, skipping lunch today. Congratulations to you, too. Quick turnaround for another mission, isn't it?"

Hayes was silent for a moment. "Yeah, I had some brownie points with the Astronaut Office, and I cashed them in. When I found out you were being considered for the mission, I lobbied hard for a spot. I told them that I wanted to be on the first launch out of Vandy. Truth is, I wanted to work with you. I could take a pass on our commander, but he didn't veto me, so here I am."

Cat knew the look and did not have time for it. She would be alongside Hayes for the next year and a half.

May 1988
Sixteen months to launch
JSC central cafeteria, Bldg. 3
Johnson Space Center

Looking for a seat, Matt saw a long-haired redhead all by herself. He put his lunch tray down across from her, asking, "May I join you, miss? How are dem institutional taters?"

"They're not as good as red beans and rice, Dr. Wallace. Please have a seat."

"Good to see your green eyes again, Lisa. Have you been spending a lot of time at JSC?"

"I've been mostly back home in Colorado, but there's an MMU on *Discovery*, STS-81B, and that's beginning to ramp up. We've made improvements in the hardware, and particularly in training, if you know what I mean."

Matt did know. Lisa Guinne was lead liaison for the Manned Maneuvering Unit program, the untethered astronaut propulsion unit that fit over the life support backpack of a space suit. Its first use by Bruce McCandless in 1984 produced the iconic picture of a free-floating spaceman above a blue Earth. The picture had taken on symbolic meanings far beyond the magnificent technical achievement. Lisa's job was to wrangle the MMU for missions where NASA needed to work away from the shuttle, such as satellite retrieval. He had learned a lot from the Martin Marietta engineer during their fling two years ago at a conference in New Orleans. It had been a dreamy affair with an implicit understanding it was going nowhere; they were both married. They were still good friends, although affairs seldom worked out that way.

Lisa had told him of an improvisational attempt to use the MMU for a satellite capture on an early shuttle mission. The effort had gone awry, with the balky satellite unexpectedly tumbling so badly it was nearly lost. "Yes, I do remember," he said. "I learned that doing something no one has trained for in the space business usually turns out poorly."

Lisa laughed. "I learned that if the Astronaut Office likes someone and he screws up, the equipment gets the blame. My equipment, in this case."

"Are you still stargazing?" Matt asked. Lisa had taught him a lot about the summer night sky as they stood on the shores of Lake Pontchartrain. The Summer Triangle of stars and New Orleans creole seafood were an exotic combination.

"I've been too busy. My telescope thinks I died. What are you up to, besides keeping the astronaut corps healthy?"

"I've been assigned as crew surgeon for STS-92A, the first Vandenberg launch. It's a whole new ballgame. You got your polar orbit, solar radiation, Centaur G upper stage, and a nuclear-powered satellite. It's a cornucopia of medical hazards."

"Isn't the Centaur G rocket the payload John Young refers to as the 'Death Star'?"

"Yes, it's a big risk. *Intrepid* will be modified with lots of special plumbing specifically for the Centaur. In the case of a launch abort, the system to flush out all the Centaur's fuel in a hurry is a single point failure."

"No EVAs planned, then?"

"Only at the unscheduled or contingency level, but for the first time ever, an EVA might be necessary on launch day. There's no MMU, so you're off the hook."

"What do you mean? Are you afraid of my Irish Setter hair on your clothes again?"

Matt laughed. "Not at all. The hitch is the commander. The rest of the crew is great, but Terry Rogers is an old-school terror."

"What's so bad about Terry?" asked Lisa.

"He's very competent, but if astronauts have a 'ten' ego, he's an 'eleven.' He's hard to work with and resistant to my excellent medically based arguments."

"Perhaps your arguments aren't as excellent as you think. What's your ego rating?"

"Seven. I'm a humble 'seven.' You do have a way with analyzing problems, Lisa."

Lisa shook her head, tossing her red hair in a way that distracted Matt from business. She said, "So, mission requirements could require them to go out the door soon after reaching orbit."

"If something went wrong, yeah. The Centaur G is like stinky French cheese. It goes south quickly. If they don't get it launched within the first few hours, they're stuck with it. NASA is getting cocky with the risks on this mission. I guess that comes from having everything go right on all the others."

"I know you'll come through with your usual Doctor Right Stuff, Matt. Gotta go, take care." As Lisa cleared her place and left, Matt was aware of a nagging premonition he hadn't felt on previous shuttle missions. *Bad commander Karma? Maybe . . .* He didn't really believe in premonitions, but he did believe in looking at risk factors and inferred there were too many.

Flight Day Two
Mission Control Center
Conference Room

"This is it?" the flight director said. "This is the best plan we've got? Stuff the hole in the wing with metal tools and hold it in place with frozen water bags?"

"We're working on a more definitive solution." the engineer said. "This is the lowest tech, immediate deorbit contingency."

"You think this would work? I wouldn't give it a snowball's chance in hell, and I picked my metaphor on purpose."

The other engineer in the room spoke up. "If we had more time, we could come up with an in-orbit repair patch. We would get it to them on a Titan IV from Vandenberg. It would require a rendezvous to retrieve the kit, but it's doable. We don't know how much time it will take or even how much time we have."

"Assume they can survive three more weeks," the flight director said. "We must believe we have the time and the know-how. Maybe we have thirty days. Full steam ahead. I want a repair kit parts list by tomorrow and a production and launch schedule in forty-eight hours. Commandeer the next suitable expendable launch vehicle from the air force and get it redirected. We don't have time to waste on this one, ladies and gentlemen. Go!"

"And who do we say authorized this?" the first engineer said.

"That depends on who you're talking to. Figure out the person two levels up from them in the NASA food chain, and tell them he authorized it. Then tell them to call me. No time for paper. We need results. Code name, Plan B."

Flight Day Two
Intrepid
Presleep, per Crew Activity Plan (CAP)

"We now know what damaged our wing," Terry said. "It was a large piece of foam shed from the external tank. It clipped us at about T+90 seconds. The Shuttle Projects Office never thought this possible, but we're proof they were wrong. Doc Wallace says Jack should be released for EVA after another twenty-four hours, so we'll do our cabin depress accordingly. Congrats to Cat for her job stowing the shaky cradle."

"The comm engineers believe the S-band system was damaged by the gantry explosion and concussion waves," Dominick reported. "I spent all day working it, and my conclusion is the best we get is intermittent communications for the . . . for the duration of the mission."

Hayes said, "I spent my day making sterile water with med equipment destined for our always-four-years-in-the-future space station, *Freedom*. No glory today; this can't help us. I did make a doc investigator happy with my great work."

As they slid into their sleeping bags, Hayes turned to Cat, "You were an artist with the RMS. I thought the cradle system was going to tip over as you brought it down."

"Thanks," Cat said. "Tomorrow's another day, another challenge. Good night, John-Boy."

Hayes laughed at *The Waltons* reference. "Good night, Grandma."

Flight Day Three
The White House
Oval Office

The NASA officials briefing President Bush had finished their presentation and sat respectfully waiting for his reaction. He'd listened to them without interrupting them, but they knew he had many questions.

"All right, now. Our shuttle is in a real pickle, and it can't come home. You think the Soviets can successfully launch this *Buran* shuttle clone into an orbit that will match *Intrepid*? The crew can transfer with space suits, and land back in Kazakhstan? Why can't NASA do the same with one of our other shuttles?"

"Mr. President, *Atlantis* is many weeks away from being ready to launch," answered the aide sitting next to the NASA administrator. "It is the shuttle farthest along in the launch readiness cycle. Unfortunately, how long it would take to move a shuttle to California and get it ready doesn't matter—SLC-6 pad can't be repaired any time soon for another polar orbit launch."

"And we can't use Kennedy Space Center?" asked the President.

"No, sir," the NASA administrator said. "A polar orbit is not feasible from there. We can't drop the solid rocket boosters and external tank over populated areas, and we don't have enough energy to do any sort of dogleg launch. Also, there's no safe launch-abort modes for that crew if something goes wrong. Lastly—and I have to say this—we need to be damn sure the same kind of damaging foam shedding doesn't happen with the next shuttle launch. We aren't there yet."

"Don't the Soviets have a space station, *Mir?* Why don't the Soviets get them to fly over there?"

"Orbital mechanics aren't my specialty, Mr. President, but I can tell you that *Mir*'s orbit is at a fifty-one degree inclination, and *Intrepid* is at seventy-six degrees. There isn't enough fuel in ten shuttles to come anywhere close to matching the orbits."

"This *Buran* thingie hasn't even carried people, has it? Isn't that a big risk? Why do they even have a shuttle?"

Before answering, the NASA administrator consulted his aide for a few moments. One of the junior science advisors standing at the back conference room wall whispered to his neighbor, "I hope the president doesn't ask why the fuck *we* have a shuttle. The Department of Defense screwed NASA good on that one."

"Mr. President," the administrator said, "the Soviets apparently started development of their own shuttle based on the concerns raised by *our* having one. They figured if the US had one for launching or grabbing satellites within one orbit, they needed one too. They don't really seem to have a special mission for it, other than going to *Mir*. They conducted a successful automated and crewless launch and landing of *Buran* in 1988."

"Don't we have any options for fixing *Intrepid*?"

"Sir, our engineers have never been tasked to come up with an option for this kind of repair in orbit; this is unprecedented. Primarily, we don't have the weeks or months it would take to design, fabricate, and launch it to them. We're estimating they have under a month before . . . before they can't go on."

"You must realize what you're asking would be a colossal black eye for American prestige," said Brent Scowcroft. "Not to mention the security risks. What are the Soviets requesting from us for this rescue mission?"

"Of course, nothing is straightforward with the Soviets, General Scowcroft," answered the administrator. "Their plan requires at least one of our astronauts, a NASA manned maneuvering unit, and NASA EMUs, that is, space suits. Their equipment is completely different, and we don't feel there is any big technology transfer or national security breach in complying with their rescue scenario."

"The manned maneuvering unit is that thing the astronauts can use to zip around outside the spacecraft?" asked Bush. "Senator Jake Garn told me he was sorry they didn't put one on the shuttle mission he flew on. Do the Russians have one?"

"Not that we know of, sir, but the MMU is not a dangerous or radically new technology."

"Here's the money question, fellas. Do we really have any other viable choices here?" The president looked around the Oval Office at the team assembled from NASA. They all shook their heads no.

Shuttle Training Aircraft
Above White Sands Space Harbor, NM
August 1989—One month to Intrepid *launch*

Matt sat in the back of a Gulfstream II bizjet configured to fly like a brick. He snapped a picture of the person seated across from him, who was next to a large rack of computers and electronics. The subject of his photo appeared to be asleep, sprawled in his seat.

Dominick Petrocelli raised an eyelid. "I saw that, Doc," he said.

"It's blackmail. I shall send your lazy astronaut picture to the director of Flight Ops," Matt said.

"Wouldn't work. He already knows I'm lazy. How's Terry doing?"

"Commander Rogers is flying 'er like the experienced pro he is. Lloyd is watching from behind the jump seat right now. If Lloyd's like me, looking out the windshield when we reach the twenty degree nose-down glide path, he'll be certain the end is near." Practicing in the shuttle training aircraft was the closest an astronaut pilot could get to the experience of landing the real shuttle in the last few minutes of its mission. It could be harrowing.

"What's scary about a twenty-eight-thousand-feet-per-minute descent?" Dom asked. "Don't worry, Doc. We always flare and pull up at the end. Haven't lost a flight surgeon yet." He stretched his arms and yawned. The two astronauts and two flight surgeons arose early to fly T-38s from Houston to El Paso, where the special G-II aircraft was based. The astronauts piloting the two-seat air force trainer jets amused themselves by observing the flight surgeons in their back seats trying to fly in military formation.

"Why don't we ever land?" Matt said.

"Lots of reasons," said Dom. "Not really like the shuttle when you land. Also, it's a mess. When Jack Lousma was forced to land *Columbia* here on STS-3, it kicked up a dust storm. They are still vacuuming gypsum grit out of her to this day. It's not sand down there; it's calcium sulfate."

"Do you think Terry will let you fly any of the approach to landing on STS-92A?" asked Matt.

With an exaggerated look around the cabin, Dom said, "I don't see any recording devices. No. No way I'll get any stick time . . . not on the first landing at Vandenberg."

Lloyd moved back into the instrumented rear of the cabin to join them. The flight engineer, who sat on a jump seat between and slightly behind the astronaut and the instructor pilot, turned around and yelled, "You're up next after this pass, Dom."

The shuttle trainer at the end of its approach made a low pass over the runway, all its high-drag mods were cleaned up, and it climbed out like a plane for the next practice run.

Lloyd sat down. "This is a hell of ride," he said. "Looks like you're going to bury the nose in New Mexico. Nothing but white dirt out the windshield. Hey, flight surgeons get to try most of the astronaut duties at least once. How about letting me fly one approach?"

"Because, Dr. Patel, although we're brave, we don't want to die," Dom said. "I've seen you fly, remember?"

Matt leaned forward toward Dominick and put his hands together. "Did you know that all astronauts aboard this aircraft speak the truth? Something about coming face-to-face with the reality of landing. What's your truth, Dominick?"

"You're a weird dude, Dr. Wallace. My reality is: a night landing on an aircraft carrier in a squall is much harder than landing the shuttle." Thinking for a moment, he added, "Okay, my truth is the Houston Oilers won't win the Super Bowl this season."

"It needs to be more profound than that, Dom," Matt said. "Although, that may be a universal and abiding truth about the Oilers."

Dom sat in silence again for a few moments. Suddenly he said, "My truth is that despite all the risks we know about, I don't really believe anything will happen to me. Despite our abstract admission of all the possibilities, most of the corps feel the same way. I know I could die, but I utterly feel I won't. Is that profound enough?"

"Yes. I want to understand the crew members for missions when I am the crew surgeon," Matt said. "It helps if things go sideways."

"If I was going to die traumatically, it would have been a long time ago. When—" Dom was interrupted as the jet entered the steep dive that signaled the end of this approach. He rose to observe, preparing to change seats with Terry. He dropped into a New Jersey mobster accent. "Have fun wid the godfadda."

After they were alone, Lloyd asked Matt, "When did you make up that bullshit about truth and the shuttle trainer? Are you going to ask the old commander, too?"

"I may be weird, but I'm not crazy. Hell, no."

"What do you believe about the risks on this mission?" Lloyd asked.

Matt laughed. "If you mean, do I believe the shuttle is as safe and reliable as NASA management does, the answer is no. They should do an unmanned test launch from Vandenberg first, but they didn't even do that before the first shuttle launch. But people who go around shouting 'The emperor has no clothes!' around here end up buck nekkid themselves, out in the street."

Flight Day Three
Intrepid

It was lunch in the middeck. Terry, the family patriarch, insisted everyone eat at the same time. "My last mission was hectic to the end," he said. "There was barely enough time to finish all our assignments. Our mission has different problems and opportunities. We have a chance to deliver excellent data to the investigators who have put so much into their experiments. If you've finished the ones that have a defined end, please get that info down to Payload Ops. If the principal investigator wants to extend an experiment to get more data, then let's prepare to do that."

"I'll be going through the orbiter and powering down everything but essential items to conserve power," Dom said. "Houston would like to be able to shut off at least one of the three fuel cells."

Jack was eager to examine *Intrepid*'s damaged right wing. "Everybody, quit asking me about my knee. It's fine. Besides, my assignment tomorrow is hang out and wait for a chance to rescue Hayes."

"No rescue will be required," Hayes said. "Just don't fall asleep, like—"

Terry interrupted. "Houston is declining once again to have us send any live or recorded video. I might do it anyway and downlink it. We aren't sheep; we're astronauts doing our jobs in a professional manner. I made my case through CAPCOM earlier as best I could on an open channel."

"I'm up for a video," said Cat. "Do they think we're up here bawling?"

"The CAPCOM actually said they are considering something for us, to make sure we didn't exceed our precious bandwidth," said

Terry. "A script was implied. CAPCOM didn't say that with much conviction, however. It's baloney."

"Maybe we can blink our eyes in Morse code to get our message out, like Senator John McCain did when he was a POW in the Hanoi Hilton," said Hayes.

◆

Later, Cat asked Hayes to meet her on the flight deck after lights-out. "Summer camp intrigue," said Hayes. "I like it."

After the sleep period began, Hayes moved past the toilet by the shuttle main hatch and then drifted "up" to the flight deck. Cat soon joined him.

"What's the deal?" he asked. He liked being alone on the flight deck with her. They were in Earth's shadow and had a glorious view of the heavens. He pointed out the windshield. "The Earthlings don't know what they are missing," he said.

"Tomorrow is Terry's birthday," Cat said. "He'd never mention it, but birthdays are a big deal for me. I smuggled a few party items onboard in my personal preference kit, and I wanted you to help me put up this sign where it won't cause a problem. Terry will see it in the morning. I got some little hats, too. By the way, what did you bring?" Cat started to unstack a string of attached letters that spelled "Happy Birthday." "It had to be something, with you."

"Me, unauthorized cargo? Hmm . . . I'll get back to you later about that. It's a great idea to give Captain Bligh a party. Hey, that's what we should video—your party."

"You're not worried that Houston would think we'd lost it?"

Before Hayes could answer, Terry poked his head into the flight deck and growled, "What the hell are you two conspiring about? We all need our sleep for tomorrow."

Hayes was about to retort, but Cat laid a hand on his arm. "Why Commander, your paranoia is showing. We're planning nothing threatening or mission critical, I assure you. You shall find out tomorrow."

"Get to sleep," he said before disappearing.

Cat and Hayes laughed. It felt good.

Flight Day Four
JSC
Medical Sciences Division, Bldg. 37

Matt was summoned off the SURGEON console at mission control for a meeting with the chief of his division, Dr. Geoff Pasternak. He left Lloyd to continue the prep for the upcoming EVA. Helen, his clinic boss, was in Pasternak's office when he arrived. Her hair bun was gone, and it was scraggly on her shoulders.

Jesus, she looks worse every day, thought Matt. The crew's slim prospects were taking her apart. He needed to give her a chance to talk about it later, doc to doc, if she wanted to.

Pasternak was a veteran of the Apollo-era medical support team. Legend had it that his hair turned white overnight after the Apollo 1 fire. "Have a seat, Matt," he said. "Good job with the bends problem. You were cool and on point in a very stressful situation. I know you want to be back in the FCR when they look at the wing."

If I haven't screwed up, why am I here? Matt wondered. "That was mostly Lloyd, sir."

"How's your Russian?" Geoff said. "I heard you speaking it at the Soviet-US aerospace medicine confab last year."

Matt looked at Helen for a clue that this was a joke; all he saw was a stone face. "I took Russian in college. I can make small talk. Better with reading it. The Russian space docs speak fine English. Last meeting, my linguistic efforts were limited to their KGB handlers, the guys in the cheap, shiny suits who were hogging the buffet table. I asked them to leave some shrimp for the rest of us."

"Glad your sense of humor hasn't left you," Pasternak said. "You're going to need it." He leaned forward in his chair. "You're going to Baikonur Cosmodrome to support a Soviet-led rescue mission for *Intrepid*. They'll be launching their *Buran* spacecraft into a matching orbit, and it will rendezvous with *Intrepid*. Our crew will transfer to the Soviet spacecraft by EVA and come back to Baikonur for a landing."

"I should be elated we have a plan, but I can't see it. When is this supposed to happen, Geoff? The Apollo-Soyuz orbital linkup in '75 took years to plan and was nothing compared to what you're suggesting."

"I know it sounds preposterous, Matt, but NASA has bought into it, and it's been approved by President Bush himself. We have carte blanche, and the goal is to get our team on a C-141 to Kazakhstan within a week—for a launch within two weeks. You're the crew surgeon, and we need you there to communicate with *Buran* and be there when the crew returns."

"I like the sound of that last part, sir, but I can't believe NASA is signing off on this shuttle-ski vehicle; it was unmanned on its maiden voyage." Matt wondered if his own hair was going to turn white before this ordeal was over.

"Coincidentally, the Russians were already preparing for their first manned launch. NASA's other practical options for saving the crew are nil. Nada. The Russians are calling the shots, and we're left with trusting them. It makes me sick, but if we get our people back, it's more than worth it."

"Has anyone briefed the crew of *Intrepid* on this yet?"

"Don't know. I got the call this morning. This is a fire drill, and that sucks—but you're in it. Your first briefing, by Mission Ops, is tomorrow at 0800. You're part of a small Skunk Works. We want it small and nimble, like the old days when NASA could do something in a hurry. If we do business-as-usual, NASA 1989 style, this deal isn't going to happen.

"I'll be there tomorrow," Geoff said, "but only to observe. HQ has wisely told all the chiefs to restrain themselves and listen to the folks doing the actual work for a change. You need to tell the people loading the transport plane what you require to help get our crew through this."

Matt sat across from Pasternak without speaking. He heard the voice of Admiral Ackbar from the *Return of the Jedi* movie in his head: *"It's a trap!"* He almost said it, but for once restrained his gallows humor.

"Matt, you look like hell. Go get some sleep. Let Lloyd cover the wing inspection. We need you 100 percent. You'll be the physician in the mob of engineers. Transferring between vehicles by EVA has never been done. The engineers have their decimal points; your job is to protect the humans."

Helen Swansen spoke for the first time. "He's right. This time, I'm going to escort you to your car, myself. That's doctor's orders. You will be no good to anyone if you are beyond fatigue. Like he said, tomorrow 0800."

Matt and Helen went to his truck. "Helen, about Jack—"

"Your job is to save the whole crew. I'm here to help you." She watched him drive off, after which he circled the space center and came back to the same parking place.

◆

Two hours later, Lloyd was sitting at the SURGEON console in the FCR with Matt next to him, waiting for the *Intrepid* EVA team to egress the airlock. Matt was crowding the public affairs officer's position, but the PAO didn't care. With a de facto news blackout about the mission, he had nothing to do. Jack had recovered, and this time all the oxygen prebreathe protocols for preventing the bends had been done correctly.

Liz was CAPCOM again. "Shuttle, Houston. EV1 and EV2 are cleared for opening the outer airlock door. Be careful out there. Nobody's trained for this one."

In the shuttle's payload bay, Hayes opened the outer airlock door and slipped his boots into the straps of the foot restraint on the end of the robot arm. He rotated his heels to lock himself in place. As he did so, Cat said, "EV1, your chariot awaits. Where to?"

With no handholds, tether rings, or anything designed for EVA out on the wing, Jack was limited to a safety backup role at the edge of the payload bay. By the time Cat maneuvered Hayes close to the fractured wing, he was at the limit of the arm extension.

"Houston, EV1," said Hayes. "The hole in the panel is jagged and irregular, with more of the bottom of the leading edge involved than the top. By illuminating the gap, I can see the anterior spar and something else. I can reach it without ripping my suit. The gap is big enough."

Hayes was videoing and taking photos, being careful not to damage the wing further. Matt hoped the video would help MCC better understand the problem, but he didn't think the photos would ever be developed. Removing a fragment of wing panel from the hole with pliers, Hayes was careful to avoid snagging his glove on the sharp edges. He held up the piece and waved it above his head before putting it into a small net bag. "Looks like about 30 percent of the broken panel. If I only had some duct tape."

When Hayes announced he'd learned all he could, Terry ordered him and Jack back inside, and they made an uneventful return.

In mission control, Matt had his own concerns. When were they going to tell the crew about the rescue mission? *It must be hell for them hanging this way. It will at least give them hope and a goal to work toward.* Astronauts needed goals.

Intrepid
Much, much later

"What attracts you most to a guy?" Hayes asked.

"Top of the list?" Cat said. "Hands, then chest and abdomen."

"I'm glad I work out. And there's a six-pack just under the surface, I swear."

"What about you and women?"

"I go for the smile, especially if directed my way. Yours is striking. Magnificent when bestowed upon me. Followed by big blue eyes."

"Then you're a most fortunate man in my case, wouldn't you say?"

Flight Day Four
JSC
MCC, Flight Control Room comm loop

"FLIGHT, we're getting another recorded video download from *Intrepid*," said the engineer manning the instrumentation and communications console.

"More video of the wing inspection?"

"Not that," INCO said. "I'll put it up on the screen."

The video screen showed the *Intrepid* crew on the flight deck, which was decorated, albeit sparingly, for a birthday party. They all wore tiny little party hats and were holding paper cut-out beer bottles as they sang the Happy Birthday song to a nonplussed Commander Rogers.

They toasted their commander, and then Dominick Petrocelli's head appeared full-screen, saying, "We're out of vino. Which locker has the Chianti in it?" Terry raised his arms in the air as if to surrender—and then the clip ended. The flight control room broke into applause.

"Public Affairs, I see you over there, grinning," FLIGHT said. "You want to put this out to the media, don't you?"

"You're damn right I do, sir. Not letting them do interviews is none of my doing."

"Run with it, PAO. We'll ask for forgiveness later. If you get fired, my uncle will let you work at his car repair shop in Kemah."

September 1988, twelve months before launch
Flight Operations Facility, JSC

"Hey there, you got a minute?" asked Hayes as he caught up with Cat in the hallway near her office.

"A minute, yes. Go to lunch, no," Cat said.

"I got that message. As far as I can tell, you never eat." Hayes paused, while someone passed them by in the corridor. "Have you had the one-on-one talk with Terry yet?" he asked.

Cat motioned for them to step into an empty room. "Yes. I'm still trying to understand why he did it. It's as if he wants absolution if something goes wrong."

"Maybe he wants one of us to quit to make room for another astronaut he prefers before we get too far along in training. But, in my opinion, he's already got the best team," Hayes said.

"Terry's concern about the increased risk of STS-92A is genuine. I haven't been complacent about the dangers, but offering each of us the opportunity to withdraw from the mission, with his full support? That's disturbing. The fact that NASA is letting Terry go to the senior management meetings means they don't believe this is a routine shuttle flight, either . . . if there is such a thing. Slick Six was built to launch the air force's manned orbiting laboratory, which was cancelled in the late sixties. Terry has closely followed the program to convert Slick Six into a shuttle launch site. There's a long history of poor-quality construction, with numerous redos and reworks."

"There were lots of challenges, which is why we're launching now instead of four years ago." Hayes counted on his fingers. "Let's see, pushing the main engines to 109 percent for the first time, really frightening abort modes with that Centaur rocket in the trunk, a helium flush fuel dump system that is a single point failure, only one decent abort site at Easter Island—did I miss anything? Yeah, new SRBs too. See, all those are launch problems. The risk after the first ten minutes is completely acceptable. Besides, you'll have me there to protect you."

"Major Humble, I feel so much better knowing you'll be there. You didn't take Terry up on his offer. None of us did. Credit goes to him for asking, but I don't want my career to be over before it starts. I've come too far to give up my dream. I said a mutiny on my part would be the end of my career, regardless of his support. I'd end up flying my desk until retirement."

"He already knew none of us would accept his invitation to bail. He wanted us to know his assessment—NASA is accepting risks on STS-92A far beyond any previous mission. No one should do this job with their eyes half-closed. I have my issues with Terry's autocratic style, but sharing his concerns with us has shown me a side of him I like."

March 1989, six months before launch
Clear Lake City, TX
Near JSC

Dawn leaked around the edges of Helen Swansen's window shades. Seeing her bedmate was already wide-awake, she said, "Some people have to get up and go to work."

"Some people get cranky if they don't get a day off," Jack said.

"Does that mean you're up for another New York adventure? Will you meet me in the city?" she asked.

"'Meet me in the city?' Are you quoting Junior Kimbrough's tune?" he said, reaching for her hand. "Deepest blue of the old delta blues artists is he. Raw and rough. He hasn't made it to CD yet, but I have his records. You need to hear him."

"Junior's not smooth as silk, like you?"

"I can jive with the best, babe, but I don't drop it around this place." He kissed her forehead and said, "I would love to sneak away to New York City again, but with only six months to launch, I don't have two nights to string together."

"I could write you a doctor's note." Gazing at Jack's face, Helen frowned. "When do you think we can show our faces together in Houston?"

"You know, I asked Ray about that last week."

Helen sat up on the edge of the bed and began brushing her hair. "Which Ray? Ray Charles?"

"I've met Ray Charles, but I meant wise astronaut Ray Gordon. Ray Charles did let me sing a few bars of "What'd I Say" with him. I was a Raelette.

"What I wouldn't give . . ."

"So sorry, it wasn't recorded." Propping himself up in bed, he said, "Ray Gordon is one tough SOB. He doesn't take any BS from anyone, especially about race. I've seen him go toe-to-toe with fearless leader Terry and win. Ray's advice to me was, 'The world may be ready for a biracial couple, but NASA is not.' They are chickenshits and don't want the kind of controversy or attention you and I would bring. We both know astronauts who were sidelined because of some act deemed embarrassing to NASA. They wouldn't say anything officially, but 'us' would have consequences. I'm not going to work for NASA forever, but I'm not ready to be sentenced to living on a shelf for the rest of my astronaut career."

Helen lay down again and snuggled Jack. "Times are changing, love. Maybe no one would notice."

"Sugar, they don't come any whiter than Swedish you. The rednecks in Texas would definitely take note.

"My crystal ball predicts biracial couples will be mainstream quicker than you think."

"The world is changing, but not fast enough for me here on the Gulf Coast," Jack said.

"It's not fair. The other astronauts can sleep around all they want if they don't get arrested in a strip joint or die of VD." She frowned. "Jack, you'd better take care of yourself on this mission. The first launch from Vandy makes me nervous."

"It's a cinch," said Jack. "I've got nothing to do but watch."

"So why are you spending so much time training for an EVA?"

"The Astronaut Office limits my free time to keep me from boozing it up at The Outpost. Seriously, we have a good team on this flight, darlin'. Terry may be a pain in the ass sometimes, but he knows his stuff, and the rest of the crew is great."

"Are you going to tell Hayes or any other of your mates about us?"

"Nope. Especially not Hayes. I love him, but I don't need to be taking advice from him on matters of the heart. He's a disaster." Jack began to nibble her neck.

"Go away, sexy distraction," Helen said as she got up. "I need to get ready. I have other lazy astronauts to take care of."

Stepping into the shower, Helen let the water cascade over her head. *I know he's worried about losing everything he's worked so hard to achieve. Will I ever know what it cost him? Will I become a casualty?*

1965
Jackson, Mississippi

The aroma of chicken stew filled Mrs. Badger's kitchen, and dust motes danced in the afternoon light flooding her kitchen table. She came to stir her dinner and saw her son, Jack—elbows on the table and his head in his hands. An open letter lay before him. Picking it up, she saw the letterhead of Senator James Eastland. Despite her son's exemplary academic record, Mississippi's congressional delegation was refusing to give Jack an appointment to the US Air Force Academy after high school. She kissed the top of his head.

"He's a segregationist devil, son. He's got no right to do this, 'cept he can. But I know you're the cream of the crop, and you'll rise to the top despite these men."

"It hurts, Mama, but I'm never giving up. I want to be a pilot. My country needs good pilots now more than ever. I'm going to write President Johnson and ask for his help."

"That's a great idea. I'll fix you some sweet tea."

Jack's appeal worked. Six weeks later an air force recruiter showed up at the Badgers' door. With his help, Jack secured a nomination to the Air Force Academy from the vice-president. When Jack graduated, he got a congratulatory letter from Senator Eastland. He enjoyed burning it.

Flight Day Five
Intrepid
Sleep, per crew activity plan

Cat awoke with her heart racing. She was dreaming of Alan, one of those dreams so real a nun who had taught her in high school called them "visitations." She clung to his fading presence, fighting arousal. In her sleeping bag aboard *Intrepid,* all was quiet and dark except for the omnipresent ventilation fans. She longed for complete silence so she could recall his breath on her neck. Alan often came to her in her dreams, held her, and told her he wanted to take care of her. He told her he loved her. It was what her soul needed; when awake, she had only herself to rely on.

◆

She had spied Alan for the first time in the waiting room of her group urology practice in Houston. He had dark hair cut short, a solid build, and a great smile. She asked one of the receptionists which doctor he was there to see. Alice had noticed him too and said, "He's here with his mother to see Dr. Garabed."

Cat was happy to hear that. The last cute guy she had noticed in the waiting area turned out to be there as her patient, precluding anything but a professional relationship. With her busy work schedule, Cat's opportunities to meet men she considered worth a second look were scarce.

"Where is his mom in the list?" Cat asked.

"Let's see . . . probably next up. Her name is Larson," Alice answered.

Smiling, Cat went back to her office. *It's almost Alice's birthday*, she remembered. *Need to get her a card.* This was her weekly block of time to do paperwork and return nonurgent phone calls. She left her door open, just in case. Mrs. Larson and her son passed by her door on their way out after her appointment. The older woman looked unsteady.

"Can I get your mother a wheelchair? It's a hike back to the front door and parking lot," asked Cat, rising from her desk.

"No, I'm fine," said Mrs. Larson.

"Oh, c'mon, Mom. Let the nurse help us out," her son said.

Nurse. I love it. Cat retrieved a wheelchair and, as her son situated his mother in the seat, she said, "I'm Dr. Riley, by the way, one of the partners in the clinic. We have several male nurses, also."

The man blushed. "Oh, I didn't mean to insult you after all your help," he said. "I'm Alan Larson, and this is my mom. I work in a practically all-male profession, and I do get accused of being a male chauvinist on a regular basis. Maybe even with 'pig' added, sometimes."

"No offense taken. What's your line?"

"I'm an airline pilot for Continental. There aren't many female airline pilots."

"Not yet, there aren't. I have my private pilot's license, but I hardly ever get a chance to fly. I own half a Bonanza, but I spend all my time staying current." *Pilot. Nice.* She verified there was no wedding ring on his finger.

Alan's face lit up. "Hey, cool. The Bonanza's a great-handling plane. I fly aerobatics for fun when I'm not working. Ever try that?"

This time, Cat's charm worked quicker on the elder Larson. "Alan, why don't you ask the nice doctor for her phone number. I need to get back home to take care of my Pookie-Dog, but you can call her later to talk flying."

"Hey, that's a good idea, Mom . . . if she will give it to me." He was grinning.

Cat handed him her card, with her home phone number on the back. "Usually, I give out the Dial-a-Prayer number, but I'll make an exception for you. I'm not often home, but you can leave a message on the machine."

Alan laughed and wheeled his mom down the hall. She closed her door and smiled. *You never know.*

◆

Cat looked at her watch, which was set to Houston's Central Daylight Time, and saw it was not long before the wake-up tune of the day. Her heart rate had returned to normal, but her longing clung to her—like it did every day if she paused in her work. She reached into her pocket for the item she had brought onboard but revealed to no one. Unwrapping an Earl Grey teabag, she held it to her nose and inhaled. It was Alan's favorite tea. *My vanished love,* she thought. She wished she had her Discman and a few jazz saxophone CDs. *I could really use some Ben Webster right now.* She wondered what they were supposed to do today.

Flight Day Five
JSC
Building 2 auditorium

At 0800 the morning after his meeting with Dr. Pasternak, Matt sat on the stage at a conference table with twenty people, most of whom he already knew. A somber Lisa Guinne sat next to him, as the group gathered. There were dozens of NASA managers sitting in the audience. Gene Kranz, the director of mission operations was at one end of the table, holding up a large loose-leaf binder. Kranz, famous as the flight director who successfully managed the near tragedy of Apollo 13, had overseen all mission ops since 1983.

"Ladies and gentlemen," said Kranz, as the waved the binder, "this is our bible, *Operational Flight Rules* for the Space Transportation System. Every possible problem we can think of is covered in this book, along with a well-thought-out response." He looked around the table. "You may as well throw it in the trash. We're in uncharted waters here, and you're the team that's going to Russia to bail out our leaky boat before it sinks."

Kranz looked toward a man in the back of the auditorium. "I have the nod from security that we're good to go. I'm going to turn this over to the man chosen to lead your team and who will travel with you to Kazakhstan in the Soviet Union. You all know him. Kurt Robertshaw, the floor is yours."

Kurt Robertshaw rose from his chair at the head of the table, his face as solemn as a judge issuing a death sentence. He was one of the old guard astronauts selected from the military in the late 1960s. He still wore a crew cut, now gray, and had the upper torso of a body builder. He had served in the support crew for the Apollo-Soyuz Test Project in 1975 and had hung on through the drought in American spaceflight until the dawn of the shuttle era. Now a veteran commander of two shuttle missions, he had reached the age astronauts retired or moved into NASA management positions. He motioned to the man sitting next to him.

"Stand up, Stas." A man stood, made a curt bow to both sides of the table, and sat down. "This is Stanislav Komarov, who has flown here to be our liaison with the Gromov Flight Research Institute near Moscow. GFRI is the organization responsible for operating and crewing the *Buran* spacecraft during our upcoming rescue mission. I still remember a little Russian from the Apollo-Soyuz days, but we also have Linda Arlinsky here to help translate today as needed." He gestured toward a short woman with outsized frizzy hair, who raised her hand.

Matt leaned over to Lisa and whispered, "I wonder what kind of TV reception she gets with that antenna on her head?" This earned him a punch in the arm.

Kurt said, "Here's the outline, version one: We will launch *Buran* with a crew of three cosmonauts. Our NASA EVA-trained astronaut, Sharon Maralow, will complete the crew. She used the manned maneuvering unit on STS-81D." Sharon raised her hand. "There will be additional space suit torso parts and gloves onboard, sized for Cat, Dom, and Terry.

"There will be a cosmonaut in a Russian space suit, and we need to figure out how to get the manned maneuvering unit aboard *Buran*. Stas tells me there isn't yet a functional robotic arm, like our Canadarm, on their vehicle. The spacecraft's internal volume and configuration are okay for getting nine people back on the ground since *Buran* was designed for a crew of up to ten.

"The Energia booster that launches *Buran* is very robust, so weight and orbital inclination are not an issue," Kurt said. "There's a direct insertion launch window of ten minutes one week from now that will give us one orbit to rendezvous. Yes, I said one week. There are other phasing orbit windows that could take days to rendezvous, but we're aiming for next week. Given our situation, there's no time to waste chasing Terry and his crew. Any questions so far?"

Matt spoke up. "Why haven't we told the crew yet?"

"That's above my pay grade, Matt. I agree that they're overdue to be in the loop on this." Kurt looked over at Kranz, who mouthed "Today." "I believe NASA wants a complete data package they can upload instead of an open comm channel marathon. The crew will know very soon. They need to brainstorm on their end, too."

The meeting moved on to Stas's presentation. His English was excellent as he went through slides of the *Buran* interior and specifications. The short little Russian spoke as if he were lecturing at a university. Stas showed a picture of the Russian Mission Control Center near Moscow, and said, "We have recently completed a new mission control room dedicated to our *Buran* shuttle program. It is next to the one used for our space station, *Mir*."

Many of the details went over Matt's head, but he did note that there were fewer nasty propellants on *Buran* compared to the shuttle. *Good for the Russians. Maybe their shuttle is well-designed after all. They are being open about a lot of data, though. Are they trying to impress NASA?*

During the break, before Kurt tackled his stack of transparencies, Matt and Lisa grabbed a coffee and moved away from the crowd. "Are you believing this?" asked Lisa. "The cockpit of the *Buran* looks like a retired Boeing 707 from the sixties."

"Have some charity; the shuttle is only seventies state of the art. Kurt's going to ask each of us what we need for this mission, and I'm going to say a miracle," Matt said.

"Even my little piece is problematic. To get the MMU in orbit and functional, I need my own miracle plus two techs, a van full of parts and equipment, and an MMU support station for their payload bay. Yikes!"

"This is going to be like the old brainteaser: A farmer has to cross a river to get to market with a fox, a chicken, and a sack of corn," said Matt. "He can't leave the fox and chicken or chicken and corn together. The fox would eat the chicken, and the chicken would eat the corn. The boat only holds the farmer and one of them at a time."

"I see what you mean. The NASA EMUs don't work out of *Buran*. The Soviet Orlan space suits don't work with the MMU or our shuttle. The EMUs haven't been fit to three of the crew. How do you get five people out of *Intrepid* into the Russian shuttle?"

"I hope Kurt will tell us."

"What's the answer for the farmer?"

"Farmer takes chicken over, comes back, gets grain across, takes chicken back to original bank, brings fox over, goes back for chicken. I thought you were an engineer."

"I am, but you're an obnoxious pedant."

"You do say the nicest things. I flunked English vocabulary, you know."

At that point Kurt knocked the table and round two began. The lights dimmed and the overhead projector lit up the screen. "This is what I will need from each of you by tomorrow . . ."

June 1989
Shuttle fixed base training simulator
Mission STS-92A-T

Cat and Hayes sat in the middeck of the shuttle simulator, safely on the ground in Building 5 of the Johnson Space Center. But they weren't alone—mission control, teams at other NASA centers, and a backroom engineer army were all mobilized like a real mission. They were doing a "long sim," an extended two-day training exercise focused on the STS-92A mission. The simulation supervisor was notably creative at raining hateful breakdowns upon the flight team and crew.

Up on the flight deck, Jack was working as mission specialist one helping Terry and Dom in a flight engineer role for the ascent and return phases of flight. Hayes took off his headset and told Cat, "You know, we should go get a nice dinner after this sim is over. The pace of training is speeding up, and you look wine deficient."

"Any deficiency is in your department. I don't want to go out with you, particularly while we're assigned to the same mission. Let's say your reputation precedes you. I don't see you asking Petrocelli out for a drink."

"Dom is not only a family man, but he's also ugly. What do you mean my reputation precedes me?"

"How many women from JSC have you dated since you've been here?"

"I don't know. I'm popular. What's that got to do with anything?"

Rolling her eyes, Cat sighed. "Hayes, I'm willing to admit I like you. However, we're a team, and I personally can't afford to be involved with you outside of work. Chill, dude. See how you feel when we get back from our mission." She tumbled back to a familiar place. Two years and her heart wouldn't accept Alan was not coming back. He died with his little halo intact, a ghost lover whose voice was always in her head. She knew she had to move on, but she couldn't get her heart to listen. *He made me feel so good. I miss him so much.*

Jack stuck his head through the hatch between the middeck and the flight deck and yelled, "Hey, Cat! Get your ears on. It's showtime."

Cat covered her mike and said, "Damn you, Bartlett, you made me miss my call. Yes, Commander. Minor technical difficulty here. Read you loud and clear now."

"Cat, what the hell are you doing down there?" Terry barked. "We need you on the RMS. You need to move the Centaur out of the payload bay, now. We'll be using the rear jets to translate us to a safe distance for firing." The Sim Sup had given the crew a malfunction in the shuttle's forward maneuvering jets.

"On station in a sec, Commander," Cat answered as she climbed up the ladder to the aft cockpit. *Hayes is such an asshole.* A short while later, she took pleasure in his obvious discomfort as he activated a script he had been given earlier to simulate a nosebleed.

◆

After the simulation was over and the crew was leaving for actual sleep, Terry pulled Hayes aside. "Bartlett, a word," he said, as the others continued to exit.

"I thought things went well today. We got the satellite off, despite all the malfunctions, and my nose stopped bleeding," said Hayes.

"Our performance was nominal despite, not because of, you. Your attitude isn't meeting the professional standards this crew needs to accomplish the mission."

"Care to elaborate, Commander?"

"Stop harassing and distracting Cat. You didn't take your medical problem seriously enough during the sim. Your behavior is reflecting badly on all of us, including me as commander."

"I wouldn't want your reputation to be tarnished, but a few jokes or talking to Cat isn't jeopardizing our mission. We're coming together as a team." *Not just an extension of your ego.* "Yes, you're the boss—" Hayes stopped himself. *Cool it, bud. I don't want to get thrown off this mission by Captain Prissy Pants.*

"I'm trying to help you make this team great," Terry said. "Think about what I've said. See you tomorrow for sim debrief. Get a good rest."

As Terry was leaving, Hayes called out, "Thanks for the advice, Terry. You have a good night, too." *You prick. Why does he think Cat needs protecting?*

Flight Day Five
Intrepid

"*Intrepid*, this is Houston. We have news to share this morning. You're going to have visitors to your neighborhood. There will be a lot of material sent to you, but in a nutshell—we've called a taxi to take you home." The CAPCOM was Doug Lewis, who was relishing the reveal of NASA's rescue efforts. "The question is, do you have enough rubles to pay the fare?"

Dominick had already moved toward the computer, as Terry said, "Houston, you caught us flat-footed with that one. Care to elaborate?" Hayes started to say something, but Terry cut him off with an index finger pointed at his own chest.

"Hold on to your helmets for this one, Terry. As we speak, a team is being assembled to travel to Baikonur Cosmodrome in the USSR, where the Soviets will launch a vehicle next week to rendezvous with *Intrepid*. You will need to take a walk to get to their *Buran* orbiter, but then you come back to Baikonur. Easy as pie."

"I can't wait to hear the details, Doug, but you've got a bunch of grinning crew faces up here right now. Whatever it takes, we'll be ready. We'll be ready."

Cat grabbed Jack and gave him a big, zero-g hug that brought Hayes over to get in line.

"Hey, me, too."

"For you, Hayes, they cost a quarter—or dare I say, a ruble?" She gave him a little hug, and then went to look over Dominick's shoulder as he received the printout for their new lease on life.

"We have lots of questions, here, Houston, but they can wait until we've read the new crew activity plan," Terry said. "Is NASA sending anyone to fly with the Russians?"

"The illustrious Sharon Maralow will be accompanying the two cosmonauts piloting *Buran*. The Russians will also fly an EVA cosmonaut. Sharon will get the ball rolling on the transfer via MMU between the two spacecraft."

Terry and Dom left the middeck to perform a scheduled inertial measurement unit alignment to keep the navigation system functioning. Jack looked at Cat and Hayes and said, "Yesterday I would have killed for a videotape of *Raiders of the Lost Ark*, but things are going to get interesting very soon. I was getting bored."

"It's the miracle I was praying for," said Cat.

"The drowning man gets tossed a life preserver. Or is it an anchor?" Hayes said.

"Don't be a negative butthead," replied Cat.

Flight Day Five
Mission Control Center

"What's the status of Plan B?" the flight director said. "Can we patch the hole with an EVA? Can we design, procure, and get the patch to them before it's too late?"

"Things are coming along well on all fronts," the structural engineer said. "The cooperation from the MIT materials processing lab has been amazing. Because of the crisis, NASA is getting a break from everybody without exception—every company and university we have contacted. They're all working on this for free, for God and country."

"Wing panel?"

"The contractor is busting ass to make a patch while bitching that NASA has been cheap in procuring spare wing panels and hasn't bought anything in several years."

"And the air force?"

"The air force is also being uncharacteristically helpful. They've redirected a Titan to us, and it should be ready by the time we are. It was supposed to be a classified satellite launch, so we're hoping there won't be any publicity. The team at Marshall is working to integrate the rescue gear into an air force 'spook' satellite case they grabbed since all these satellites are being designed now to be retrieved by the shuttle should they need repair."

"This deal is still bootleg, as far as the higher ups are concerned," the flight director said. "Don't let anything slow you up. Somebody gives you lip, send them to me. I don't trust the damn Russkies any farther than I can throw one."

January 1986
Enroute Lafayette, LA, at nine thousand feet

Alan Larson looked down at the barge traffic plying the Intracoastal Waterway east of Houston. It was a beautiful South Texas winter day, cloudless and comfortable—unlike the oppressive humidity and heat of a typical summer day. "I hardly ever see the world from this altitude anymore. Either I'm at thirty-one thousand feet, or I'm landing and too busy to look. If I'm in my Pitts biplane, I'm upside down." He looked left to the pilot of the single-engine aircraft and said, "It's also refreshing to be the passenger instead of the pilot."

In the left seat, Cat adjusted the boom mike on her headset. "I hope you're enjoying the view. I ordered a no-turbulence day for our trip to Louisiana."

"When I told the crew on my last trip I was going flying with a doctor in a Bonanza, they were horrified. They were sure I wasn't coming back."

"You'll be fine. They myth of the arrogant surgeon crashing his Bonanza only applies to *male* doctors. I'm an excellent pilot and immune to that prejudice." Cat's Bonanza was flying on autopilot. "Would you like a little hands-on stick time yourself? No loops, though. We aren't certified for that."

"No, thanks," answered Alan. "I truly am enjoying being your passenger."

They were interrupted by a call from air traffic control, and after Cat checked in with the next controller, she said, "I can't wait for my Cajun relations to meet you. They'll love you. They'll also give you the third degree about your intentions and tell untrue stories about me."

"I'm sure the stories are true. I look forward to hearing them."

"They'll want to know if you're 'the one.' They swore at my medical school graduation, that was it. No more graduations; the next one had to be a wedding. Don't be intimidated."

"I promise not to cut and run from the aunties. On the other hand, it is easy to be intimidated by you, Cat."

"Why would a successful, handsome man be intimidated by little ole me?" Cat said, batting her eyelashes.

"I have fallen—am still falling—in love with you, but you're a little scary. Strong and scary in a nice sort of way. I know you understand what I mean. You can be intense, and the flip side of that is wonderfully passionate."

"It's possible that former boyfriends may have mentioned being intimidated by me. It's been an excuse for ending a relationship, so there may be a little truth to it. I don't mean to be intimidating. I see others do that on purpose all the time, and it makes me mad."

"It's not because you're trying to dominate people, Cat; it's the person you are—beautiful, smart, witty, compassionate, accomplished. What do you need a man for?"

"You left out I'm also difficult. Why would I need a man? Oh, to love me, want me, and take care of me. Maybe fuck me every now and then."

"Stop that. I'll get a hard-on under my seat belt."

"Not my problem. I'll change the subject. I know I don't have a blizzard's chance in Houston, but I have applied to NASA to be an astronaut. You know I've always been crazy about space, and they've opened the selection process for a new class."

"Cat, I can't think of a better candidate. I'll bet ten dollars you get in. No, make that twenty dollars." Alan smiled and blew her a kiss.

"Twenty dollars! That's quite a vote of confidence from a cheapskate like you."

"Damn right it is, darling."

The controller on the radio interrupted them with a vector for their descent into Lafayette Regional Airport. "Okay, got to focus on flying . . . right, Captain?" Cat said.

"You're the captain today, and that's right. I'll shut up and anticipate a delicious crawfish étouffée."

Astronaut quarantine
Four days until STS-92A launch
Vandenberg AFB, CA

Hayes entered the crew quarters lounge, grabbed a coffee, and asked, "May I join you, or is this a private conversation?"

Jack said, "Have a seat. You know better than us that we gave up any shred of privacy long ago, and we're about to get even cozier."

"At least we have our own bedrooms here," Cat said. "But this building doesn't seem ready for us. It doesn't feel like the astronaut crew quarters at KSC—all the history, the signed patches, and the traditions at the Cape. I always saw myself walking out of those double doors of the O&C Building and riding to the pad like every other astronaut who's ever flown. Looking happy and confident of course."

"You'll always be the first woman in the first crew to go out these California doors. You can do KSC next time," Hayes said. "You know what I miss? The Beach House at the Cape. I don't think they can replicate that here at Vandy. The house sits fifty yards from the sea between two launch complexes, and space crews have been chilling there with their families since Apollo days. And it's part of the quarantine zone before launch."

"I walked down to the Point Arguello Lighthouse when we came here to tour Slick Six. There's no beach to be found," said Jack.

"I didn't get to the Beach House on my trips to KSC," Cat said.

"It's just an old sixties tract house that was saved from demolition when the space center gobbled up a subdivision. But it's a rare spot for astronauts to be normal. I took my brother's family there with his four kids before my last mission. It was the normalest I'd felt since NASA selected me," Hayes said.

"Normalest is not a word," Cat said while shaking her head.

"It's as good a word as 'normalcy,' which Warren G. Harding misinvented in the 1920s because he didn't know any better," said Matt. The crew surgeon for STS-92A had come into the lounge and stood behind Cat.

Cat jumped and turned around. "Don't sneak up on me like that." Matt sat down and she said, "I relinquish my role as mission grammarian to you. Any other tidbits?" She took a long draft from her coffee. *Our crew surgeon seems destined to continually irritate me.*

"I was happy to report to the FCOD that the biometric data I collected for the FC HSP here in the West Coast ACQ at L minus four is A-OK," said Matt. Silence followed. Enjoying his own joke, he translated, "Everybody's temperature was normal this morning before you started guzzling coffee."

Cat rolled her eyes.

"I'd like to report the exercise facility here stinks compared to the Cape," said Jack.

"We're all trailblazers," Matt said. "You'll need to work a little harder to keep that body in shape for another four days. I'm sure NASA will gradually upgrade the facilities as time goes by. The next time you're here you'll have a *Pac-Man* in the lounge." Looking around he asked, "Where's our commander and pilot?"

"They're doing tabletop simulations again," Jack said. "Terry is wound up tight about this mission, since we're the guinea pigs for this launch site."

"Speaking of concerned, my fearless leader of the Flight Medicine Clinic, Helen, is flying in for an inspection. She'd like to talk safely to all of you from eight feet away later today. She has to go back to Houston for the launch but wants to see *Intrepid* on the pad at Slick Six in person."

"I hope she comes early," said Jack. "I have permission to take a car up to Tranquillon Peak, where I can look down on Slick-Six. I want time for a little solitude before we launch. Maybe we should put our R and R astrocabin up there."

Matt looked at his watch. "She'll be here in about two hours. I need to round up the cockpit crew."

"Go save Dom from Terry's flogging," said Hayes.

♦

Back in her room, Cat gazed out at the hodgepodge of military architecture on the base. She saw herself reflected in the windowpane. *You made it. Look down from heaven, Alan, my love. And pray for me to not screw up. And to make it home in one piece. When I'm back, grant me peace, okay? Help me move on, will you?* The phone rang—it was time to meet Dr. Swansen.

♦

"Must you drive like a Formula One racer at Monte Carlo?" Helen asked.

"Yes," Jack said easing up on the gas. "It's in the astronaut rule book. Plus, it's good clean fun. This is a great road." At the wheel of their vehicle from the base motor pool, Jack was driving them up the twisting service road that led to Tranquillon Peak in the Lompoc Hills. "But for you, I'll slow down."

"Thanks, I was getting queasy."

"Matt gets an attaboy award for managing to sneak you out for this ride," Jack said.

"He's goofy and annoying sometimes, but he has a good heart. And I'm his boss," said Helen from behind her surgical mask. Jack was masked up as well to maintain a semblance of quarantine.

They rode in silence a short distance farther until Jack found a place to pull over. "No sense going to the top. It's a collection of boring comm antennas and tracking radar dishes." They stood by the side of the road in the stiff breeze and took off their masks. "Look down that way. The mobile service tower is backed away, and you can see our fully stacked bird at the pad, ready to make the leap into space."

"This is so beautiful, Jack. It's perfect. The sun is shining and glinting off your rocket. There's a big marine fog layer just offshore, and nothing but chaparral for miles."

"Romantic spot, don't you think?" Jack took Helen into his arms. "Forget the germs. By the time I get sick, I'll be back."

Helen followed her heart and hugged him back. "I have tried to stealthily quarantine myself in hopes of getting to see you."

"Helen, I owe you an apology. I called NASA chickenshit about its potentially bad reaction to you and me getting together, but I'm the coward. I put my career and getting this flight ahead of us. I'm sorry—you deserved better."

"Oh, Jack." Helen's mouth was dry, and her heart was racing. "I understand completely. You've spent years treading lightly in a world of racist white men. It's their system and their game. I never held it against you. And I know the cost of the anger you've been tamping down all these years. I want to help you with that."

"Anyone's opinion about me or us is a moot point now. I got my reserved seat into space. I don't care what anybody says or does. I want to be with you." He kneeled and opened a ring box he took from his flight suit. "I don't deserve you, but fuck NASA or anyone else who disagrees. Will you marry me, my love?"

Helen caught her breath and then smiled. She kept him waiting a moment as she looked into his big brown eyes. "Can you try that again without the 'fuck NASA' part?"

Jack put his hand over his brow in embarrassment. Looking up, he said, "Helen Kristina Swansen, will you marry me and be my love forever?"

"Yes."

Masks dropped, they kissed and held each other a long time. Jack slowly pulled himself away and said, "We've got to get back. Matt told me where to drop you off. Suddenly, I've lost my burning desire to leave this planet."

"You will get on that rocket and you will have a wonderful time. And I want you to take my ring with you, so it'll be even more special when you bring it back. I don't think I can wear it yet. I'll be too busy for those inevitable questions."

"One well-traveled, hypersonic engagement ring to be returned to you, madam."

Flight Day Eight
Intrepid

Lounging on the flight deck and looking at the big blue marble helped pass the time, so Cat was Earth-gazing with Jack. Shuttle veterans said a crew timeline was so packed with objectives and activities that a mission seemed to pass in hours instead of days, but marooned in orbit, they had run out of things to do waiting for mission control to uplink a detailed timeline for their rescue. Their routine housekeeping duties didn't provide much of a distraction.

"You can't beat our amazing planet flashing by for entertainment," Jack said. "Every minute is a different show. I thought I wouldn't have time to sight-see, but now it's all I do."

"My favorite is the cities on a clear night," Cat said. "Bright diamonds strewn on a black tablecloth, like you could reach out and pick them up."

"Staring out the window isn't our job, though," Jack said. "Lurching from one uncertainty to another is wearing on me. I want to get on with it. If *Buran* misses its direct-insertion-to-orbit launch window next week, we'll be doing even more of this."

"Idleness has made me notice how cramped the middeck is, even without the constraints of gravity," Cat said. "And messy, too. I like it better in the cockpit."

The law of orbital mechanics was a cruel mistress—if a phasing orbit was necessary, it could add days to the rendezvous process. There would be no way to speed up *Buran*'s chase of *Intrepid* if it didn't launch at the perfect time. The medics had instructed the crew to observe a low metabolism, twelve-hour sleep/wake cycle to minimize carbon dioxide production. None of them could sleep that much. They were not running low on food, but in unspoken agreement, they ate less.

Hayes stuck his head into the flight deck. "Cat, can you help me video this material processing experiment?" he asked. "We can take video now and more before we leave. That'll give the principal investigator more data on his crystal's growth. The data can be set up to download while we sleep."

"Good idea." She joined him in the middeck. There was a video camera in the corner of the middeck that watched a plant experiment on the wall for signs of germination. It was on a twenty-four-hour loop to be stopped at the proper time. She pointed at the camera. "This videotape won't make it home."

"I feel sorry for those investigators who are going to lose the experiments they've labored on for years," Hayes said, "but we can salvage other people's hard work."

"There's not much we can do for the murine gestation experiment," Cat said. "These little mousy guys and gals aren't going to make it back to the elementary school kids in Omaha."

"We should still feed them," said Dom. "That'll give me something to do. A lot of these competitive school kid space experiments are public relations puffs, but I like this one." Dom had put himself in charge of sticking additional mouse chow on the inside of their enclosure and checking the air flow to make sure their waste products were sucked into the filter.

"You realize, those little creatures are also making carbon dioxide," Cat said.

"In that case, we'll all go down together."

"We can downlink whatever extra payload data we have on the next comm pass," said Hayes. "NASA will let us do that, at least."

Everyone chafed under management's decision to bar live crew video. Their silly birthday clip was all NASA had released so far, with the explanation that the crew was too busy.

Hearing the noise of the teleprinter, Terry grabbed the output. "Here it is at last: how we're going to get home."

◆

Terry briefed the crew after they'd all read the plan. "Everything about this orbital rescue rendezvous is going to be tight, but I know each of you can execute your part. They want *Buran* to be the primary maneuvering craft. Then Dom and I are baggage. I'd hoped to be the last one off the ship, but it makes sense that Dom and I evacuate first. We'll configure *Intrepid* for a ground-controlled deorbit burn that takes her to a safe, watery resting place. Jack does a solo EVA to rendezvous with Sharon, who is bringing our suits from *Buran*. While we are suiting up, Jack and Sharon will wait outside. They'll help us transfer when we exit the airlock."

"Cat drives Jack on the RMS outside," Hayes said. "Sharon's in her MMU, and I help Cat don her suit as the last ones out. Turn out the lights when we leave." *I like the idea of loading Cat into her EMU, but it's not going to be easy for both of us to suit up and get into the airlock with nobody helping us.*

"We have another list of items and systems to power down to conserve our oxygen—that includes all the remaining payloads, Dom. It's titled 'Extended Orbiter.'"

"Aw, c'mon, Terry," Dominick said. "I'll rig up a separate power jumper to keep their little fan going, and they don't breathe *that* much. If the mice die, it's really going to be gross."

"We've got lots of other things to do first, Dom," Terry said. "We've also got to conserve our maneuvering fuel for our transfer to *Buran*.

We need to give Hayes and Cat a crash course in driving *Intrepid* with the thruster jets. We shouldn't need to adjust the orbiter attitude at the end, but I can't leave the ship without someone onboard who can man the tiller."

Flight Day Eight
JSC / Phone call

Deputy Director of Operations, National Space Transportation System: "Art, I've got to go to NASA headquarters in Washington this afternoon to explain to them, the White House, and God knows how many congressmen what's going on with the *Intrepid* rescue. I just got off the horn with the Center director, and he's hopping mad about all the calls he's getting about rumors of a secret rocket rescue you are cooking up. The press is calling, air force generals are calling—you know he hates to be blindsided. So, what the hell are you up to? Did you think you can keep any secrets at NASA?"

Flight Director: "Mission Operations is exploring sending up materials they could use to fix the wing. We had to develop this in hard parallel, in case this Russian thing blew up. I've talked to the air force reconnaissance group and many others. The administrator won't get a bill until it's over."

Deputy Director: "Does Kranz know about this back door? Does your boss support this?"

Flight Director: "Yeah, I've mentioned it to him. He's been busy with the *Buran* rescue ops. I told him it wasn't costing anything but sweat equity at this point."

Deputy Director: "Look, I've got a plane to catch. Short and sweet, is this a viable option?"

Flight Director: "We think so if the clock doesn't run out for them. Of course, the Russian rescue is going to go perfectly, right?"

Deputy Director: "Right. I told the Center director I would handle this, and that it was good you had looked at other options. I said I would tell you to cease and desist. So, I'm telling you. You heard it. You know at NASA it's better to follow the lines of authority than to be correct, so keep that in mind. If his office bugs you, tell him you talked to me."

Flight Director: "Yes, sir. Have a good flight, and good luck in DC."

May 1987, Two and a half years before STS-92A launch
Pad 39A
Kennedy Space Center, FL

"Hey, it's a Cat on a catwalk."

Cat turned to see Matt get off the elevator that had brought him to the 195-foot level of the gantry at KSC's launch pad 39A. Behind her, the space shuttle *Atlantis* stood majestically bathed in the ultrawhite, ultrabright beams of the pad's xenon lights. "Dr. Wallace, long time, no see. As you can see, I made it to AsCan status without resorting to a padded bra or voodoo love charms." She hadn't seen Matt since her candidate exam, but she remembered his quirky personality and felt like giving him a jab.

"I knew all along you had the right stuff," Matt said to Cat.

Crinkling her nose, Cat made a face. "If one more person says 'right stuff' to me, I'm going to puke. I wish Tom Wolfe had never written that book. Good book, but not my inspiration. Besides, I got no stuff. I haven't done anything yet."

"You've made it to the pad where the Saturn V launched Apollo capsules to the moon, and you have a space shuttle to play in. That's quite an accomplishment."

Cat gazed out to sea. "What a beautiful view, with a clear night sky and a warm breeze from the ocean."

Matt laughed and said, "Even better, you're a couple of hundred feet above the voracious KSC mosquitos. I thought they were going to carry me away. Are you ready for this drill?"

The simulated emergency would require the crew to evacuate themselves from the *Atlantis* cabin during an aborted launch on the pad. *Atlantis*'s planned launch had been scrubbed because of a serious engine problem that required it to be taken back to the Vehicle Assembly Building for repair. NASA decided to make the best of it and run a mix of rookie and experienced crews through a few evacuation simulations while prepping the VAB for a rollback of the shuttle.

"The escape route is more frightening than a launch emergency," answered Cat. The crew's exit off the tower involved jumping into a large metal basket and riding hundreds of feet at high speed down a wire to the ground. They would then retreat to a bunker or escape in a modified Vietnam-era armored personnel carrier.

Most of the astronauts felt the most likely launch pad failure modes would not leave anyone alive to evacuate. Nonetheless, it was their duty to evaluate and practice. They were here tonight to work out kinks in the system.

One of the five baskets was released as a demo, and it whizzed into the night at fifty miles per hour until it was snagged at the bottom by a net and jerked to a stop. It was all over in sixteen seconds. Cat turned to Ben Pollard, who was commander of this pretend mission, and said, "That basket goes like a bat out of hell. How did they man-rate that thing?"

Ben laughed. "I believe they used sandbags, although I'm told the Apollo astronaut Stu Roosa rode one like it—once. No one's been crazy enough to go down since. I've ejected from an F-4 and ridden two solid rocket boosters into space, but I'm not going down in it, either."

Cat had flown to the Cape with Ben in an air force training jet, the astronauts' personal transportation of choice. The NASA T-38 Talons were white with a jazzy blue stripe, and it was established tradition for astronauts to fly them between Houston and the Cape.

Ben was a smooth pilot, and he let Cat have some stick time as they flew over the Gulf of Mexico.

This was Cat's first time in a live shuttle and not a simulator. *Focus, girl. Don't get giddy. You're one step closer to your dream. Don't blow it.*

The exercise supervisor gathered the mock crew together, and along with four other KSC close-out crew members they crossed the orbiter access arm walkway into the white room in front of the *Atlantis* hatch. The crew were inserted into their seats, lying on their backs. Cat was seated in the middeck with Sharon Maralow, a veteran spacewalker.

Sharon was next to the hatch and, as it was closed, she said to Cat, "You and I got the cheap seats, honey. No view, except the tiny window in the hatch. We're in the exit row, though, so last in, first out. I don't want anyone climbing over me!" Sharon had a deep midwestern drawl, with a husky laugh to match.

As Cat waited for the alarm, she looked around the middeck. Even without the lockers along the walls, it was not a very big space. *It's different in orbit, where every wall's a floor in zero-g. S*he would be stepping on the space toilet door on the way out.

The tone for the evacuation sounded, and Sharon climbed out of her seat and cranked the handle to open the hatch. She cracked it to confirm the access arm had moved back into position. Shoving the hatch open, she was out in a flash. Once on the platform she turned and yelled, "Better boogie out, sweetie. Those guys are right behind you."

Cat and the rest of the crew acquitted themselves well, but it still took several minutes to get to the escape baskets. Cat got to slap the paddle releasing her basket but had no desire to get in it. The drill brought home how dangerous this job was, but the risk was worth it. *I want to take that big ride.*

The next morning, the team met for a breakfast debriefing. Matt made the point that sooner or later, somebody needed to go down in the basket, with suitable protective gear. He was not volunteering.

He spoke to Cat after the meeting. "What did you think of the orbiter?"

"I think it'll be much more comfortable in orbit, Matt. Heading back to Houston?"

"I have one more day here with medical meetings. Then I drive my rental car across Florida to Tampa tomorrow. I have a cheapie NASA contract airline flight back to Texas."

"Oh, you poor guy," Cat said. "Couldn't you find a T-38 seat?"

"Flight surgeons are far down the list for that, Cat, but I do get them back to Houston after a shuttle launch. Sometimes, I get a round trip to El Paso for a flight in the shuttle training aircraft, if an astronaut doesn't need the back seat to bring back taco chips."

"Then you better be nice to everybody, Dr. Wallace."

"Always, Dr. Riley, always."

Flight Day Nine
USAF C-141 Starlifter
Enroute to USSR

The Starlifter carrying NASA's go-team had left Ellington Field near JSC at 0800, with a planned arrival at the Soviet Union's Baikonur Cosmodrome the next morning. Somewhere over the Arctic, Matt tapped Lisa on her shoulder as she dozed, stretched out across several of the Spartan military transport seats. "We're doing an aerial refueling, and there's still enough light to see it, if you want to watch," Matt said.

"Catch me on the next one," Lisa mumbled.

"Don't know if there'll be one. Pilot says it depends on the winds. Sleep tight." Matt lingered to look at her peaceful face, nearly asleep. It took him back to their time together in New Orleans. *It's so nice to have her on the team and so hard to keep it professional. I hope we have time alone to talk about something other than this FUBAR mission.*

After watching the aerial ballet of a midair refueling from the back of the cockpit, Matt went back into the cavernous belly of the Starlifter. It had the cool, musty smell of military transport webbing and $100-per-foot rope. He sat down next to Stas Komarov, who was reading Tom Clancy's novel *The Cardinal of the Kremlin*. The Russian liaison looked professorial, with a bald pate and a little goatee.

"What do you make of your travel accommodations?" Matt asked in broken Russian.

"Ha, Dr. Wallace," Stas said in English. "This would be first class on Aeroflot."

Matt continued in Russian, "I've been wanting to ask you about the . . . air door . . . on *Buran*. You didn't say much about it in your talk."

"Air door? Oh, you mean air lock. We got something from Soviet Navy."

Alarmed, Matt's Russian failed him. "You got a diving airlock for this mission?"

"My little joke, Dr. Wallace. You're always making them, no? Soviet technicians are installing an airlock designed for use with docking to *Mir* space station."

"By that, you mean—designed and built, not tested?"

"Much on this mission is not tested. It has been pressure tested, of course. We are not docking, anyway."

"I wish we could, Stas. That would make things so much easier. What does the Kremlin think of Tom Clancy? Do you need to hide that book when we get to the USSR?"

"The KGB loves your Mr. Clancy. His books tell them much about your CIA. I'll give this one to them when I finish."

That wasn't the answer Matt was expecting, but he didn't know much about Ronald Reagan's "Evil Empire"—nor could he ever discern where Stas's facts ended and his sarcasm began. He seemed to always be smiling. Matt did not feel like smiling much of the time. The USSR and USA were cooperating on this rescue, but he needed to be mindful of what he said, did, and saw.

"Your English is much better than my Russian, Stas. I hope you will be around for the launch and recovery."

"Definitely, Doctor. After all," Stas said with an impish grin and a finger point, "I am supposed to watch *you*." He added in Russian, "I also believe you understand my language better than you let on."

♦

Before trying to get some sleep, Matt met with Lloyd, Kurt, Sharon, and Linda to review their plans after landing. Kurt was squinting at the sheaf of papers in his hands. "Why is it so dim on these damn transports?"

Matt said, "Kurt, put on your reading glasses. You and I both know you need them. It does not diminish your super astronaut status one iota. Even John Young uses them."

"Yeah, but he walked on the moon. Awright." Putting on his cheaters, Kurt ran through the day of landing. "After we land—somewhere—we're shuttled to our accommodations in Leninsk, which is the nearest city to the Baikonur Cosmodrome."

"We'll be exactly twelve hours ahead of Houston—maximum jet lag," added Lloyd, with his eyes closed. Noted for being able to fall asleep anywhere and anytime, Matt thought he was already slumbering.

Kurt shook his head. "Lisa and her two techs need to hit the ground running. Our launch window is only four days after we arrive. Stas says their launch crew needs a minimum of two days with the vehicle erect on the pad, and they've got to railroad it over to their pad whatever . . . launch complex 110." He pointed at a spot on a map of the cosmodrome he had in his papers. "A few kilometers away is their Yubileyniy runway complex, where the vehicle will land."

Matt laughed. "So, they named their runway 'Jubilee'? I'll be extremely jubilant when I see the crew back on Mother Earth."

"I sure hope me and the suit techs get the time we need with this *Buran* vehicle before launch," Sharon said.

She had her unruly mane of hair pulled back in a ponytail. *How does she get that hair stuffed into her space helmet with any room left for her head?* Matt wondered.

Kurt turned to him and asked, "Have you decided who is going to Kaliningrad?"

"As crew surgeon I will stay at the cosmodrome to be there when *Buran* returns. Lisa, her crew, and cameraman Randy stay with me. Lloyd and everyone else should be at the Soviet mission control. They call it 'the TsUP.' At least you'll have good communications there."

Sharon chuckled. "I'm going to be doing a lot of pointing and drawing if those *Buran* guys don't speaka da English."

"Stas knows who they picked for the crew, but he isn't sure about their language skills yet, Sharon. We'll meet them soon enough," Kurt said.

We are going to need Sharon's good humor on this mission, Matt thought. *Plans made in haste usually don't go well in the space biz, but she always makes everyone feel like things are going to work out.*

Flight Day Ten
Intrepid

Hayes looked into the payload bay from the aft cockpit station. He was getting his lesson on how to pilot a space shuttle in orbit from Dominick. Hayes gently pulled on one of the controllers for a few seconds. The shuttle began to flip, tail over nose, until the payload bay faced earthward.

"You overshot, but not bad for an army guy," said Dom. "I'll mail you your diploma."

Hayes turned to Dom. "I've been numbed by what's been happening to us, for self-preservation reasons. It's real to me now; we may get out of this alive."

"I know what you mean. I'm grateful we now have plenty to keep us occupied until the rendezvous."

"There's still a lot to do. In fact, it's time for EMU school, starring Jack and Hayes. See you on the middeck."

Hayes disappeared through the floor hatch. He saw that Jack was already pulling his space suit out of its storage spot in the airlock. "I'm glad mission control decided not to plan this rescue by cramming three EMUs into the airlock. They said they tested it in the WETF, and it could be done. But doing it with two first-timers *ever* in the suits would not be a good idea."

Jack started unfolding his EMU. "That does leave me outside with the airlock door shut, but I can make a run for the Russians if I get a suit issue. I'd say that is the least of our worries."

The commander and pilot floated in. Terry did not look enthusiastic. "How are you going to fit a big guy like me into that little suit?"

Flight Day Eleven
Baikonur Cosmodrome
Kazakhstan, USSR

"The Soyuz rockets launch from a different area than Energia, don't they, Stas?" asked Kurt. The NASA group was riding in a troop carrier on its way to the *Buran* processing building for a careful look at the vehicle. No one had been able to accomplish much yesterday after their long flight, although Lisa and her team had woozily scoped out the Soviet space vehicle's payload bay before jet lag forced them to retire.

"Yes, Soyuz launches are from different launch complex. The Soyuz system is very good, very reliable . . . but for me, there is also sadness to speak of them. My father was Vladimir Komarov." Stas looked around. "I see you do not recognize the name. He died in the first Soyuz manned mission, in 1967—not long after your Apollo 1 fire that claimed the lives of three of your astronauts."

Lisa leaned over and touched his arm. "I'm so sorry, Stas. We had no idea. The early Soviet space program wasn't well publicized in our country, especially if something went wrong. What happened?"

Kurt spoke up. "His parachute didn't open, and his Soyuz capsule crashed to earth. That's about all we ever knew."

"You are correct, Lisa. There was much secrecy in the early days. Everyone was in a hurry; the Soyuz capsule was not fully tested or developed, but the Politburo was caught up in the moon race and under much pressure to launch. Everyone knew it, my father included. He asked for an open casket funeral before he left."

Good lord, only the Russians are that fatalistic, thought Matt. "I do remember your father now, as the first in-flight space fatality. What a tragedy; he was a real hero. Most people feel the Apollo 1 fire happened because of that same kind of programmatic pressure. Americans today don't see the moon race for what it really was—another battlefield in the Cold War."

"Everything went wrong on my father's flight," said Stas. "There was supposed to be a second Soyuz launch and rendezvous the next day, but a solar panel failed on my father's ship, then his navigation system. He overcame everything, but on reentry the main parachute did not deploy, and the manual chute became tangled when he released it. The retro rockets were firing after the capsule hit the ground!" Stas was visibly upset by revisiting his father's death. "I became a space engineer to honor him and to make sure no other brave cosmonauts suffered his fate at the hands of clowns."

"You are certainly doing your part to save a crew of space travelers now," Matt said.

"Perhaps." Stas looked away. "We are at the MIK OK, the processing building. Ladies off first. Your team has twenty-four hours, Lisa, before we must move *Buran* to be mated to the Energia rocket. It will be much easier to work in this building."

"Did you give your techs the specs on our power requirements for a battery recharge?" she asked.

Stas made a fist wrapped around his opposite index finger. "They are making an adaptor as we speak. Your little MMU cradle needs to be installed quickly. We still must take the *Buran* stack to the fueling facility before it can go to the pad."

Matt was gazing up at the vehicle that was eerily *not* his country's space shuttle. *This is surreal. Neither country has done anything like this.*

"Stas, we must be honest with each other," Kurt said. "How much pressure is this direct-insertion-launch mission putting on your timeline? Are you hurrying things as much as it looks?"

"We are moving along at the proper pace, Kurt. Our launch will be fine. After that, it is up to the gods of space."

"And those would be?"

"Gagarin, my father, Grissom, and all the others who have given their all for spaceflight," Stas said.

"I plan to do my part," Sharon said, "unless somebody gets in my way. When do we get to meet the crew?"

Stas pointed at three men who had just entered the servicing bay. "Here they are."

The three men wore flight suits with a military bearing, but each broke into a broad smile upon seeing Stas. After the obligatory Russian hugs, Stas said, "Ladies and gentlemen of NASA, meet the crew for the *Buran-Intrepid* rescue mission. Commander Nikolai Kondakova, pilot Colonel Fyodor Titov, and EVA specialist Gennadiy Tokalev." Each man gave a nod and a bow as his name was announced.

Titov, the pilot, spoke first. "We are all very pleased to meet you, and though these are difficult times we are still glad for the opportunity to help your astronauts. I speak English okay, good enough I hope to help Astronaut Sharon and the *Intrepid* crew when we are all together in *Buran*."

The commander said something in Russian to Stas that neither Matt nor Linda could catch. "This would be a good time," said Stas, "for everyone to get a tour of *Buran*. Lisa and her team can work while we take turns going into the crew module. Sharon can stay for a longer briefing when we are done. I would suggest she and translator Linda talk with Gennadiy to get acquainted. He and Sharon will be outside together, and I am sure they have much to discuss."

"Sounds good to me," said Sharon. "I need to show him our fantastic titanium telescoping rescue pole. I betcha they don't have one of those."

"Are you coming, Dr. Wallace?" asked Stas.

"Wouldn't miss this for the world, Stas. Lead on." *This sure isn't NASA,* thought Matt. *Having a bunch of greenhorns crawl around in the shuttle a few days before launch would not be allowed. Different culture entirely.*

July 1988
Thirteen months to launch
Kennedy Space Center
Banana Creek viewing area

Cat was elated, but exhausted. She and her cousin June were trying to manage a boisterous group of special needs children at the VIP shuttle launch viewing site in the dark. *Only seven minutes until Columbia lifts off.*

Cat was there to fulfill the promise she made to June during astronaut selection week the year before. June was a teacher in Orlando for kids with developmental problems, and as soon as she learned of Cat's selection as an astronaut, she began lobbying for a special event for her pupils. "Cat, what good is having an astronaut relative if you don't get to see a launch up close?" June had asked. The Banana Creek viewing site, with its bleachers and giant countdown clock, was about three miles from Launch Complex 39, and the closest anyone could safely watch a shuttle launch.

Although her training schedule for STS-92A was brutal, Cat wanted to see a night shuttle launch and decided to combine that with her cousin's field trip request. Cat admired June for the work she did with her students. *How does she keep up with them every day? I'm pooped, as usual. Why don't I ever save anything for myself?* She had asked a fellow astronaut to fly her to KSC in a T-38 that afternoon. He devised a reason for a short mission to the Cape, and here she was, chasing seven-to-ten-year-olds around in the dark.

"Now, Audrey, don't go too close to the water. There may be alligators down there," Cat said.

"Alligators! I wanna see them," Audrey said, aiming toward the creek.

June came to Cat's rescue. "All right, children, it's nearly launch time. Look at the big clock. It's time to sit down."

Cat had been taking care of others as long as she could remember. First it was her parents, and later, as a physician, it was everybody. She was always an afterthought to her parents, compared to her brother, their golden boy. When her older brother was drafted and later killed in Vietnam, her parents—and their marriage—fell apart. Nobody noticed that Cat was still alive as her parents drank and fought their way into early graves. She slavishly took care of them, even taking a semester off from college to try and keep the family intact. The only people that ever cared for her were her Louisiana kinfolk. Being close to them was a big part of why she had remained in the Houston area.

The joyous anticipation of June's kids was contagious, and for a few minutes Cat forgot the cost for her good deed. She loved children and mourned the brother who never lived to have any kids. *If you don't have your own kids, nieces and nephews are a good substitute. Will I ever have my own?*

Cat had promised to go to dinner with her loquacious astronaut colleague, even though all she wanted was a bowl of cereal and bed. And she had to be back at JSC by noon the next day for training. *No rest for good old me. You silly girl. Does this make you forget you are alone? When is somebody going to take care of me?*

The countdown approached zero and the crowd hushed, leaving only the sound of crickets and frogs. The shuttle was hidden by its gantry, but at lift-off the pad exploded in light to reveal the smoke and fury of the launch. In the first eight seconds after clearing the tower it rose at under one hundred miles per hour before leaping into the sky. Fifteen seconds later, Cat and the kids felt as much as heard a chest-rattling rumble as the sound pressure waves finally reached them. This was not an undemanding sound—it grabbed you by the shoulders and shook you. By the end of the first minute, the shuttle was lighting up the night and traveling at 1,000 mph.

Oooh yeah! I can feel that in my tushie. I so want to ride that beast. I can't believe my ticket is already punched. She smiled but felt drained as she helped June herd the little ones out to their bus. *When I make it through dinner, I can get some sleep.*

Flight Day Twelve
Baikonur Cosmodrome
Kazakhstan

"This ride is worse than a worn-out Jeep," Lisa said as they bounced down one of the cosmodrome's numerous interconnected roads. Lisa, Stas, and Matt were in a Soviet military vehicle, driven by a young soldier.

"You Americans are so soft," Stas said, turning around from the front seat. "This is a great ride. In any event, we don't have far to go. You will get the tour backwards. Our first stop is the landing complex site, where *Buran* will land on its return."

They couldn't arrive soon enough for Lisa. As her butt was reaching its limit, the six-story command center for *Buran*'s landing phase, the OKPD, loomed before them. She would be in its control room with Matt and Stas after the launch to monitor the flight and coordinate with Kurt and the rest of the team at the Soviet mission control outside Moscow.

"The high-quality runway is four and one half kilometers long," said Stas. "Piece of cake to land, as you say."

"What a coincidence. That's the same length as the Cape's Shuttle Landing Facility runway, aka gator tanning facility," Matt said.

"Not coincidence," said Stas. "We will come back tomorrow, so you can set up your postflight medical area."

"You don't have one already?" Matt asked.

Hesitating, Stas said, "We think it best if you set up your own area. Next stop, the Raskat launch complex."

The driver detoured from the direct route to pass by two shrines to the Soviet Union's most cherished space pioneers. Stas pointed at a tiny house with a green roof. "The Gagarin cottage is where Yuri stayed before becoming the first human to orbit the Earth. Next door cottage was for Sergei Korolev, the rocket engineering genius who made Gagarin's flight possible. They both died too young," lamented Stas, "like my father."

Lisa whispered to Matt about how run-down the cosmodrome looked, but she couldn't say much without Stas hearing them. She was still unsure when the little man was joking, and when he was honestly proud of what he was showing them.

When they reached the Raskat launch complex, Stas said, "Raskat means 'thunderclap.' You will believe name when you hear and see the Energia rocket launch, with *Buran* strapped on its back."

"A lot of this equipment looks like it's been here a long time, Stas. What was here before?" asked Matt.

"This site was built for the N1 lunar rocket program before it was cancelled. If Korolev had not died in 1966, there would be a Soviet flag on the moon, too. Maybe even first! As you know, with *glasnost*, our country has been more forthcoming about our sometimes inglorious space history. The N1 rockets kept blowing up."

"What are those giant tubes?" Lisa asked.

"Those are the escape chutes for the *Buran* crew, like the baskets at Kennedy Space Center for your shuttle. They lead to a big room underground, with lots of mattresses. Would you like to go down one? The guards do when they get bored."

"I'll pass on that, Stas. Can you take us to the orbiter processing building now? I need to check on my techs." Lisa looked at her watch.

"Certainly, Lisa. I hope they are done soon. *Buran* will be mated to the Energia rocket tonight and rolled to the fueling facility tomorrow."

"We can see all the hard work, Stas, and we're grateful."

"Some duties cannot be omitted. Please join us tomorrow for the ceremonial tree planting behind the cosmonaut quarters. Every Soviet crew does this before a launch. You can see Gagarin's tree, how big it has grown. Also, it is important to put a few coins on the rails, to be flattened as the *Buran* stack is rolled out to the launch pad. The crew is not allowed to see this—bad luck."

"I can't tell you NASA doesn't have its own superstitions," Matt said.

"Ah, yes," said Stas. "Apollo 13, whose command module exploded on April 13. No more thirteens for you! For similar reasons, we cannot launch anything on October 24. Two rocket explosions occurred on that date. There is also a tradition regarding the bus that takes the crew to the pad, which I need to advise Astronaut Maralow about."

◆

After Lisa checked on the technicians working to integrate the manned maneuvering unit with *Buran* for launch, she and Matt were returned to their hotel. Jeff and Rick, the techs, volunteered to stay in the primitive Soviet housing of "Proton City" back at the cosmodrome. Lisa and Matt would recharge at the better—-but still seedy—tourist hotel in nearby Leninsk. It was near the cosmonaut quarters, where the *Buran* crew were staying.

Both Lisa and Matt were still suffering from maximum circadian disruption, and as a countermeasure, Matt recommended they eat when the locals did. They did not feel hungry but had their driver stop by a small market for a takeout.

Everywhere they went, they were stared at. People would approach Matt and Lisa and ask if they needed anything or any help. The novelty of having real enemy Americans on display was the best entertainment in town. When asked why they were there, Matt always said, "Scientific exchange program."

Sitting down in Matt's room with their meal, Lisa asked, "What is this stuff, anyway?"

"A goat and cabbage local specialty, I believe. Don't ask—eat." This was the first time he and Lisa had been alone in a long time. "Nothing to compare to the cuisine in New Orleans." Lisa relaxed. She had been under tremendous stress, feeling the heavy responsibility for the MMU piece of the rescue scheme jigsaw puzzle. "Try a little local vodka. It can't make us feel any worse." He poured each of them a shot. "Lisa, how have you been? How's your family life in Colorado? You told me you wanted kids."

Lisa looked down at her strange meal, in an even stranger land. When she looked up, she said, "Actually, Barry and I are getting a divorce. We got married young, have grown apart, have different ideas about kids. You know, the usual. If I knew all the reasons, it might not have happened."

"Lisa, I'm so sorry. It's always sad when a marriage breaks up. There is no 'usual.' Why didn't you tell me this before now?"

"I really like you. I didn't want to suggest I wanted to"—she started to reach her hand across the table but stopped—"rekindle the fire we had."

Matt reached across the table and took her hand. "There's something I didn't tell you. My wife, Marion, died in a car wreck last year. I have nothing left but my work. There was no one to stop me from jumping on a plane and coming to this godless place and no one to go home to."

Lisa knew they were both exhausted. Neither was hungry, and they sat for a few minutes, gathering a measure of strength from each other as they held hands.

Buran launch
Baikonur Cosmodrome, Pad 37

The bus carrying the space travelers to the *Buran* launch stopped on the way to the pad. As the three cosmonauts prepared to leave the bus, Titov said, "Sharon, every cosmonaut gets out to"—he searched for the right word—"stops here to urinate on the right rear tire, in honor of Gagarin, who began the tradition. It's good luck, but women are exempt."

"Fyodor, Stas warned me about this. This is in the same category as the optional enema I was offered, per your standard procedure. I can tell you right now I'm not about to freeze my ass cheeks for y'all's entertainment. I'm not watching either, so don't you worry."

The cosmonauts took quite a while to unzip their suits and perform their ritual. Sharon used this time to look at her ride—the gargantuan rocket stack ahead of her. The main Energia rocket was taller than the shuttle's external tank, and there were four strapped-on boosters instead of the shuttle's two solid rocket boosters. The sky was clear, and the wind was howling. Apparently, it was always howling on the central steppe of Asia.

The *Buran* close-out personnel strapped the crew into their seats lying on their backs, the same as a shuttle launch. The Soviets called their flight deck the "command compartment," and there was a seat for Sharon. The switches labeled in the Cyrillic alphabet baffled her. *Nice to have a seat with windows, for a change,* she thought.

Titov had briefed her on what to expect at launch. She wasn't going to worry about what she could not control—her thoughts were about what would happen in orbit. *We're comin' to get ya, gang. Hang in there.*

Sharon was seated behind the commander and pilot, with Gennadiy Tokalev seated on her right at the flight engineer's station. She was surprised at how calm she felt. The crew were Russian, but they were her brothers. *I have more in common with these guys than most Americans.*

At T-9.9 seconds, she felt the four liquid hydrogen/liquid oxygen core rockets ignite, and six seconds later the four strapped-on kerosene/liquid oxygen engines kicked in. With more thrust and payload than the US shuttle configuration, the heavy stack lifted slowly from the launch pad, but accelerated rapidly. The vehicle performed a roll maneuver to the proper heading after clearing the tower and was on its way to meet *Intrepid*.

Plenty of shaking, but a smoother ride without solid rocket boosters, thought Sharon. She felt the g-forces increase to three times that of Earth. *Please, God, let this thing get me to the church on time.*

After about two and half minutes, the strapped-on boosters fell away. Stas had told Sharon the Zenit rockets parachuted to a soft landing on flamingo nesting territory, but the birds' breeding season was over. She was surprised the Russians gave a hoot about where their rockets landed, beyond landing in the Soviet Union. *Right now, I don't give a damn. I have a job to do.*

The central Energia rocket shut down shortly before the eight-minute mark. The Soviet orbiter separated from the Energia core, leaving the spent rocket to land somewhere in the Arctic Ocean. *Buran* was in orbit and on the chase. Sharon knew from experience when she was free to leave her seat and help with the on-orbit chores. She was going to do her part, and they were going to get this rescue done.

Flight Day Fifteen
Intrepid + Buran *formation*

"Howdy, strangers." The crew of *Intrepid* heard the voice of Sharon Maralow over their UHF radio system. "We got yer pizza delivery. Exact change only, please."

Intrepid was tail first to its orbital path, as the orbiter routinely flew "backward" to protect the windows from any space debris in its path. As it chased them, *Buran* had grown from a tiny speck to a spaceplane while remaining in the same spot through the front cockpit window. This was visual confirmation it was on a rendezvous course with *Intrepid*.

"Sharon, so good to hear your Okie twang," Dom said. "The Russians will apparently let anybody fly. Are—"

Terry cut him off. "Houston, can you confirm radio contact with *Buran* through Russian mission control?" He was seated in the cockpit, ready to maneuver *Intrepid*.

"Yes, *Intrepid*. Real-time translation back and forth to Russian control in the TsUP. There's a time delay, but we've been working with it." Again, Liz was on the CAPCOM console in mission control. The wake-up music that morning was *The Blue Danube*, recalling the waltzing space vehicles of *2001: A Space Odyssey*. The two spacecraft in orbit were in a choreography demanding perfection by both dance partners, dance partners whose governments had been locked in a Cold War for forty-five years.

Buran had burned its orbital control rockets to match the orbit of *Intrepid*. The Soviet orbiter progressively slowed its approach and aimed for one hundred meters below and behind the US shuttle.

Neither vessel had a computer program onboard for what they were attempting.

"Good day to you, Commander Rogers," said a new voice on the radio. "I'm looking forward to shaking your hand. This is pilot Colonel Fyodor Titov of the spaceship *Buran*, at your service. Commander Kondakova will be bringing our ships together."

"Colonel Titov, I also look forward to meeting you face-to-face," answered Terry. "*Intrepid* and her crew appreciate your efforts on our behalf, and we're ready to go to work. We'll monitor your approach with radar and call out our relative positions."

Sharon came back on. "Houston is worried we will get confused out there, so they want call signs: Gennadiy Tokalev is 'Snow1' and I'm 'Snow2'. Hayes and Jack will keep EV1 and EV2. We'll stick with names for the short crossover of Terry, Dom, and Cat. Got that?"

Hayes replied, "Roger. I am no longer confused. We look forward to your delivery, Snow2."

Commander Kondakova slowly brought *Buran* into trail of the American shuttle, matching *Intrepid*'s speed without approaching too closely. Both commanders knew the limits of their maneuvering fuel and conserved every gram.

"We're getting our act together over here, *Intrepid*," said Sharon, "reconfiguring the cabin for the upcoming EVAs. The TsUP in Russia is happy, and we're all going to eat, sleep, and get ready for tomorrow's special activities."

"*Intrepid* and *Buran*, Houston. Everybody's cleared for EVA prep for tomorrow. Loss of comm signal in about two. Any questions?"

I've got lots of questions but none you can answer, Liz, Cat thought.

Flight Day Sixteen
Intrepid + Buran

"*Intrepid*, Houston." Liz was back as CAPCOM after the crew's sleep cycle. "You are go for final rendezvous with *Buran*. Keep it cool, guys, and have a good time."

In the middeck, Hayes turned to Dom. "Liz left out 'good luck.'"

"No wave-off or go-around on this one," said Dom. "We get one shot, but we're damn ready."

They helped Jack get into his EMU and sealed him in the *Intrepid* airlock by himself. NASA flight rules prohibited such a procedure, but it was only the beginning of the unrehearsed and perilous practices required by this rescue.

"EV2, this is EV1," said Hayes. "How copy?"

"It's lonely in here, EV1, but I can't wait to get outside," Jack said. "I have a hot date. Are you on the loop, Snow2?"

"Loud and clear, EV2," answered Sharon. "Hey, I wish I had Snow White for a call sign—always wanted to be a princess. I'm rarin' to go, inside our hosts' docking module. Their airlock can extend to make it bigger. We'll use the hatch that goes into the payload bay. Gennadiy, Snow1, is here, too. It's a tight fit with our goody bag, but we're ready."

At the RMS station, Cat said, "With all those suit parts and the radar-assist mat, it would be snug in there. I can see the tunnel extension sticking out of the payload bay, as you get closer." Every muscle in her body was knotted. *I need to relax before I get a cramp.* She watched the slowly approaching *Buran*. It looked nearly identical to the shuttle, creeping closer in absolute silence, like being trailed by their own ghost. *It'd be nice if we could mate.*

Intrepid's payload bay faced the Earth and was orbiting in an attitude that was ninety degrees off its direction of flight, with the right wing leading the way. The Russian vehicle was coming up from a slightly lower orbit, with an attitude that would leave it clocked at ninety degrees to *Intrepid* when it finally stopped, with their payload bays facing. This configuration would prevent the tails from striking, keep each ship's maneuvering jets from impinging on the other, and bring the airlock hatches within meters of each other.

Mission control called the commander before losing communications. "We know you'll be shutting down your antenna soon, so if you have a question, relay it through Snow2. We're all going into breath-hold mode now, so let us know to exhale ASAP."

Cat brought the RMS over to the airlock, and Hayes came up to the flight deck. The spacewalkers on both vessels began their egress, with Jack taking up a spot on the RMS foot restraint and Sharon donning the MMU. The Russians wanted to install a mat with radar-reflective markings on the floor of *Intrepid*'s payload pay. The markings would allow *Buran*'s navigational computer to automatically station-keep with the shuttle. Although they were only meters apart, the two spacecraft were still in different orbits, and *Intrepid* was orbiting at a slightly slower speed.

Sharon said, "Snow1 is going to stay tethered and will be responsible for the extension of the rescue pole." The pole would be a telescoped out from *Buran*'s bay toward *Intrepid*, and although flimsy, it provided a place to tether a space suit.

With her MMU checked out, Sharon slowly approached Jack until they almost touched. "I can't shake your hand in this MMU, much less give you a hug," she said. "But it sure is good to see your face."

Jack was grinning ear-to-ear. "Miss Maralow, I've never been so happy to see another person's face. Welcome aboard *Intrepid*." They gazed intently into each other's eyes, and Jack saw Sharon's determination. Hundreds of miles above the earth, it was a tiny celebration of the best of humanity.

Terry's voice broke their reverie, "EV2, Snow2, get that mat going! We need to optimize propellant use while in formation." Addressing the others in the cockpit, he said, "The mat's a goddamn waste of time. They are showing off their tech." Terry was frustrated at ceding control of the situation to the Russians, but his job was to observe and breathe from a portable oxygen tank, in preparation for his spacewalk. He and Dominick took turns manning the rear flight deck station, ready to move *Intrepid* at the first hint of a problem.

Jack unfurled the two-meter-square mat, fastening it to the payload bay floor with Sharon's help. Gennadiy unstowed the large bag of EMU parts from the *Buran* airlock. By the time the radar mat was installed, they had already been outside an hour.

Inside *Buran,* pilot Titov announced, "Standby *Intrepid*. We are initiating autopilot radar-based navigational control. Very low power; no one gets cooked." There was a small puff of *Buran's* control jets, and the vehicle moved a few meters closer to its crippled partner.

Gennadiy extended the rescue pole toward *Intrepid,* and Cat brought Jack to him. They couldn't speak to each other directly. Jack thought a wave would look silly, so he gave a salute, which Gennadiy returned. After Jack had tethered himself to the bag of EMU gear, Gennadiy released his own attachment. Cat brought Jack and bag back to the airlock.

"We put extra LiOH canisters in the bag, too, in case the cabin was getting a little stuffy," Sharon said. "Putting on an EMU is hard work." Jack put the equipment into *Intrepid's* airlock and sealed the outer hatch door, cutting off any emergency return if he developed a suit problem.

Inside, Terry and Dom got ready to put on space suits for the first time. They would need at least another hour of suit checkout before they left the airlock. After Dom had put on his cooling and ventilation undergarment, he went to one of the middeck lockers and pulled out a transparent EVA contingency container. He had placed the mouse experiment in it and obviously intended to seal it up and take them with him.

Terry, struggling with his own gear, noticed Dom after Hayes started laughing. "You—Are—Not—Going—To—Take—Those—Rats!"

"They deserve a rescue, too. They belong to those kids in Nebraska. At only a 10.2 pressure differential, they can make it over in a vacuum without this sack popping."

Hayes grabbed Dom by the shoulders. "What is it with you, Dom? Did your mom forbid you a pet rodent?"

"Yes, but that's only part of it."

"As you pointed out, Terry, time is of the essence," Hayes said. "I know Dom will promise to jettison these little guys at the first sign of any interference with our mission, which is saving our asses. Let's get your lower torso on."

Cat heard the exchange on the intercom from the flight deck. *We need to get out of here. We're all going crazy.*

◆

Still on the Canadarm foot restraint, Jack attached a tether to the D ring on Dom's waist as he exited the airlock. "Welcome to the outside, Dom," Jack said. He immediately noticed Dom's murine bandolier, and that the mice seemed to be tolerating the trip. Jack started to say something about Dom's cargo but thought better of it. He didn't want the *Buran* pilot to become distracted and start asking questions.

Cat moved them both over to the escape pole. Dom transferred his tether to the pole, and with Sharon backing him up, he moved toward the *Buran* airlock. She said, "Dom, Snow2. Snow1 will help you enter the airlock."

While Dom was entering the Soviet docking module, Jack helped Terry out of the *Intrepid* airlock. Terry's suit fit was not as good as Dominick's. "I'm sweating," he said, "and my visor has started to fog."

"Let's do a suit purge; that will improve things." Jack pushed the commander's purge button to run a high flow of oxygen through his suit and past his visor, as Cat moved them to the pole. "Can you see well enough to move over to the docking hatch? Snow2 can help you."

"I can see better now—but I won't be satisfied until all my crew is in one place again," said Terry.

"We're right behind you, Terry," replied Jack. "Only a few more logistics to take care of." Jack waited outside with Gennadiy while Sharon crammed into the *Buran* airlock with the other two Americans. Sharon needed to remove the life support backpack from Terry's suit and attach it to Cat's smaller suit for her crossing with Hayes.

Cat watched as Sharon, their commander, and their pilot entered the *Buran* airlock hatch and the door was sealed. Jack was working his way along the pole from *Buran* back to *Intrepid*.

Cat noticed the nose of *Buran* pitching away from them, slowly at first, but accelerating. Hayes's reaction time was fast enough on the *Intrepid*'s tiller to break formation and keep *Buran*'s tail from striking his vessel. He could not move fast enough to prevent *Buran*'s wayward rotation from whacking the rescue pole against the side of *Intrepid*. The pole bent but did not break, and its recoil sent the tethered Jack to the end of his line like a child's paddle-and-ball toy.

The next seconds spiraled into chaos. Cat heard Sharon, now back inside *Buran,* yell, "A thruster's stuck open!" There was shouting in the background as Nikolai and Fyodor struggled to stabilize their ship. As *Buran* gyrated, it brought Jack—at the end of his tether—back around to *Intrepid.* Hayes struggled to maneuver faster, but it was too late—Jack's head slammed into the Ku-band antenna deployed from the side of *Intrepid.* Cat and Hayes felt the sickening thud as Jack's helmet was breached. Unconscious, Jack's life ebbed away in the vacuum of space. Hayes wanted to suit up, go after him, something, anything . . . but he dared not leave the controls. The relative motion of the two vehicles briefly spared them the gruesome view of Jack's body.

The impact with Jack broke *Intrepid*'s dish-shaped antenna off at its base, and it drifted away. Cat and Hayes watched as *Buran* slowed its rotation. Nikolai was using all the vehicle's thrusters to counteract the rogue unit blasting away at full bore. They heard Sharon sobbing over the UHF radio, "Jack! Jack! What happened to Jack?"

◆

Kurt Robertshaw and his crew were listening to the TsUP communications, with the help of Linda, the translator. Kurt was tense but optimistic, as things had been going smoothly so far. His team's feed to mission control in Houston was intermittent and went down every few minutes. Then the quiet order of the Kaliningrad mission control center was obliterated as all the controllers in the TsUP erupted, shouting into their mikes.

"Linda . . ." Kurt said, but she held up her hand.

"It's hard to understand," she said, listening to her headset. "Something is wrong. Thruster stuck open . . . Vehicle spin slowing now . . . How long can it run? Twenty minutes and it melts . . . Fuel draining away . . . Options . . ." Linda shook her head. "I'm not able to fully follow the conversa—Cross-range landing at eastern abort site possible if deorbit now . . . Will not get another chance . . . Astronaut killed . . . Pull him in, jettison pole, close doors . . . Abort now. Synchronize retrograde burn to vehicle rotation . . . Dump propellant when aerodynamics . . ." Linda looked in horror at the Americans with her. "They're aborting the rescue. Their own vehicle is in trouble. Someone is dead!"

"What about *Intrepid*? Did Cat and Hayes get off? They couldn't have . . ." Kurt fell back in his chair. Houston was completely out of the loop. Their line was dead.

◆

Hayes had successfully moved *Intrepid* a hundred meters from *Buran*, which was slowly turning end over end. All of *Buran*'s maneuvering thrusters were firing, causing the vehicle to look as if it had grown whiskers fore and aft. Nikolai and Fyodor were regaining control. Sharon's strained voice returned over a background of barked Russian. "*Intrepid,* the Russian's are pulling the plug. We have to deorbit now or never. Maybe we can make it to some goddam Siberian runway and survive. If I thought it would make any difference, I'd whack 'em all with a two-by-four, but I don't know if we can even save ourselves." There was a low thumping background noise as *Buran* fired its ODU engines to begin the deorbiting process. "Hayes, Cat, don't give up! There's always a Plan B. Houston won't give up! God bless you. See you back at the base." Her voice belied her words.

Cat watched with Hayes as Gennadiy—who had managed to stay inside *Buran*'s payload bay during the disaster—reeled in Jack's body. *Buran*'s left payload bay door was already closing, and the orbiter rapidly began to fall behind *Intrepid*. They saw its ODU engine fire again. Hayes and Cat had not spoken to each other since Jack's death.

"Hayes, Cat, this is Terry. Before we lose comm . . ." Their commander's voice was fading into static as the handheld radio moved out of range. "I let you down. I'm sorry. I should have been the last to leave."

Cat keyed her mike. "Commander, it's been an honor serving with you. Please make it home safely with our blessings."

"Bad things sometimes happen to good astronauts, Commander," Hayes said. "Godspeed."

Terry's reply was garbled static. Cat and Hayes moved together and held each other tightly. They floated in the cockpit for a long time.

"Pray for the mice, Hayes," Cat whispered. "May St. Jude get them home." She could not mention the names of her friends.

Flight Day Sixteen
OKPD Control Center
Baikonur Cosmodrome

At the *Buran* landing site, Matt knew there had been an abrupt change to the mission status, without a full understanding of what the controllers were saying. He had been talking regularly with Patel, Kurt, and the others at the TsUP outside Moscow despite frequent dropouts and redials. Matt hailed them on the line. "Lloyd! Kurt! What the hell is going on?" There was no reply.

Matt looked to Stas for an answer. Stas was listening intently to the comm loops and slammed his fist down on the table. The mask of control dropped from his face. "One of *Buran*'s forward thrusters is stuck open. It's out of control. They are using all the other jets to try and regain stability. This is very bad, very bad." He turned to the cabinet behind him and pulled out a bottle of vodka. Unscrewing the top, he took a long drink, offering it to the Americans paralyzed by shock.

"Events are happening quickly. *Buran* cannot be in this state for long. They must abort now if they can."

Lisa managed to ask, "What about the people doing EVA? What about *Intrepid*? Cat and Hayes are still onboard!"

Stas ignored her questions, while he spoke rapidly into his headset. Randy, the photographer, began taking pictures of the control room, including the screen showing the positions of *Buran* and *Intrepid* as little cartoon shuttles moving across the map. No one paid any attention, and no one stopped him.

Stas took another swig from his bottle and slammed the bottle down. "Idiots! The generals are idiots! I told them so. I tried to warn them!"

Matt was stunned but forced himself to grab Stas's arm. "Stas, what about our crew?"

Stas calmed himself, but his voice was flat and intense as he said, "One of your crew died outside the vessels. Two are left onboard your shuttle. The rest seem to be safely inside *Buran*. The immediate deorbit burn gives *Buran* a chance to land at our eastern alternate runway, a place called Khorol, which is two hundred kilometers north of Vladivostok. It will be at the very edge of our vehicle's cross-range capability. Fyodor and Nikolai must get our shuttle under control if they're to make it to the runway. Otherwise, God only knows where they will end up."

"Who is dead, Stas?" Matt's voice was weak.

"Your Colonel Badger, I think. I'm so sorry. I hope the others can land safely." They looked up to the screen showing the cartoon shuttles separating. "The controllers here will try to help. There is specialized navigation equipment at Khorol Aerodrome to help guide *Buran*. Khorol is at least 3,500 kilometers away from us. There is nothing else we can do." He took another long draft of vodka.

"Stas," Matt said, "what did you mean you tried to warn them?"

"It doesn't matter now . . . this mission . . . the original mission . . ." Stas was struggling with what to say. Finally, he blurted, "This was supposed to be an unmanned mission again. *Buran* is not ready. During test firings of the *Buran* thruster propulsion module six months ago, the valves did not close properly. The thruster was stuck in firing mode. They claimed it was fixed, but I know they were too rushed. It happened again today."

"If you weren't ready for man-rating, Stas, why make the offer you did?" Lisa asked. She could barely speak between sobs.

"Politics. Stupid little men and their politics, always in a hurry. Just like what killed my father! Chairman Gorbachev came to visit

Baikonur again last year. He was not impressed with the *Buran* program. Money is tight. Generals and directors at Gromov Flight Research Institute were worried their project will be cancelled. They were probably right. Then, your shuttle gets marooned in space. Gromov chief tells Gorbachev, 'Hey, we can go get them with *Buran*. Americans will look weak. We will look like great Soviet Union.' Great Soviet bullshit! The chairman believed them."

One of the Russian flight controllers came over to speak to Stas, but Matt could not hear what they were saying. Stas was red faced. He put his bottle back into the cabinet. "One of the big shots I talked about is coming over to sit with us while *Buran* is landing. It will all be over, one way or the other, in about an hour. Please don't mention my . . . explanations. It doesn't matter now. It is what it is. Besides, NASA was desperate. It wouldn't have made any difference."

Like hell, it wouldn't have. Matt was seething, but now was not the time to boil over. His throat was so tight he could scarcely breath. He still couldn't get his friends in Moscow on the line. He wanted to know what happened to Jack. He couldn't accept that Jack was dead. A guard came over, confiscated Randy's camera, and escorted him from the building. Lisa was crying more softly.

January 1990
California Institute of Technology
Pasadena, California

Richard Feynman answered the phone in his Caltech office. "Professor Feynman, Howard Baker here. We met once, many years ago, there in California. How are you?"

Feynman had been expecting to hear from the former senator. "I'm okay, thank you, but I know you did not call to inquire about my health."

"As you know, Professor, I was recently appointed by the president to chair the commission tasked with looking at the causes and consequences of the recent *Intrepid* shuttle mishap."

"Mishap, yes. That is putting it mildly. I am sure NASA as well as the president would like to know all the reasons why *Intrepid* was lost."

"That's why I'm calling, Professor. I'd like you to be on the President's Commission. Former astronauts Sally Ride and Neil Armstrong have already accepted."

"I've already turned down this invitation from the NASA administrator. I've spent my life trying to avoid Washington and politics, Senator. I will be honest with you. I have not been well. This would be asking a lot of me at this stage in my life. It could do me in."

"I won't bullshit you, Professor. We need you. There's going to be a lot of pressure to whitewash this situation. I need someone who is not political, not ex-NASA, and who has a scientific mind to look at the fundamentals that others cannot see. I think you're uniquely qualified in this regard."

"I have heard that you are a good negotiator, Senator. All right, I will accept. I owe it to my country. I hope you won't regret your decision."

"Why would I do that, Professor?"

"If I don't think you're doing a good job, I'll say so."

"I hope you do, Professor; I really hope you do."

PART TWO

Flight Day Sixteen
Intrepid

*B*uran was gone. Jack was gone. At eight thousand meters per second, they weren't going anywhere. Silence enshrouded them on the flight deck. There was no communication with Houston. Hayes was doing everything he could to reconfigure the cockpit audio panel, but there was no response. The loss of the Ku-band dish antenna when Jack was killed had been the final blow to their already crippled comm system.

"Houston, *Intrepid*. Do you read?" he asked for the hundredth time.

Cat floated in the neutral body posture humans naturally assume in zero-g with her back, knees, and elbows slightly flexed. In a happier moment, Jack had joked that it resembled sitting in an invisible recliner chair watching television. Tears were welling up in her eyes, fogging her vision. She shook her head violently.

"Hey, it's raining in here," Hayes said. He pulled a handkerchief from his pocket to wipe her eyes. She moved her head away but took the cloth and wiped her face.

"If you don't need any help, I'm going to the middeck. I need to be alone. Can you leave me be awhile?" Cat moved through the deck hatch without waiting for an answer.

Cat needed to escape from the vortex of despair that was swirling around her. She usually tried never to feel sorry for herself. Didn't have time for it. *Damn it, that's all I have now—plenty of time to dwell on things. I can't believe Jack died. Alan is dead. Mom and Dad are dead. Now me.* She took deep breaths and slowly stopped crying, using a wipe to wash her face. *Stop it! I cried, and I'll grieve, and I'll get on with my job.* She was a survivor and would not curl up in a ball and passively await her fate.

Later

"I can't believe that after everything we've been through, it's come to this," Cat said. "With no comm, we don't even know if our crewmates made it home."

"I admit our situation is off nominal right now."

Cat smirked. "That's one way to put it, Major Understatement. Staying on that page, what is your revised NASA-approved contingency plan?"

"I fall back on my sports hero and noted philosopher, Yogi Berra. 'It ain't over till it's over.' New York Mets, 1973—bad start, but went on to win the National League pennant. Who's your sports hero?"

"Baseball is boring," she said. "My hero is Larry Bird. The Celtics are my team."

"Not the Houston Rockets? You do live there."

"I went to Yale Medical, but Boston is my town. Irish me loves the place."

"Okay, what's your favorite Celtics game so far?"

"I haven't had the time to watch recently, but Bird did play to perfection in game six of the NBA finals in '86—and beat the Rockets, by the way. My favorite game, though, is game seven of the 1981 conference finals against Dr. J and the Sixers. Boston had come back from a three to one deficit in the series and won the final game at the buzzer. They beat the Rockets in the finals that year, too."

"Wow, you really know your Celts."

"My dad was a big sports fan. I learned it from him. And you have a male chauvinist look of surprise on your face." This time she gave him a wry smile.

Ignoring her jab, he said, "There's your answer, then. Do the Celtics ever give up? Does Larry Bird quit? Aren't we still breathing, thinking, and hypercompetent humans? We have nothing to fear but—"

"I get it. We pick ourselves up and keep going. We have nothing to fear but a painful death from carbon dioxide poisoning or suffocation or maybe a quick incineration on reentry."

"We can't go into a tailspin, Cat. That's not us. Without communications, we don't know what options NASA may have left to help us. The Russian rescue preempted everything. Our job is to stay alive and do whatever we can for ourselves. Like keeping up with the shuttle housekeeping duties to the best of our ability. We're due for an IMU alignment now. We keep this bird alive, and she'll do the same for us. Until she runs out of gas, so to speak."

Cat sighed deeply. "Of course, you're right—we'll go down fighting. But if mission control had a viable alternative, they would've used it, instead of accepting help from the Soviets. We do have the extra LiOH cartridges that Jack and Sharon brought over, and with only two of us, we can make them last. We'll have plenty of time to choose how we go if it comes to that."

"We get to pick our end, like in *Ghostbusters*? I pick the marshmallow man."

"You do remind me of Bill Murray, and that's not a compliment."

"You are much sexier than Sigourney Weaver; that is a compliment."

"You should do the IMU alignment. I'll fix dinner." Cat disappeared into the middeck.

As Hayes ate his rehydrated creamed spinach and beef steak, he reviewed their options. "I keep coming back to a repair of the leading-edge panel. We only have one EMU and no parachutes, so no bailing out. You should eat more."

"Aren't you the one with the aeronautical engineering degree? Do you think *Intrepid* is going to crack open gently like an egg at forty thousand feet? No bailout—you got that right. Any other brainstorms?"

"We don't know anything about how the orbiter might fail with a breech in our wing panel—-nothing. That brings us to the lame idea that mission control sent up first: stuff the hole in the busted panel with every piece of sacrificial metal we can find. I still have Jack's tool kit. God, I wish we had Jack, too." Hayes grief silenced him. He looked directly into Cat's bright blue eyes and, taking a deep breath, he said, "We hold the metal filler in place with frozen water bags, and we have a piece of broken wing panel to stick back on somehow."

"I think your duct tape idea would hold about a millisecond after we hit the atmosphere."

"I don't believe Houston thought much of the filler scheme, either. Your turn. I know you've thought of our end game. Please, eat your applesauce."

"Don't tell me what to eat," Cat said. "You're right, we don't know exactly what will happen on reentry. Superhot plasma from our entry is going to wreck our right wing, but we don't know when. We implement the wing stuffing plan. We make sure we have our navigation straight, and do a deorbit as planned for Vandy but make sure we're over water—even if we must move the track west. We get to a low enough altitude to have control by aerodynamic surfaces, turn towards Vandy. You and I land it. No problemo, señor. If not,

♦ Ruthless Sky ♦

we scare some Canadian moose and land in the drink without hurting anyone." Cat ate a carrot and said, "These veggies are going bad. I don't know why they stuck the fresh fruit and veggie storage up by the heat of the avionics bay. We should finish them now."

"Don't tell me what to eat. I'm okay with our only scheme, but I don't want to pull the trigger on deorbit until we run out of resources. We should consider aiming for Edwards. It's only a little further inland, and its runways and dry lakebed are more forgiving than Vandenberg. Your hair looks great, by the way."

"Thanks. I put a lot of thought into a shorter hairstyle that wouldn't look like a human mop in zero-g. The pictures of Sharon Maralow and her long tresses in orbit make her look like the bride of Frankenstein. Guys have it so easy."

"No, guys do not have it easy, Cat. We live with women. Beautiful and difficult women like you make it even harder."

"No sympathy from me, Major Lothario. Edwards sounds fine, except we don't want to be coming apart over Los Angeles. Don't you have to go do a wastewater dump, or IMU alignment, or some such?"

"Yes, Captain Bligh. You do the dishes." Hayes went to the flight deck. Despite their circumstances, he felt oddly content.

Later

"I need to know something," Hayes said. "I'm not sure I want to, but I need to—did Jack suffer when the side of his helmet got knocked off? We train that a suit depressurization is survivable, if we can get repressurized quickly. Was he out there all alone, slowly dying?"

"I understand your concern, but are you sure you want to talk about this?"

Hayes nodded.

"I don't know if Jack got knocked out when his visor cracked open, but in any case, he was unconscious within fifteen seconds," Cat said. "All the air was sucked out of his lungs . . . and other unpleasant effects—but he never felt anything after the first few seconds of it. Didn't you ask during EVA training?"

"No. We were told only that we had a few seconds to fix the problem. What else happens?" Hayes asked.

"Are you thinking about taking a walk without your EMU?"

"It would leave more air for you. Buy you more time. And what if we can't deorbit? I don't want to suffocate. I want to know what happens."

"I don't need your air, thanks. Being in a vacuum is ugly. All the water boils off your tongue and mouth, and everything gets bulgy. That's all I'm going to say."

"I'd get a nice cremation when I reentered the atmosphere."

"I think Yogi Berra would be disappointed with you, not to mention Larry Bird." She touched the side of his head. "You didn't say it, but I know what's in your mind. If you had been at Jack's side, you couldn't have saved him. You need to believe that. You might've died, too."

"It's a relief to know Jack went quickly. He was such a generous, forgiving person. When I reached my limit with NASA, which was often, he let me bitch and rant with a sympathetic ear. He always came back with a snarky comment that brought me around. Most people didn't get a chance to hear his self-deprecating humor. If he were here, he'd say, 'As the only black crew member, I was the expendable one, like the *Star Trek* red shirts,' and then he'd laugh." Cat looked at him disapprovingly. "Truly," Hayes said. "He would have said that."

Cat wanted Hayes to continue despite her own heartache about Jack's death. "I never heard him complain about racism, at NASA or otherwise," she said. "He must have felt it keenly."

"He kept a certain distance, but we were friends," Hayes said. "I figured he never dated because, in NASA-world, with his schedule, he never met any eligible black women. He was very aware of being in redneck Texas cowboy land. We used to ride bikes together around Clear Lake in the early morning to avoid being fried by the Texas sun. One morning, we pulled up to a crosswalk near a school, and the auto traffic stopped for us to get across. I remarked it was nice of people stop for us. Jack said, 'They didn't stop for us, they stopped for you. I've been here many times and had to take my chances getting across.' Switching to his Mississippi country boy voice, he said, 'Ain't nobody ever stopped for me, brother.' That's the only time I ever heard him mention anything about racism. NASA is not a place for that kind of self-expression, and Jack had a stoic ethos."

"If Jack were here, he might say you're talking ignorant bullshit about things you know nothing about," Cat said. Mounting pressure in her chest made her ready to change the subject. "I'm not a stoic, but there is something Jack and I had in common. Both of us have lived and worked our entire lives in the world of white male privilege. It gets old. It gets really old. I beg you, do not start singing James Brown's 'It's a Man's World,' please."

Another Flight Day
Intrepid

"Men have always tried to control me," Cat said, as she turned to face Hayes.

"I see a thunderhead in your eyes," Hayes said, releasing her shoulders. They were on the flight deck, watching Earth pass beneath them. He had come behind her, and for a moment, she had been sitting in his lap. He began to put his arms around her. "Is that what you think I want to do—control you?" They were still very close.

"Yes, that's the nature of men, and you are definitely a guy."

"Have you always felt this way about men?" Hayes drifted away from her.

"That's been my life experience. It started with my father, a depression-era Irishman who made a success of himself. He didn't know what to do with me. Fitting me into his mold didn't work for either of us. I was tough, just like him. The counterculture of the sixties drove us apart."

"My father and I didn't see eye-to-eye about Vietnam or the hippies, either, but we did reconcile," Hayes said. "My going to West Point had a lot to do with that."

"I was never able to come to an understanding with either of my parents," Cat said. "When my brother was killed in the Battle of Hué during the Tet Offensive, they never recovered. They died of heartbreak and alcohol—in that order. At the end, Dad went out raging, as did my mother. Mom had always been an alcoholic, but Dad caught up with her quickly. I gave them a lot of my life—first, trying to please them, and then trying to save them."

"Please them? They weren't satisfied having a spectacular person like you for a daughter? What was wrong with them?"

"I've asked myself that question countless times. For years, I thought there was something wrong with me. Maybe it was my lack of a male sex organ."

"By all standards, you've overcompensated for that," Hayes said.

"Touché from the kettle, Mr. Pot. Doesn't that apply to all astronauts? What was your motivation? What were you trying to prove?"

"I was trying to prove I could be worthy of a woman like you," Hayes said. Chastened by Cat's "Really?" expression, he said, "I was trying to impress everybody, especially women, and, above all, avoid embarrassing myself. I liked the challenge of aviation and space, and I play to win." He held up his arms in mock surrender. "But then I slammed into your brick wall. I don't understand why you never let me get close enough for you to know me. You're not a cold or self-obsessed person." He paused. "There have been rumors about Sally Ride, about her living with another women after her divorce. If that's the case with you, I need you to tell me."

"Does that make Sally any less amazing? Do you have a problem with that?" Hayes shook his head. Leaning toward him, Cat lowered her voice. "Very well. Under the circumstances, I know I can trust your discretion." She whispered loudly, "I'm the most heterosexual person you'll ever meet. How egotistical to think the only reason a woman might not go for you is she's gay. What were you saying about self-obsessed?" She laughed as the heat rose in Hayes's face.

"Oh . . . that felt good," she said. I'll make a deal with you. I'll tell you my lonely hearts story if you go back to work on the radio."

Hayes frowned. "I've worked on that damn radio today until my eyes are crossed." Cat's face was wearing the look he classified as *Well, what then?* "All right, it's a deal," he said.

Cat took a deep breath. She opened her mouth but closed it again. Finally, she said, "I'm in love with a phantom. His name is Alan, and he's dead. I know he's gone. But my heart has its own agenda." Her eyes began to glisten. "He died two months before I was selected for the astronaut corps. He crashed his stupid little Pitts aerobatic airplane close to Ellington Field. The NTSB decided it was g-induced loss of consciousness. Doesn't matter if something broke on his plane or he passed out; he's still dead."

"That's a long time to grieve so deeply," Hayes said.

"Yes, I understand that intellectually. I've seen a good psychologist although I had to sneak around NASA so I wasn't labeled as a nut case. Alan was an airline pilot, and we were deeply in love. He treated me like a person, not a nice-looking woman. We weren't even together long enough to have a good fight and make up. In my darkest times, I wish I had gone down with him. I feel like a vile beast chewed up my heart and spit it out."

"You did crash with him. I can't compete with dead perfection. I'm an irresistible Romeo only in my own mind." Hayes shook his head. "I've never had to go through such a crushing tragedy. I hurt for you."

"The rest of the psychodrama? I feel vulnerable and couldn't stand to go through losing a love again—blah-blah. Plus, most professional men I meet are selfish jerks. It's much easier to devote my soul to NASA and my work. It was a pretty good plan until this mission."

Hayes reached for her hand, and she let him hold it. "Now would be a good time to let go of your pain. Let those memories go to a better place. Your heart is still frozen. It needs to thaw out. We've trained together for almost two years. Time enough for me to know you as a sweet and giving soul. You're a jewel, with so many facets. Let me love you, Catherine Riona Riley. I can promise you one thing."

Cat said nothing and raised her eyebrows.

"You won't regret it."

Cat said nothing.

"I won't leave you alone," Hayes said.

"Of course not—we'll both be dead," Cat said with mock disgust. Then she smiled. "Frozen—maybe—yes, but not frigid. Don't ever call me that. That's what presumptuous men say after I refuse their demand to sleep with them."

"You are the hottest woman in the solar system; I know there's a long line of suitors. But your mind is as beautiful as your heart. Few men are smart enough to keep up with you."

"Ah, but you can, Major Ego? You should be warned that most men who really get to know me discover I am trouble, capital T. Difficult, as you previously mentioned. Many suitors run away. Not worth it. Now it's time for you to go to work on the radio. I need to be alone."

Hayes went to the middeck to pretend to fix the unfixable as he, too, wanted to be alone with his own thoughts.

♦

Cat stared out the windows at the clouds over equatorial Africa. She could see desert to the north and thought of Alan. She smiled as she noticed the ache in her chest was diminished. *Maybe it's time to stop feeding the hole.*

Another Flight Day
Intrepid

Hayes extricated himself from deep in the middeck avionics bay. Somersaulting over to Cat, he said, "I wish this mission hadn't been so damn weight limited. I would have brought my ham radio walkie-talkie, and we would have some comm backup. There are thousands of amateur radio operators down there who could relay for us."

Cat was cleaning the cabin air filter. "I knew you were a ham, but not in the radio sense."

"WD5IAE, at your service: Dit-dah-dah. Dah-dit-dit. Dit-dit-dit-dit. Dit-dit. Dit-dah. Dit."

"I already knew you were ditzy."

"It's a sweet Morse code call sign using a telegraph key. I've worked all fifty states and many foreign countries. The space shuttle is a very desirable station to work—hams would line up for a conversation. No radio contact is more exotic than low earth orbit."

"Hams build their own radios, don't they? Can't you get creative here with *Intrepid*?"

"In my own defense, the shuttle's avionics are not designed for end-user tinkering. The designers used redundancy, not repairability, as a guide. One of the two audio central control units is fried. When Jack . . . When we lost the Ku-band dish, it may have caused more damage. I'm patching into the military AM/EVA radio to make blind calls. It's not tunable, but it does have the emergency military 243 MHz guard frequency built in. Lots of facilities monitor that."

"Range?" Cat asked.

"Hard to say. There aren't any trees in the way, but there isn't much power in this rig, and the antennas are probably fucked up. That's where the Morse code comes in. It can be heard when voice is unintelligible." Hayes floated around to behind Cat. "Can I borrow your barrette? The metal clasp will make a telegraph key of sorts."

"Okay, MacGyver. You're the ham."

Cat gave him her barrette, and Hayes fluffed her hair. He began to fiddle with the clasp. "Our best chance is over North America or Europe, but I'll take anybody, anywhere."

"What will you send?"

"CQ CQ SOS SOS DE *Intrepid* shuttle SOS SOS DE *Intrepid*, and then listen. I may not hear a reply right away, but next time around they might transmit back. Too bad we're not over any one place for very long. And our polar orbit means we don't often cross over the same spot. I'm going to complain about that in my report when we get back. I can't automate the transmissions, but I can put on a recording loop to listen. I used to have a good 'fist' for code, as they say, but having only your hair clasp as a telegraph key will cramp my style."

"And you having my barrette is cramping my hairstyle. We can take turns monitoring the frequency. If I hear something, I'll get you."

"We are over ocean a lot, so we shouldn't be tied up too much." Hayes started to go back to the flight deck to work with the audio controls.

"Before you go, help me clean up this mess in the middeck. It's starting to bug me."

Turning, Hayes said, "Looks okay to me. Your obsessive-compulsive side is showing."

Grabbing his shirt, Cat got in his face and said, "Listen, asshole, the last thing you ever do with an obsessive person is call them OCD. Deal with it. Never mind—get lost while I do it the right way."

◆ *D. K. Broadwell* ◆

The humbled Hayes retreated through the hatch to the cockpit while Cat turned back to the cabin filter and suppressed her laughter.

Another Flight Day
Intrepid

On the flight deck gazing at the Earth, Cat watched a line of thunderstorms rolling into the dusk of East Texas. The silent lightning flashes were nearly continuous. Unbidden, peals of thunder pushed into her mind to accompany the fireworks. *Memories of my life as an earthling*, she thought. She turned to see Hayes.

"Quite the show," he said.

"We've got great seats." Cat touched his arm. "I've been thinking about what you said. I've taken for granted that you are open and communicative. That's uncommon with men. You have an unexpected sensitivity."

"Thank you for noticing. I've worked hard to get there. I read a lot of Dear Abby. I knew that to have a chance with you, I would need to up my game. Being a 'self-absorbed doofus,' as someone called me once, would not cut it."

"I have decided to go on a date with you. Tonight. Pick me up at 1800 Houston time."

"Be still my heart. May I use the middeck to clean myself up?" Hayes was grinning from ear to ear.

"After you get to a stopping point on the comm work. I need to do some repair work too. Somebody stole my hair clasp."

"Please don't change clothes on my account. I signed up for this mission to see you in your cute space shorts and T-shirt. Having your sweet ass in my face has been an exquisite view."

"I reserve the right to change into anything I want. Remember, gentlemen are not oglers."

Promptly at 1800, Hayes rapped on the hatch between the two decks. He was carrying paper flowers cut out from the reams of printer paper sent to *Intrepid* before their links went dark.

"Come in," Cat said. She had put on a pair of pink socks she'd been saving for their reentry.

"What lovely socks, Dr. Riley. I'm so glad you had time to see me this week."

"We're having spicy macaroni and cheese. I hope you like that."

"I would sell my mother for a glass of wine to share with you right now."

"If you can trade her for a full-bodied California Chardonnay, I endorse your plan."

They started their meal with a quiet awkwardness that surprised Cat. "Tell me about your necklace," Hayes finally said. "It's always floating around your face, but you never take it off."

"That's Mary, my Miraculous Medal, and I pray to her every day to redeem us from our predicament. You know I'm Catholic. What about you?"

"I'm a registered backsliding Baptist. God and I have had a few disagreements. I want to believe in him, but the twentieth century has been rough on the old guy. Joni Mitchell sang about the heaven full of astronauts and God on death row. That's us, by the way. Bush people in Indonesia are praying to us as our little light goes by."

"I don't believe you're that cynical," Cat said. "God has a plan, and we don't know it, but we'll be taken care of. *Sanctus Dominus, pleni sunt cæli et terra gloria tua*—Holy Lord, heaven and earth are full of your glory. I guess that includes glorious us."

Hayes said, "It's easy to believe God loves me when I'm with you." A timer alarm went off. "I need to go do some switch flipping. I shall return. Please don't go away."

A few minutes later, Hayes came back to the middeck. "Come up to the flight deck. I rolled *Intrepid* into a good view of the stars for a while."

Cat and Hayes floated under a sharp and glorious full moon impossible to view from Earth. They gazed in silence for minutes until Cat asked, "What's your sign, Hayes? I'm a Virgo. Very much a Virgo."

"You're into astrology? Isn't that a conflict with your astronaut-doctor-scientist-Catholic self?"

"No, I don't limit my spirituality. There are lots of systems that work. So, first date, what's your sign?"

"What sign is irresistible to Virgos?"

"You can't pick your sign. When is your birthday? I know Terry's, but I never knew yours. Would you like some nice fresh after-dinner water?" She squeezed her container, and a water blob drifted toward him.

"Taurus, May 12." He gobbled the water.

"That's not too bad. You are stubborn and a hedonist. Where is your moon?"

"My moon is right there outside the windows. I can see it."

"What's your moon *sign*?"

"Don't know." Hayes rotated so their bodies were 180 degrees apart. "Your face is beautiful upside down, too. What a lovely neck."

"You've never had your full horoscope done? Your moon sign is very important. I'll put 'get horoscope' on the list for when we get home. Taurus and Virgo—that can potentially work. I need more information."

"I'm a stubborn hedonist, so Virgos are . . .?" Hayes rotated back into her attitude, took her water container, and squirted a globule back at Cat.

"Virgos are—*slurp*—me."

"Let's see," Hayes said. "Quick mind, lots of integrity, temperamental, good-looking, attention to detail, sexy. Shall I go on?" He moved closer to Cat. Their knees touched.

"You can leave out the physical attributes although I appreciate the compliments. Yes, that's a nice capsule. There are less flattering aspects to Virgos, too. People have referred to me as exacting, picky, and overly critical—maybe even obsessive."

"Obsessive is . . . good in our line of work. Attention to detail is good."

Hayes put his arms around Cat, who reciprocated. They had not held each other since Jack's death and the *Buran* disaster. It was different this time. They were a man and a woman hugging each other like two lovers in the parking lot outside their favorite bar.

"Hayes, you're shaking!" Cat said.

"I love you. I can't help it. You move me to my core." Hayes kissed her, and she kissed him back. *Intrepid* rolled on through the dry hostility of space.

Cat's Journal (excerpt)
Intrepid

Hayes and I have decided to keep journals, although whether they are for ourselves or posterity is an open question. Before my life became so "interesting" that I could no longer record any of it, I frequently wrote in a journal. Hayes says he doesn't care who reads his journal because if they do, he'll be dead. A disturbing comment, but true.

What do you write with a future like ours? Anne Frank knew her situation was perilous, but she wrote about the moment, her present. The tiny bubble Hayes and I inhabit has much in common with Anne's tiny apartment. No Nazis outside—only don't-give-a-fuck-about-you Killer Space.

I don't want to die, but I don't fear death. My faith tells me that I will find another home in God's heaven. Whatever His plan, His love will redeem me.

I have another record I keep with carbon dioxide levels and other data of interest to flight medicine, but this is my journal. I want to read it years from now because that means I'll be alive and can recall the intensity of my life at this instant. Maybe this is what being in a foxhole with bullets flying is like—very alive but close to death. We could perish any day, and I'm falling in love. That's too dramatic—I'm allowing myself to become infatuated. Yes, that's better. Lord, may we live long enough to fall in love.

I didn't date this entry because I don't carry the date or the mission elapsed time in my mind anymore. Time seems suspended. Hayes and I look at the stars, and the Earth passes below us in a never-ending, gorgeous panorama, and my roomie and I talk. It turns out we have a lot to talk about.

I have a spaceship, and I have a man. We don't have much of a future, so falling in love is a fine way to exist. Hayes has been courting me in his macho, goofy way for forever, but I couldn't be bothered until now. I've stopped my rush to the next task and listened to him, noticed him, and given myself permission to open my heart. Hayes said my heart had been frozen. I kept telling myself my heart was full of Alan, when really it was a void. The echo of Alan made me feel warm and empty at the same time for two years. My hiding in his memory has distracted me from getting on with my life. I'm going to find a way to make tea with my Earl Grey teabag. No one will ever know drinking it is my farewell to my beloved. I think he would approve.

Familiarity should breed contempt, but I'm content to talk to Hayes about mundane things. "Mundane" means "of the world," doesn't it? A strange term to use as we orbit it in our little coffin of love. We have our shuttle housekeeping duties and our routines, just like an old married couple. Men being attracted to me is nothing new, but it's fun and flattering to hear how he first noticed me: seeing me jog around JSC with my ball cap, tank top, and my bouncing dark-haired ponytail. Love at first sight, he said. Do I believe in that? More like lust, I'd say, but lust is the sponsor that brings humans love if we have the time and inclination.

I've certainly never intimidated him. His ego is big enough for both of us. I do arouse him, and my body feels like it's waking up from a long sleep—desire as an antidote to despair. Why not?

Hayes's Journal (excerpt)
Intrepid

I've never kept a diary, but Cat and I agreed to do it for our last days in-flight. If our journals survive us, they'll answer some of the inevitable questions earthlings will have about our final days. Self-expression has never been my forte, but I will make the effort. Don't expect me to embarrass myself, Mr. Nosey Reporter. Fire away.

— No, I have not given up. I'm still trying to contact the ground, and we have a deorbit plan that acquits us honorably in our duty to get home or bust.

— Yes, I believe I'll be dead in a week or so. I feel very calm about our pathway. I would much rather go down fighting than lapse into a coma in my sleep from hypoxia or carbon dioxide poisoning.

— Why am I not despondent? I'm happy because the woman I love has finally stopped treating me like a friendly tool and has started paying attention to me as a man. I can't stop fantasizing about her. Yes, there is a sex drive in space, even if NASA ignores it.

— Yes, I've been told I think I am God's gift to women. I know that's not true, but Cat is God's gift to me, if she'll have me. She says her faith makes her content to meet her maker, and I believe her. I'm not sure about the hereafter or what I even deserve in that department. I'm damn sure that I want more than ever to keep living and have a life with her. In the meantime, I'll enjoy every second. Two days ago, we had our first date, and yesterday she really started to flirt with me! Guess what I'm thinking, Mr. Nosey Reporter.

• *D. K. Broadwell* •

Today we passed the time with another long discussion about Star Trek. Captain Kirk is her ideal hero. He did charm his way into a lot of alien pussy, I'll give him that. She's being, to use her Cajun term, canaille. Naughty and mischievous, trying to make me jealous. This includes comparing me to her other heartthrob, Mel Gibson. I don't want any starlets. I want her. But our time is running out.

Star Trek was wrong about "Space, the final frontier." A frontier is a place on the edge you reach, populate, and move on. Space is like the sea. Astronauts are star sailors. Like the sea, space is vast and unfeeling, with a hundred different ways to kill you. You can do everything perfectly and still enjoy a random death. At least ours will not be anonymous or unnoticed.

Cat said she feels like Jonah in the whale, but I disagree. It's much more complex than that. Intrepid is our Moby Dick, a great white disaster.

Another Flight Day
Intrepid

Cat couldn't sleep, which was becoming a problem. Physical inactivity and stress were dragging on her, but she was reluctant to use the sleeping pills in the med kit. A dark voice was telling her, *Save them. You may need them at the end.* Exercise options were limited. Many shuttle missions carried a small treadmill but not STS-92A.

Hayes was asleep. *Men always sleep better than women. Women worry for everybody, men just for themselves.* She looked at Hayes in his sleeping bag, arms through its holes. In zero-g his arms assumed a neutral posture, floating in front of him as if he were casually reaching to embrace something. *He looks like a zombie with his eyeshade on.*

Cat's head was throbbing, and she had a sour taste in her mouth. The queasy stomach she felt when upset came sliding in like a nosy neighbor you can't get rid of. She went to the flight deck, taking deep breaths. It was dark, but she could see daylight Earth a few minutes away. One of her astronaut comrades had been in special ops warfare early in his career. He was fond of saying, "Hope is not a plan." *Where is our fucking plan?* She buckled herself into the commander's seat, took out her journal, and wrote furiously:

If nothing survives me but this, understand—*I have no regrets.* The choices were mine. I accept the consequences.

I do have disappointments. I wanted a child. I would have been a great mother—certainly better than my own. I'm disappointed to die so fucking young, but when I chose this career, I knew mortality was never far away. Death is always trying to get your attention, but you can't do your job if you give it to him. And I wanted the job, I wanted to go to space, and now I'll go out flaming across the Big Sky. Literally. British Columbia, California, maybe empty ocean. Don't know, but I hope someone sees us.

No regrets about my performance. I have devoted my life to being so fucking good that NOTHING ELSE WOULD MATTER. But I couldn't save us. Nobody could.

After the shitstorm of investigations and righteously indignant finger-pointing is over, I want everyone at NASA to know I forgive them. Death will release me to my Heavenly Father. He will separate the self-serving and liars from the heroes. Oh yeah, I'm pissed off. The pompous bureaucrats who fucked up can burn in hell.

That covers brain and soul; last, as always, is heart. Always last. I am disappointed I didn't live long enough to fully enjoy the ecstasy of falling in love again. It's been such a long time. Of all people—the horny Major Hayes. I can't help but smile. My friends would laugh out loud.

Cat smiled when she wrote about Hayes. She looked up from her journal, as *Intrepid* passed through the terminator line separating night from day on her home planet. She gazed through welling tears at the glorious, constant sunlight flooding the cockpit. She grabbed her ever-present hankie and cleared her vision enough to see Louisiana sliding silently by. *My kinfolk are down there, waiting.*

"Fuck you, space," she said aloud. *I'm going home to give everyone my report in person.* She ripped the page from her journal, balled it up, and crammed it into a trash bag. Crawling back into her bag on the middeck, she fell into a deep sleep.

Another Flight Day

With no alarm and no duties, Cat no longer thought *What time is it?* when she woke up. She saw Hayes floating nearby writing in his notebook. He turned to her with a smile. "Good morning, sleepyhead."

"Good morning. What are you grinning at?"

"A beautiful damsel trapped in a high tower."

"Trapped with you, I might add. Get me some coffee, please."

After her coffee, Cat joined Hayes on the flight deck where he was sending his Morse code SOS blind and hoping for a reply. "How's your ham fist doing?" she asked.

"My spacewalker hand is pooping out, and so is your barrette. Do you have another one?"

"Sure, it's in that third suitcase I brought along. Sorry, no, I didn't plan my wardrobe for any of this." She rubbed his right hand. "There now. Give it a rest and watch the stars." They held hands and gazed at the wonder of the universe.

Cat looked at Hayes. "You said you loved me. Have you ever been in love before, deeply in love?"

"No. Maybe a little. Nothing like what I feel for you. Relationships were a fun game for me, and I never let myself get hurt by caring too much. Too much at stake to get involved."

"I'm sure you hurt a few women along the way with that attitude. Why should I be different, aside from possibly being dead very soon?"

"I thought you were optimistic about our chances."

"My mood about that swings around faster than we orbit Ma Earth. You avoided my question."

Hayes pondered a moment. "Explaining true love is a reckless proposition, but I'll try. You're forthright, honest, spiritually deep, brilliant, and caring, which is not a package I ever found in any woman. And you're as beautiful and sexy as they come. As I said before, you have many fascinating facets. When we get out of this mess, I see loving you for the rest of my life."

"Since we are going home, loving me for the rest of your life might turn out to be harder than you can imagine, Major Cyrano."

"My turn," said Hayes. "Tell me one of your romantic fantasies."

Cat laughed. "None of them include being trapped in orbit with you. But I'll give you something. Close your eyes." She took both his hands. "Imagine a fireplace. A sheepskin rug. A bottle of champagne—must be French to be real. And music."

"What kind of music?" asked Hayes.

"Slow and moody saxophone jazz. Art Pepper. Ben Webster."

"I'm there. Sign me up for that club."

Cat put her arms around his neck. "Invitation only." They kissed.

Hayes kept his eyes closed. "Your kisses get hotter every day."

"Maybe you need to check *Intrepid*'s environmental control settings."

As if on cue, the ship's master caution and warning alarm system sounded and a light on the panel in front of them lit up: FUEL CELL PUMP. Hayes blurted, "Christ Awmighty. Let me look for the right info screen." Without the fuel cells, there was no electrical power. They settled into the commander and pilot cockpit seats.

"I'm looking for the right checklist," Cat said. "Is that on a cue card? Hang on."

"It's going to say shut the motherfucker down before it blows up, and we only got two out of three fuel cells running now. Where's that screen? Okay, fuel cell one is the culprit; cooling pump pressure low; stack temperature already rising with pump down."

"Here's the checklist."

Hayes and Cat looked at the emergency checklist together and read a procedure they had never practiced. Cat said, "By the time we find all the right cockpit switches and panels we'll be cooked. Where is the R1 power panel? I forgot."

"At your right elbow on the side. Let's switch seats," Hayes said. "I'm going to do something not on the list first. We already powered down fuel cell three to save resources. We can't put all the electrical load on one fuel cell. We can't afford to kill the good one. I'm going to untie the buses." He put his hand on the switches that linked the good and the sick fuel cells, which powered every circuit drawing current on *Intrepid*. He hesitated. "If everything goes dark, we're fucked. But here goes." Breaking the connection between the two fuel cells, one of the cockpit screens went dark, but most of the lights stayed on—they still had one healthy fuel cell running.

Hayes and Cat completed the bad fuel cell shutdown checklist and did what they could to put it in a safe mode. Through call and response they methodically ran the checklist to bring the mothballed fuel cell back online. Retying the electrical buses, the orbiter was back to two functioning fuel cells, as it was before the crisis.

"Where's a goddamn shuttle pilot when you need one?" Hayes asked.

"And where's Jack when you need him?" asked Cat. She felt her eyes moisten and the familiar pain in her chest. She turned her head away from Hayes. *I've got to keep it together better than this. I'm useless if I'm bawling all the time. Lord, give me strength.* Taking two deep breaths Cat said, "Jack sat in the mission specialist one seat behind

Dom and trained as a flight engineer to help with these emergency checklists. I wasn't even on the flight deck."

"Are you still complaining about that? I told you before we launched I would swap with you on descent so you'd have a cockpit view."

"Now we're both going to get great views. Best seats in the house. Any idea what happened to the fuel cell pump, Major Engineer? Was there something we missed?"

"I'm sure there are plenty of orbiter housekeeping things we messed up, but I was watching the fuel cells. All the automatic fuel cell purges have gone off great, twice a day. Every piece of this orbiter sets a record for on-orbit longevity each second that passes. We didn't need this. If we get another fuel cell problem, I don't know if we can deorbit. There's no MCC to help us sort that kind of problem out."

Cat gave him a hug. She took his wrist and counted his pulse. "Not even above a hundred. We did a great job for a space suit guy and a robot arm girl. Now I have something else to pray about: let's not lose another fuel cell."

"I want to go home. We need to take this heap out of orbit soon, come what may, before something else breaks."

"Hush. She'll hear you."

Another Flight Day
Intrepid

"Status report, Ensign Chekov," Hayes said in a stern voice.

"You're not Captain Kirk—not even close," Cat said, in the middle of life support resource calculations.

"That was my Mr. Spock voice."

"Okay, Spock. *Intrepid* has a beefed-up cryo tank system, so with power management and only two of us, liquid oxygen and hydrogen are doing well. LiOH cartridges are still an issue. For max life support, we need to push the CO2 levels. We defer change-out until one of us gets a headache. We have maybe ten to twelve days, depending on how frisky we are."

"I'm feeling very frisky. How are we doing on coffee?" asked Hayes.

"We are low on that, too. Both of us like coffee. All the coffee pouches with cream are gone. I let you have the last one. Black from now on."

"You are both beautiful and generous—an irresistible combination. I get a headache with coffee withdrawal. I wouldn't want you to have a headache."

"I know what you want. We have caffeine tablets if we run out of java. Too many astronauts were going cold turkey off coffee before flight and regretting it, so they added that to the med kit."

"And I need to proceed on the kludgy wing fix so we can deorbit without carbon dioxide toxicity."

"We've gathered all the hole-packing metal we can without removing a critical piece of shuttle hardware. Maybe you can salvage pieces from the payload bay."

"My EMU is refurbed, but I've been wasting a lot of time sending Morse code to a deaf planet. Doing it makes me feel useful. I don't know what NASA or anyone else can do for us, but I want to know what happened to *Buran*." He pulled a paper from behind his back. "I made you a drawing," he said, giving it to her.

"It looks like a kid's Christmas drawing. There's a fireplace, music notes, a bow and—"

"A sheepskin rug, lush saxophone jazz, and a champagne bottle."

"Live for the moment, they say. Come here, you." She held out her arms.

Hayes floated gently into her open arms. They kissed and let their bodies intertwine as they floated around the middeck. He kissed her chin, then unzipped the jacket she was wearing. She was bare underneath. "Your breasts are beautiful . . . perfect," Hayes said, pulling off his T-shirt. It floated away.

"Thank you, Major Romance."

He kissed her shoulders and lips and nuzzled her long neck. "You smell so sweet up close."

Cat kissed his nose. "I found a little something to put on. You . . . you smell very, very manly. Men are messy. Got a plan for that in zero-g?"

"I have a condom. That's my stowaway contraband you asked about. I brought one last mission, too. A certain Earth lady was very impressed later by its provenance."

"You brought only one? Or do you say that about all your little raincoats—that they are space condoms?"

"I'm insulted. I'd never lie about something like that. I'm an honest man. Mostly. I'm smart enough to know I'm not clever enough to get away with it. You I couldn't fool."

"Glad you qualified that. You are male, after all. I've found that in matters of love and lust men are mostly dishonest."

"When you're born, the doctor whispers in your ear, 'It's okay to lie to get pussy.'"

Cat laughed. "And you are telling me this not so secret because you think we're going to die?"

"No, to make you laugh. And it worked."

"Hayes, honey, before we get too carried away—I'm not sure what to do. I can't go stick on the wall somewhere. NASA didn't send up the Velcro–and–bungee cord astronaut intercourse kit."

"I have given this a lot of thought, my darlin'. I was thinking about the sleeping bag, with some external strapping. But that's a tight fit."

"I'm too claustrophobic for that," Cat said, biting his earlobe. "I was freaked out about getting into the space suit for our rescue."

"I thought that might be the case. Next, I remembered the seats. They're stowed while we're in orbit, so I'd forgotten them. The flight deck has a nice view, and they have a five-point harness—maybe with proper padding behind you, with me holding the seat sides . . ."

"Won't work. The buckle for all the other straps is on the crotch strap. That's the promised land." Their teasing kisses became longer and deeper.

"You're overthinking this," Cat said. "You should have put as much effort into fixing the radio. Mother Nature needs only a tiny boost here in zero-g. Which locker has the foot restraint assemblies?"

"Locker down by the floor deck." Hayes pointed with his foot but didn't release his embrace. "I don't ever want to let you go, Cat. Holding you is already paradise found. I'm not sorry I came on this cursed mission. I get to have you all to myself." Slowly, they released their clasp and applied themselves to the making love problem.

Cat retrieved six of the foot restraints and affixed two to the deck slightly aft of the middeck lockers. Hayes waited until she could slip her feet into the loops, and then set his between hers. Hayes placed two loops on the middeck locker wall at about arm height. "Aren't you glad we decluttered the place?" she asked.

Hayes said, "Your long and sexy legs are a perfect fit." He slowly pulled her shorts and panties down to her ankles, and with a little kick from Cat, the clothing floated away. She slipped into her foot restraints, pulling off his pants and briefs as he floated in front of her. She kissed the very tip of his cock, and Hayes gave a small moan.

"Aren't you forgetting something?" Cat asked while holding him in front of her face.

Hayes reached into his pants before they drifted away and retrieved his condom. He settled into his own foot restraints. "You're so beautiful. I could only imagine your nipples, your breasts, your thighs. My imagination failed me." Closing his eyes, he took a deep breath.

"Here, let me help," Cat said. "Give me your little raincoat." She slowly rolled it over him, taking her time. "There, that's better." She pulled him inside her—an easy job in microgravity. *It's been so long. Exhilarating to be so loved.* She felt both safe and terrified.

Hayes emitted a low growl. He placed one hand in a locker loop and the other around her bottom as he began to gingerly move his hips back and forth. "What about foreplay?" he whispered.

"We've been doing that for weeks, silly." She looked into his eyes, losing herself in the moment.

Things went very well after that. They wrapped their arms around one another, curling their toes in the foot loops. At his climax, Hayes whispered into her ear, "I love you, Cat-uh-Reen."

"You can call me your ti' cher bébé. My relatives in Louisiana did when I was little, and it made me feel safe."

"You're my cher bébé, forever. I want only to look into your bottomless blue eyes."

"*Your* eyes have gotten brighter, my darling," Cat whispered.

They drifted out of their foot loops, still locked in love's embrace. Without gravity, the touch of each other's skin was their only sensation. Hayes grabbed his floating T-shirt to dab the halo of sweat droplets that was forming around his forehead. He then carefully disposed of his condom in the wet waste container.

"Thanks," Cat said. "We don't need those little spermies zipping around here in zero-g. You look a little worked up there, Major."

"You ain't seen nothing yet, my sweet gal." He gave her nipple a long kiss. "Your breasts seem to be doing very nicely in zero-g without a bra. Why wear one?"

"Same reason you wear your tighty-whities. I don't want any unscheduled mammary excursions, to use NASA-speak. Perhaps more importantly, I don't want you staring at my boobies all the time with a beatific grin on your face. You would run into something and hurt yourself." While they kissed, Cat fondled him.

Hayes turned Cat around and steered her back into her foot restraints with her face toward the lockers. He pulled himself up against her.

"Hmmm, sweet buns. Don't worry, I'll get you a MAG."

She reached between her legs and pulled him inside. Hayes slipped out of his foot loops and did a slow cartwheel behind Cat, staying inside her as he rotated.

Cat was laughing. "That's different; can you spin around faster?"

"I'm not a figure skater. I'd get dizzy." Hayes returned to his foot restraints, placing one hand in a loop on the middeck locker. While they slowly made love, his other hand caressed her as he nuzzled her neck.

When they were done, Cat turned to embrace him. They floated free in the middeck. "I could ask 'Was it good for you?' to make conversation, but your expression makes that a ludicrous question."

"How about you, my hot astronette?"

"I prefer to remain a mysterious woman. You can guess if I liked it or not. Also, to get medical, I don't need one of your gross EVA diapers. A tampon will do."

"They have space-rated tampons? I suppose that's not something you wave around."

"They're *regular* tampons. Menses works normally in zero-g—still a pain to deal with, just like Earth."

"If you think you can cool me off with your medical talk, it won't work. I also haven't seen you take any birth control pills."

"Ha, now he asks. Typical male." Cat squeezed his butt as they drifted. Her legs were wrapped around his hips, and she moved her own hips provocatively over his crotch as they meandered about the cabin. "That's because I can't take them. They give me migraine headaches. You should have brought more condoms."

"We were weight-restricted, remember? If you get pregnant, you'll have to marry me. I'll ride around on my riding lawnmower in my John Deere cap. All our kids will run through the sprinkler and look at the mountains. Mmm . . . my, that feels so good."

"I don't have to marry you, and the kids will be in the surf because our house is on the beach. Don't forget, they'll also be raised Catholic."

"If you aren't sore, I do believe I have another notion." Hayes was pulling himself over to the locker wall when they were startled by a Morse code transmission that erupted from the middeck speakers.

Hayes held Cat by her shoulders. "Don't worry," he said. "This will be recorded. I hope." He looked around the middeck. "Damn, I need a piece of paper. S-C-O-M-S-K-E-D-S-K-E-D-V-O-X—oh shit, it's numbers. Can't do Morse numbers that fast. 'Sked'! Cat, they're setting up a schedule." By this time, Hayes had made it to the flight deck. He played the Morse code recording a few times and transcribed it.

Cat came behind him, having put on his T-shirt and her shorts. She brought him his pants. "You're leaving a trail, Major. You have very active Cowper's glands." Hayes made a quizzical face as he dressed. "Your beautiful cock is leaking. No need to gum up the avionics."

"Aw, it's not that much. You got me excited."

"Put a sock on it, while I clean up. What's the message?"

"It's from Hanscom Air Force Base near Boston. They do a lot of military electronics work there. Maybe they've been waiting for us to go by a place with the equipment to beam a transmission to us. It gives a time in military Date Time Group format for a voice radio call on this radio. It's in about three hours. They heard us!" Holding Cat, he said, "It also means that you and I may be the first humans to make love over the North Pole." He spread his arms to encompass all the stars in the night sky visible from the flight deck. "I don't know why radio contact makes me so happy; it's anticlimactic after our lovemaking. I doubt it'll change our status much."

"At least we can find out about the *Buran* crew." *Maybe I could really love you if we live long enough.* Cat put her head on his shoulder. "It's much more impressive to make wonderful love in zero-g than over the North Pole," she whispered.

Suspended on the flight deck, they were reluctant to release each other and break the spell. Finally, Hayes said, "I ain't dead yet, and neither is Cat-uh-reen Bird, my Irish cher bébé. Let's get cleaned up and get our ears on."

"Okay. We can name our kid 'Thirty-three.' That's Larry's jersey number."

"Only if it's a girl. First boy is 'Hayes.' I'm famished. Let's eat something and get ready for our comm."

Two orbits later
Over California

"*Intrepid*, this is Houston. Short window. Next sked DTG 8910111432. Acknowledge."

Hayes had the comm. "This is *Intrepid*. Next sked 8910111432. Over."

CAPCOM: "Crew status? Estimated resources remaining?"

"We are fine." Cat held up all her fingers. "Estimated end of mission is nine or ten days."

"Do not maneuver or change vehicle state vector. A cargo capsule is in a phasing rendezvous orbit and will arrive in your vicinity in twelve hours. It has some autonomous rendezvous ability, but Cat will need RMS to retrieve it. It's coming right at you, V-bar. No safety margin. Unload it via EVA."

"Copy capsule coming, V-bar," Hayes said. "Contents?"

"Repair kit. Radio. Lithium hydroxide. Tools. The chase SR71 comm ship will lose you soon. Talk—"

What happened to Buran? Cat thought.

"Shit, they're gone," said Hayes. "I mean, hallelujah!"

Cat put her hand on Hayes's shoulder. "There's something else in that package. Hope for another chance. But better than hope, we have a plan that we didn't have before."

Hayes could scarcely believe what he had heard. "Truly," he said to Cat, "this has to be the luckiest day of my life." He squeezed her hands. "It would have been anyway, even without our good news. I have already depressurized the cabin for EVA, since I was going to attempt our lame wing fix. They must have had an air force Blackbird shadowing us at Mach 3 with a beam antenna or other spy electronics to relay to Houston. That sounded like Liz."

"When is our next comm opportunity?"

Hayes looked at his notes. "About six hours."

"Tell me what V-bar is again," Cat said.

"V-bar is the reference frame for our movement in the velocity vector—ahead or behind us in this orbit. Neither of us is a certified orbital mechanic. Or shuttle driver. Liz meant they've done a capsule burn that will cause it to collide with us from behind or maybe slightly ahead. That's why they told us not to do anything to move *Intrepid*. I hope we get rendezvous advice on the next comm sked. We're going to need it."

"We'll be ready. I know it. I think we need to double-check our power consumption. I just noticed that the camera for the plant experiment was still powered up, so I unplugged it. There are probably more power parasites we can trim." Cat put her finger on his nose. "We also need to go to maximum carbon dioxide tolerance on the canisters and minimum oxygen uptake. EVA's eat up O2. That means no more hot lovin' for Major HB. For now."

"I think I can wait until we get home," Hayes said. "I'm no longer in imminent danger of blowing up."

"You've exploded enough for one day. Let's try and get a nap. Our sleep/rest cycles are going to get disrupted when that capsule gets here."

That's a good idea. "I'm feeling uncharacteristically tired, my sweet babe."

Flight Day Twenty-Three
Intrepid
Over Western Pacific

CAPCOM: "*Intrepid,* Houston. How copy?"

"Five by five, Houston," Hayes said.

"Great. This is Doug, brought to you today courtesy of our friends on the USS *Theodore Roosevelt.* Two Hawkeye AWACS planes from 'Big Stick' are doing a relay that should last five minutes. Your cargo capsule is in trail and should catch up to you in about six hours. Do you have any Ku-band radar capability?"

"Negative, Doug. The whole antenna is gone. Please, tell us what happened to *Buran*. What do you know?"

"Dang—no rendezvous radar. I'm happy to tell you the *Buran* crew made a successful emergency landing at an abort site near Vladivostok. Everyone is still on their way home from Russia—that's a long story, but they're all well. Moving on, these communications opportunities are difficult to arrange since *Intrepid* is deaf as a post on the radio. We're going to try for a sked at 2345 CDT. The capsule should be visible by then. We'll use ground radar to pinpoint it and give you rendezvous data. We named it "Chirp" by the way. C-H-R-P—Cat-Hayes Rescue Pod. Any questions?"

"You know how we lost the Ku-band antenna, don't you? Jack is dead, isn't he?"

"Yes, Jack is gone. The EVA cosmonaut Gennadiy Tokalev, who was still outside when *Buran* bucked, recovered Jack's body and made it inside to safety. Jack gave his own life to save his crewmates."

"What are we supposed to do with our Chirp?"

"Stay alive. Work outside and fix your wing. Come home. You will have food, an RCC wing patch kit to install, more tools, and a comm fix so we can talk to each other better."

"All right, then. Why didn't we do it this way the first time?"

"You're entitled to a frank answer on that. No one thought we had the time to do it. Probably wouldn't have if the full crew were onboard and breathing. Next step—get that pod. Let me talk to Cat."

"I'm here, Doug."

"Chirp is a repurposed satellite. It has grapple fixtures on either end for the RMS to grab. The satellite will be slowly rotating, but these fixtures gimbal. You can capture either end. It won't entirely fit into the payload bay with the rocket cradle there, but you don't need to bring it home."

"What about the spin?"

"When you have it captured, you can grapple a side bar to stop the spin and bring it into the payload bay. Spin should be under point five degrees per second. It will not overtorque your RMS. It's not any worse than the grab of the Solar Max satellite on STS-41C."

"Ah, T. J. Hart's grab. My hero."

"Coming up on loss of signal. You're going to be a hero, too, Cat."

"Till we talk again. *Intrepid* out."

Flight Day Two for Buran
Breaking formation with Intrepid *after Jack's death*

Fyodor yelled from the *Buran* cockpit, "Sharon, you must retract the airlock. We can't close the payload bay doors like it is now! Help Gennadiy!"

Jesus Christ, Sharon thought. *Jack must be dead. Shake that off or we'll all be dead.* Still suited, Sharon turned to the two astronauts she had escorted inside. "Terry, you're closer. The retract button is inside where the airlock extension takes off. Big red guarded switch. Hit it, man."

Terry scrambled into the airlock, fighting the jerks and jolts of the ship's gyrations. He flipped the switch and sealed the inner airlock hatch so Gennadiy could reenter the airlock. The NASA astronauts struggled out of their EMU torsos and pants, never an easy or quick task. Terry pulled himself from the habitation compartment to the *Buran* command compartment. "What can I do?" he asked.

All the *Buran* maneuvering thrusters were still being called on to counteract the rogue control jet that was blasting away. Nikolai and Fyodor had been able to make a short main engine burn to begin the deorbit process, and they had stabilized the ship enough to give a longer, calibrated burn.

"Commander, you can unstow the seats that are beneath the floorboards. We're on our way down, and we'll need them." Fyodor waved vaguely behind his pilot seat at the compartment floor. The Russian craft's seats needed to be set up before reentry, same as the US orbiter.

"Will do." Terry fumbled with the latches on a vehicle deck similar to yet different from his own vehicle's.

Sharon entered the cockpit clad in her EVA cooling garment. She gave a one-liter bag of water to Terry. "Thought I better give you this while I can. You need to fluid load as much as possible for reentry." Turning to the pilots, she asked, "How long till your thrusters burn up, Colonel Titov?"

"Another ten to twelve minutes, maybe. Who knows? We'll only use them after our de-orbit burn until we have enough control, uh . . . until air pressure lets ailerons work. We'll dump the fuel as soon as we can safely do it—if there's any left."

"Ya know, if one of the shuttle's RCS thrusters gets too hot, it melts a wahr and the damn valve shuts off," Sharon said.

"What's a wahr?" asked Titov.

Terry spit out, "She means a wire, like a fuse wire that cuts the power to the valve."

◆

In the habitation compartment, Dom opened the inner airlock hatch and saw Gennadiy had retrieved Badger's body. The astronaut's visor was half gone, and his head was puffy, with bulging, open eyes. Dom thought he was going to be sick. Sweating and nauseous, he helped Gennadiy shut the inner airlock door.

"Gennadiy says he's going to leave Colonel Badger in the airlock for reentry," said Fyodor over the intercom. "Dom, please help him out of his suit, and he'll show you how to set up the seats."

◆

At an altitude of ninety-five kilometers, *Buran* experienced the loss of radio signal with the ground that all shuttles did. The superheated plasma engulfing them blocked all transmissions. Terry was seated behind the pilots, next to Gennadiy, who was in the flight engineer's seat behind Fyodor. In other circumstances, he would have delighted in watching Nikolai mirror his own job. He tried to focus on every phase of *Buran's* reentry, but the malfunctioning vehicle's uncertain future and the death sentence for Cat and Hayes made that impossible.

"This should be very familiar, Commander Rogers," Titov said. "We have enough air pressure to have aileron effectiveness and all the thruster fuel has been consumed. No more problem."

"That's good news, Fyodor." Terry watched as the pilot and commander conversed in Russian. By their headshakes and other nonverbal cues, he knew the situation was not yet under control.

♦

In the lower deck, Sharon and Dom had managed to don the pressure suits used by the Russians for launches and landings. She said, "Drink up on that water, there, bud. These cosmonauts are nice guys, Dom, but they are not as slick as you NASA pilots. I get the feeling they're not as well-trained as y'all are."

"Who can train for this kind of mission, Sharon? They've probably never landed at this abort landing site, either. From where we did our deorbit burn, I think it will be dark, too."

"Always in the dark on the middeck, Dom. You've never had that experience. Did you know NASA once had a personal rescue enclosure prototype for astronauts, like the little transfer ball you used for the rats, except people-sized? I got volunteered to try it out, and it was gawd-awful. It was claustrophobic and running out of air would not have been pleasant. Glad it got ditched. Say, what's the deal with those rats, anyway?"

"They're mice, and I got attached to them. They—"

"We're ten minutes out," Fyodor said over the intercom. "Communications restored with the TsUP after the blackout, and we're getting good navigation signals from the landing site. The autopilot is functioning normally."

Dom felt the increased g-force pushing them into their seats as *Buran* rolled into a tight turn. The vehicle was flying a descending circular course to lose altitude and line up with the runway.

♦

Same as the heading alignment cone we fly for landing, thought Terry. "Field lights in sight," he said from force of habit. He felt empty, a ghost observer of *Buran* as it mimicked what his own shuttle should have been doing to land.

As *Buran* glided to the field and aligned itself to the runway, the autopilot computer raised the vehicle's nose in a flare, slowing its descent. Terry recognized gear extension. After the nose wheel touched down, three small drag chutes deployed, and *Buran* rolled to a stop. He had no clue where on Earth he was, other than somewhere in the Soviet Union.

The habitation compartment passengers broke out in restrained applause. Their vehicle sat on the runway in the dark. Terry congratulated the crew on their landing, then said to Fyodor, "You weren't confident this was going to turn out well, were you? Have you ever practiced landing here, in a training aircraft or simulator?"

"We have not trained so much for alternate landing sites," Fyodor said, "but we were most concerned that the special navigation system here at Khorol would not be fully operational. Out here in the dark, it would have been disastrous without that to guide us in. It worked perfectly."

Buran sat on the runway making creaking and pinging noises as it cooled, and after a long twenty minutes a military convoy rolled out of the darkness and pulled up beside it. Soldiers wielding AK-74s surrounded the vehicle as a rusting airstair was rolled up to it. A spotlight was set up, aimed at the hatch. The US astronauts had not expected anything like the small army of NASA support workers in protective suits that greet a landing at the Cape, but they were shocked at the unfriendly looking soldiers encircling them.

Gennadiy went to the hab compartment to open the hatch. A cold wind shoved him back into the vehicle. Sharon had changed into a NASA jumpsuit, but Dom and Terry were still in their pressure garment reentry suits. They had not had time to unpack the flight suits Sharon had brought for them. The three astronauts descended the stairs first, and a young soldier gestured with his rifle, herding them toward one of the trucks. After over two weeks in space, Terry and Dom were feeling the effects of returning to one-g and were unsteady on their feet. Russian soldiers grabbed their elbows and dragged them to the waiting truck.

As the three cosmonauts reached the tarmac, a heated discussion erupted between Nikolai and the military officer in charge. Fyodor tried to approach the astronauts but was blocked by a soldier. He shouted to his space comrades as they were loaded into the back of the truck, "General Secretary Gorbachev isn't happy with us. He is impounding *Buran*. Don't worry, everything will work out."

The three astronauts had no answer, and their truck pulled away. They had been prepared to die in space or in attempting to return. They weren't prepared for this reception. Sharon looked with disgust at the soldier guarding her and said to her companions, "It's gettin' to be where a gal is safer in orbit than on our pathetic little Earth. I thought the damn Commies wanted to help us, not arrest us."

"What about Jack?" Dom asked, his thumbs pressing his temples in an attempt to stop his feeling of spinning. "He deserves honor and respect. We're not going anywhere without him."

Same Day, after rescue abort
Baikonur Cosmodrome

Sitting with Stas in the *Buran* control center, Matt and Lisa were joined by a high-ranking Russian officer. He grunted an introduction as he came to join their group. He spoke few words to Stas during the tension of *Buran*'s deorbit. Stas had begged Matt and Lisa to remain quiet during the reentry. Matt had managed to sit silently so far, but his pulse was racing, and his face was hot and flushed. Stas's blurted revelation that the Soviets had not been fully prepared for this mission had left him angry and despondent. In desperation, NASA had fully bought into this scheme. *This mission is the true fucking meaning of Russian roulette*, he thought, *and the chamber was loaded.*

The control center atmosphere verged on panic. Every one of the controllers was on the phone, shouting at someone on the other end. Matt was certain some of those people on the other end were at the TsUP, and he hoped Kurt and the others knew more than he did. Mission control in Houston was probably even more in the dark about *Buran*'s status.

Silence dropped like a curtain. During the Soviet shuttle's communications loss of signal during reentry, the controllers waited for the spacecraft's emergence from the hottest part of its journey home. *This is the part that the crippled* Intrepid *cannot survive*, thought Matt. Lisa was clutching his hand under the table. "They have to get cross-range almost to the Pacific Ocean," Stas said, "but they have sufficient energy for that. Conditions are favorable."

The voice of Commander Nikolai Kondakova crackled over the speaker, as he checked in with Russian mission control once *Buran* exited the blackout. The room's chatter reasserted itself.

"If it's like our shuttle, there's only eleven or twelve minutes to go," Matt whispered to Lisa. He listened carefully. A few minutes later, Nikolai reported navigation and autopilot function as nominal. It was bittersweet for Matt when *Buran* reported it was stopped on the runway. The Russians erupted in cheers. The NASA group was relieved to have three of six US crew members back, but one—and most probably two more to come—were lost. Matt rose from his seat and forcefully told Stas, "I need to get to my crew. Get me to my crew. And what the hell happened to Randy?"

Stas held up his hand to cut Matt off, and he and the Russian officer moved away to talk out of earshot. Matt and Lisa were standing, ready to go. When Stas returned, he said, "Your crew and ours are many hours away, even by jet. General Grekov assures me that they will be well cared for. Unfortunately, General Secretary Gorbachev himself has taken note that this mission did not . . . go as planned. He has requested an immediate investigation. Your colleagues are requested to stay at the Khorol base for now as they recover."

"Perhaps you didn't hear me, Stas. I need to be with my crew," Matt said. "We also need to reestablish communications with our group at the TsUP and with Houston."

Tightening his lips, Stas raised himself up as much as his small stature would permit. "That is not yet possible at the moment, Dr. Wallace. It is best that you and your staff return to your quarters and await further developments."

Lisa grabbed the little man by his arm. "Now you're the one spouting bullshit, Stas. How can you do this to us? You know what we've lost! We need to talk to our people."

Lowering his voice, Stas said, "I have no choice in this. Let me work on it. I do understand. I'll try to put Kurt through to you on a call to your room. Come, I'll drive you." They found Randy outside smoking, and they all left the OKPD and the Jubilee runway where they had expected to see their friends return to Earth.

Flight Day Twenty-Four
Intrepid + *Chirp*

"I can see it. I wish we still had our range radar," Hayes said. He and Cat were watching from the aft flight deck, where beyond the payload bay a small speck was chasing them from behind and below.

"How are we doing on our fuel?" asked Cat.

"It's got to be close to deorbit redline. I probably wasted a lot. I don't know how much of an OMS burn we need to get home. That's an MCC question."

"Don't be so hard on yourself, Hayes. You're a helicopter pilot."

"I'm *your* helicopter pilot, and you are the world's greatest Canadarm gal. You're going to grab this thing and save our bacon." Hayes gently kissed the back of her neck.

"My seventh cervical vertebra thanks you," Cat said, "but you need to focus."

"*Intrepid* is depressurized, aligned, flushed, and dumped. I'm killing time until the Chirp decides it's close enough for us to do something. I'd like to already be outside, but I'm the only student driver you have left." The Chirp was still gaining on them.

"Somebody really burned the midnight oil to get this deal put together," Cat said. "Can't wait to see what's in it. It's exhilarating to be working again. After . . ." Her voice trailed off.

"You're a girl who needs to be active," Hayes said. "We're going into night. By next daylight, I hope the Chirp has closed on us, and we can go for it."

"I've been checking out the arm. Thank goodness, I was able to stow it during the disaster. It's undamaged."

"I'm going to close my eyes for a few minutes on the middeck," Hayes said. "We're out of synch with our sleep cycles."

"NASA used to go to great lengths to avoid having the crew do critical actions at the wrong time in our circadian rhythm cycle." Cat yawned. "If—when we get back, it will take them a year to debrief this mission. Nothing has been normal."

"I'll set my alarm. Ciao."

◆

Houston advised *Intrepid* that the Chirp would flash a blue light when it had reached its proximity limit to the shuttle. "Primitive, but effective," said Hayes at the tiller in the aft flight deck, as he verified that the nearby Chirp looked nearly stationary.

Next to him, Cat said, "I love blue lights. When I was little, my father used to take me to a small rise above the airport, and we would look down at the blue taxiway lights. That's where I caught the flying bug. Dad was a WWII pilot."

"Here we go," said Hayes, "and easy does it—only the verniers. When you're this close, I've been told, it's eyeball the target and shoot for it. I'm still an apprentice but without a mentor." The distance between the two orbiting bodies closed at a quarter meter per second. *Patience*, Hayes said to himself.

A few minutes later, the Chirp was looming in the cockpit window. Rotating slowly, it was a cylinder the size of a small van. Hayes attempted to take out the relative motion between them but ended up backing away very slowly.

"Damn, this thing is touchy. Worse than a TH-55 training helo at Fort Rucker." Hayes slowly added enough input to bring *Intrepid* abeam the satellite. "We're still drifting, but I can't fix it. Can you grab the pod?"

Cat was already working the RMS to bring her grabber attachment over the grapple on the end of the Chirp. "It would be easier if we weren't moving, but here I go." When her wrist camera showed the RMS end effector was lined up, she let it bump into the grapple. She rotated the end effector ring, and three wires tightened at its center and clamped the Chirp's grapple. *Intrepid* and its new cargo were now one vehicle.

Cat brought the still-rotating Chirp closer to the payload bay. Since it was now orbiting at the same velocity as the shuttle, she could release it and move to the last rendezvous step. She needed to grab a fixture on the side of the Chirp and stop its rotation. If she bumped it too hard the wrong way, it would start to tumble or wobble away. She placed the satellite where she had plenty of travel in each of the Canadarm's joints. Tracking the satellite's rotation, she closed the capture wires once more. The arm shivered, and the Chirp stopped. It was completely theirs.

Hayes left his seat and gave her a hug. "You have the best hands of any woman I've ever met. Congratulations."

"You're welcome. Now it's your turn to perform. By the way, don't give up your EVA job for a pilot slot," Cat said, giving him a small shove. As they passed into darkness once more, she turned on the cargo bay lights to illuminate their new guest.

◆

CAPCOM radioed at the next available opportunity. "*Intrepid*, Houston. Another short one. Do you have the Chirp captured?"

"Affirmative, Houston. Cat has the panel marked "Open Here" as close as she can get to the airlock outer hatch."

"Hayes, once you have the door open, the intravehicular items are first, then a military-to-S-band transverter radio to upgrade your communications, oxygen tanks, and, finally, the repair kit and tools. There is also another handheld radio. They all have tethers."

"Roger. While Cat holds the Chirp, I pull myself and everything else around with tether lines."

"That's the idea; it will be obvious what should stay in the payload bay and what should come inside. You should be able to get it done in a short EVA. Once the Chirp is empty, you can jettison it. You will need the arm, with its extension, for your repair work."

"We should have asked Sharon to leave her MMU before she so rudely departed."

"You'll do fine. When you get back, you can tell us how you did it. LOS soon; bye until next sked."

◆

Once he had the airlock outer hatch open, Hayes made the short leap to the base of the robot arm. "Nailed it first time," Hayes said as he slowly maneuvered his way to the end of the RMS.

"My poor Canadarm is taking a lot of abuse on this mission." The arm was not designed to be slammed from the side. "Your two-hundred-something kilos of mass are not gentle."

Hayes attached a second tether between his suit and Chirp to avoid having to make another unguided jump. As he unlocked the door panel, he said, "I keep seeing Jack out of the corner of my eye. He should be here, dammit."

"That's his spirit here to guide you."

"Thank you. I would like to believe that."

By the end of his third hour, he had everything sorted and was able to load most of the Chirp's contents into the airlock. He was ready to close the hatch and reenter *Intrepid*'s middeck. "Without Jack, there's enough room in here for all our supplies. If he were here . . ."

No time for us to grieve. Cat prayed. *Lord, let us live. Let us live long enough to get home and grieve.*

◆

With Hayes back inside, the first item they checked out was the portable radio from the Chirp. "Houston, *Intrepid*, on our new handheld radio."

Cat was relieved to hear CAPCOM reply. "*Intrepid*, signal is better than before. Hope the payload bay transverter will get you back to full speed with communications. How is the unloading coming?"

"All done," Hayes said. "We have the schedule for comm opportunities to ground stations over the next few days. The new radio, with the antenna stuck to the cockpit window, will make chatting with home much easier. We may not make all the schedules if we are busy. And FLIGHT, EGIL, and everyone else needs to know we are down to two fuel cells. Number one is toast."

"Understood. You're going to get questions on that and a lot of advice. Have you looked at the wing repair scheme? Any questions?"

"No questions yet. On my next EVA, I will do a run through of the procedure and start to work. After I install the wonderful new transverter."

"Hey, this is Cat. How many EVAs will it take Hayes to get us ready to fly home?"

"Our WETF simulations took two six-hour gigs," CAPCOM said. "But Hayes will tell you it's easier in a vacuum than in a swimming pool."

"Yeah, right," Hayes said. "Is anybody back from Russia yet? How are our mates?"

"We think they're okay. Update on next comm pass. LOS. Houston, out.

Buran *Landing + One Day*
Leninsk, Kazakhstan

Hours before dawn, Matt rolled over in his creaky proletariat bed and fumbled the phone up to his ear to choke its ringing. Exhausted, he and Lisa had been sleeping in each other's arms to stay warm. "Matt, is that you? This is Kurt Robertshaw. Where are you?"

Stas had come through on his promise of a call, albeit not too conveniently. "Kurt, yeah, this is Matt. I'm in my shithole hotel in Leninsk. All of us are still here. Not prisoners, but no longer honored guests, either. What the fuck time is it where you are?"

"Watch your language, doc. You know they're listening. Here in Moscow, we're getting the same treatment. We are all in the Prophy, the same dorm building in Star City I stayed in during the Apollo-Soyuz days. What do you hear about the *Buran* crew?"

"Nothing since they landed. My demands to be taken to the landing site were refused."

"Same frustration here—we can't get any kind of answer out of anybody. I've seen this before. The Soviets are embarrassed and can't think of a way to save face—not yet at least. Gorbachev is not getting the PR boost he was counting on; it's exactly the opposite."

"Have you talked to mission control?"

"Yeah, told 'em what little I knew. They were asking me to do all kinds of things that, of course, I can't do. We only have the Soviet's word that the crew are okay. Until we can lay eyes on them, we both have the same worries about the truth."

"Can't we send a plane from Japan or South Korea up to Vladivostok and pick them up? That can't be more than a few hours away."

"You know that can't happen without permission from the Russians. As I told you at our briefing, Matt, we all have our pay grade. This problem is way above our heads. NASA needs to work it through channels to retrieve the surviving crew and get them home."

"Two souls are still on board *Intrepid*."

"No one has forgotten about Cat and Hayes. During my call to the MCC, the flight director hinted that NASA does have another option. He didn't want to get into it on the phone line for obvious reasons. It's not another shuttle launch from anywhere. That's still impossible. Unfortunately, we've lost all comm with the shuttle. We can say it's in a stable orbit. Everyone's working to reestablish contact."

"Cat and Hayes must be going through hell. My only contact here at Baikonur is Stas, who's trying to be helpful. I'd give anything to be able to talk to the crew—the ones in orbit and the ones back on Earth. Maybe you'll have better luck. I don't see why they won't let us do that."

"I hope it's their military bureaucracy fumbling around and not a more alarming reason."

"Don't say it, Kurt; don't even think it. Can you call me again?"

"I can keep asking. Regards to Lisa and the rest of the gang."

"Tell Patel to get his arse in gear and take care of his crew. It's good to hear your voice, Kurt."

"You can tell Lloyd yourself. He wants to talk to you. Hang in there."

Lloyd came on the line. "Matt, I don't know when we'll get a chance to talk again, and there's something you need to be aware of. I did get a line to flight medicine and talked to Helen. Or tried to. Matt, she was hysterical talking about Jack. I've never, ever seen her lose her cool like this, no matter what was hitting the fan. I told her to go home. Don't try to call her anytime soon."

Matt's thoughts flashed back to a quiet conversation with Helen several months ago. She'd had a bad premonition about STS-92A. She needed a relief valve, and trusting his discretion, she had confided her fears to Matt. He was happy he could help her and Jack get together at Vandenberg before the launch. Now her worst fears had come true. Swept up in his own problems and those of the crew, Matt hadn't considered how Jack's death must have shredded poor Helen. "Lloyd, thanks for letting me know. Is there someone who will be with her?" Matt waited for an answer, but the line was dead.

Matt hung up the phone and put his arms around Lisa, who was wide awake. He narrated the Moscow side of the conversation for her. "This wasn't the time to reveal Stas's confession about *Buran* not being ready."

"I'm happy to be warm next to you," Lisa said, "but I can't cope with our situation—the crew's situation. My mind keeps going between Terry, Dom, and Sharon, and then Cat and Hayes. What must it be like to be marooned in *Intrepid*? What are they doing?"

"They're doing what the best-of-the-best do," Matt said. "They are trying to stay alive as long as possible and keep their ship going, too. What happened to their communications system? Being cut off from any ground support is unprecedented and beyond awful. I am sure Cat and Hayes are also working on that." Matt began to dress. "Skipping a bath today with the especially frigid water. I need to go find Stas. He's somewhere in this pit of a hotel."

A knock sounded on their door. When Matt opened it, he saw Stas impeccably dressed and holding his large briefcase.

"Good early morning, Dr. Wallace," he said. Leaning to one side, he also doffed his cap to Lisa, who was still in bed. "Good morning to you also, Ms. Guinne. I am pleased to inform you that we are all going to Moscow to be reunited with your team. Please get your things together. I will wait in the lobby, but please hurry. Our transport plane will be here within the hour. Rick, Jeff, and Randy are already at the airport."

Matt nodded and said, "What of our astronauts at the Khorol base, Stas?" Exasperation colored his voice.

"Dr. Wallace, I am told they are fine and still in debrief. We'll know more when we get to the TsUP."

Matt knew Stas well enough to tell when he was hedging. As Stas turned to leave, Matt muttered, "More bullshit."

Eastern alternate aerodrome for Buran
Far Eastern Russia
Khorol, Primorsky Krai

The soldiers escorting the three *Intrepid* astronauts unloaded them at a dingy barracks near where *Buran* had landed. The guards were intent on separating Sharon from the men, a division the astronauts weren't going to permit without a fight. Terry and Dom held Sharon between them and shouted at the soldiers in a futile effort to communicate that Sharon was staying with them.

Before things got violent, a Russian officer appeared. In broken English, he asked, "You want woman stay with you in small room? Two beds, one bathroom, okay?" he managed.

"We need to speak to our people at NASA, sir," said Terry. "We need to speak with Fyodor Titov."

"Everybody is tired. You rest. Talk tomorrow. We will bring you food now," the officer said.

"We need some clothes, please." added Dom.

"Da, clothes, okay." The officer nodded.

They were locked into a room with two chairs, a table, two cots, and a small bathroom. "Thanks for saving me from those goons, fellas," said Sharon, as she sagged into one of the chairs. "I didn't want to go down that road."

"Wasn't going to happen, Sharon," Terry said. Looking around, he said, "I've envisioned many fates for myself, including blowing up, but these past few hours have been like nothing I could ever imagine. What the hell are these people doing?"

Dom lay down on one of the cots, still in his reentry pressure suit. "They weren't expecting us at this base, but anybody can see what happened today. Are the locals incompetent bozos or are they following orders?"

Terry grabbed the back of a chair and then collapsed into it.

"Are you okay, Terry?" Sharon asked.

"Yes, thanks. Inner ear getting used to one-g again. Our special treatment must be endorsed by the Soviet government, but they can't keep us here forever. Gorbachev, or at least their space program, is feeling embarrassed. You would think saving three astronauts and three cosmonauts is worth talking about, under the circumstances. We're not all dead . . ."

"Yeah, but Jack is, and we all know what will happen to Hayes and Cat." Tears welled up in Sharon's eyes. "Damn, we were doing it! It almost worked; I was looking right into Jack's eyes; I could have touched him." She bent over, with her head in her hands.

The door flew open, and soldiers brought in meals on trays, fatigues for the men, and an additional cot. One of them saluted wordlessly before they were left alone again.

"I'm bustin' out of here tomorrow if I have to walk to Houston," Sharon said.

Flight Day Twenty-Five
Intrepid

As Cat rehydrated some of their dwindling food supply, she asked, "You're the aeronautical engineer. Do *you* think this wing fix will work?"

"Let's take it for granted I can install the patch perfectly..."

"It must be wonderful to be so confident of one's perfection. Just splain to poor Lucy how it's supposed to work, Ricky." She shoved his dinner in his general direction.

Hayes caught his tray and said, "That's a little harsh. I'm trying to be optimistic like you."

After eating a few bites, Cat said, "Sorry I snapped at you. I feel like somebody's been using sandpaper on my nervous system. I'm waiting for something else to go wrong."

"Your one-man support group is feeling it too, my love. We need to wrap this mission up, don't we?"

They finished eating in silence, and then Hayes showed Cat the diagrams for the wing patch plan from the Chirp. Hayes said, "A key part is the bolts—they are made from brittle but heat-resistant tungsten. They're very long and must have been a bitch to manufacture. Tungsten softens as it nears its melting point of 6,200° Fahrenheit, which may or may not be good, since the wing flexes a lot. The wing panel patch piece is fragile because it's brittle, too, and big, and the edges taper down to a very thin edge to blend into the wing."

"I understood most of that. Yes, extreme optimism is in order. It's a very complex Band-Aid."

"In an odd way, we're fortunate. The hole is at the very front edge of the wing. I need to drill a bolt hole straight through the RCC panel on either side of the gap. But I don't have to drill through any internal wing structure, and I don't need a three-foot-long bolt, because the wing is thin at the front. Then a nut goes on the end of each bolt, the patch is snugged over the opening, and we're all set. Another key is trying to make the patch smooth. The shockwaves on reentry create a boundary layer . . . Never mind, I'm going into the weeds. Simply put, my concern is my lumpy, bumpy repair will let the 10,000° plasma get too close to the wing, and it will still burn up."

"Are you going to lie awake tonight thinking about this?" Cat said.

"No, I lie awake at night thinking about you. I want us to have a future."

"Don't worry, my mother was a witch, and I inherited many of her skills. I've decided we're going to be fine."

"What would the Pope say about that sort of attitude?" Hayes asked.

"He doesn't know, and it won't hurt him. There are a lot of things *you* will never know about me, but they won't hurt you . . . because they're none of your business." Cat pushed on Hayes's chest, and he floated away. "Let's tidy up and get you outside after our shuttle housekeeping chores are done. Big day today."

"Once that hole is covered, we're headed for home."

♦

After exiting the airlock, Hayes checked Chirp for any items he might have missed and crammed the now-empty pod with shuttle trash and spent LiOH canisters. When he was done, Cat gave it a farewell shove with the Canadarm and it moved away from *Intrepid*. Her RMS was now free for the work ahead. *Wonder how long until Chirp burns up on reentry?* She watched as their rescue pod silently diverged from them, like a canoe drifting away from a dock. *Will we burn up first?* She shook it off. *Hell, no.*

Shortly into the installation of the radio transverter/repeater in the cargo bay that would turn their weak radio signals into a strong microwave signal and restore communications with the ground, Hayes muttered, "Goddamn Murphy's Law . . ."

"Yeah, 'What can go wrong, will go wrong.' Why did they name that for an Irishwoman, anyway?" asked Cat.

"The power plug for this new radio is supposed to match the plug already here for the Centaur launch cradle. But, oh no, it doesn't match. That would be giving us a break. The pins are all wrong. Someone got the wrong drawings. I'll have to jumper it."

"Don't get your ham radio dander up. Let it go. You don't have time to work this problem now; the wing fix is what's on the critical path. You said yourself we don't need MCC right now, except to answer a question." Hayes didn't reply, so she added, "The backup handheld radio will be fine. Let's get you to the wing breach. You have everything organized." No answer was forthcoming. "Hayes Bartlett, listen to me. I can't be your lover if I'm dead because you obsessed about your damn radio, and we ran out of time."

Hayes turned to face Cat through the aft cockpit windows. "Okay, you got my attention. Are you always right, besides being beautiful? Don't answer that. You're correct about this. I need to move on. Move me over to my wing-repair-kit pile. I'll refocus my astronaut laser beam attention. And just out of curiosity, has anyone ever been foolish enough to call you a bitch?"

"No one who wanted the airlock hatch unlocked. Yes, an occasional loser prick has applied that repulsive name to me. One or two of them still have their balls intact."

"I phrased my question very carefully. I'm aware that you know your way around male genitalia, surgically speaking. Stop here; this a good spot."

Despite the time crunch, Hayes needed to practice run-throughs of the sections of the repair checklist that could only be done in the payload bay. There was no margin for error once he was out on the wing. There would be no hours of underwater simulation until it was second nature. For Hayes, there would be no do-overs.

An hour later, Hayes was smarter about the wing patch and more worried. "Cat, I've got a problem. I need to drill holes through the intact part of the wing to bolt on the wing patch. I need it a to be straight and true. The patch is predrilled, and it's got to match. On Earth, drills have a little air-bubble level on the end, so you look down and level yourself up before you drill."

"You have a steady hand there, mate. Are you sure you can't eyeball it?"

"I'm a confident worker, but I only get one chance. I need a level—a reference trick."

"Like a magic helper? How about a gyroscope?"

"What?"

"One of my middeck experiments has a small, battery-powered gyroscope. We mount that to the end of your drill, and you set the drill perpendicular to the wing without a bit in the chuck and turn on the gyro. After that, it would hint when you went out of plane."

"I like that better than any of my ideas. You're a smart gal."

"That's the Cajun way, Hayes. Use what you got—might be a piece of cane, a hook, and duct tape."

"To do what?" he asked.

"Catch a gator, cher."

♦ *D. K. Broadwell* ♦

"How long have I been out here?"

"You've been out nearly six hours. Grab your drills and I'll bring you back in. You'll need a full seven-hour EVA next time."

"You are becoming the de facto commander. Ingressing . . ."

"Glad you figured that out, Major."

Eastern alternate aerodrome for Buran
Far Eastern Russia
Khorol, Primorsky Krai

Rattling blinds jerked Sharon out of her restless sleep. A puff of frigid air cascaded down the wall onto her cot from the tiny open window in their locked room. She had noticed that when the blinds moved, it indicated someone had entered the ramshackle barracks where they were being held prisoner. She rose from her cot and hissed, "Guys, we may have visitors."

"I'm up," said Terry.

"Me, too," said Dom, picking up a chair and moving next to the door to the hallway. They had been locked up incommunicado for three full nights, a clear message their fate was still being decided. Plenty of time to speculate on what was being planned for them, and many scenarios did not end well. The stifling, musty room was a dungeon to them.

The door cracked and a flashlight shone through, followed by Fyodor's head. "Comrades," he said, "leave the lights off and keep your voices low." The *Buran* pilot entered, followed by the *Buran* commander, Nikolai.

"We need to talk," Fyodor said. "Gennadiy is guarding our back. The stupid guards are passed out from all the vodka we gave them, but there may be others." He dangled a ring of keys. Nikolai stayed in the doorway, watching the hall. "Are you okay?"

"Yeah, we're fine, except: What the hell is going on?" asked Terry. "We know zero."

"The *Buran* generals are covering their fat asses right and left with all kinds of stories putting blame on *Intrepid* crew. The three of us have been restricted to this base, too, with no outside communication allowed. Of course, that hasn't stopped us from talking to our cosmonaut friends."

Dom said, "Everybody knows we're still alive, right? Is the army planning to lock us up or worse?"

"The world knows you were saved, but the party line is that the *Intrepid* and its crew caused the rescue to fail," Fyodor said.

Sharon said, "That's—"

Fyodor held up his hand. "Yes, their story is lies, but they do not want anyone to contradict it. Like you three. Or us."

The space travelers looked at each other in silence until Terry spoke. "I get the picture. What do we do about it? What about our NASA team here in the Soviet Union?"

"We know not much more than you. I think your team from launch site is back in Moscow. We considered hijacking an aircraft from this decrepit base and flying all of us out, but that won't work. We would need too much help from ground crew. But know we are watching and will not leave until we know you are safe. They'll have to arrest us—"

Fyodor was interrupted by Nikolai, who backed into the room and quietly shut the door. He whispered something and Fyodor translated.

"Someone is coming."

It was Gennadiy, who half-opened the door and spoke with Fyodor before disappearing. "We need to go," Fyodor said. "The worthless guards are getting restless."

Terry gripped Fyodor's shoulder. "You risked your lives to save us, and you succeeded. We can't ever repay that. Thank you from all of us."

Fyodor reciprocated the gesture. "You would have done the same for us, my space comrade. We are so sorry about the friends we had to leave behind and the death of your friend."

• *Ruthless Sky* •

After the cosmonauts left, Dom said, "Do you think they can do anything to help us?" Terry shrugged. "At least we had a chance to thank them. Let's try to get some sleep."

Buran *Landing + Seventy-Two Hours*
Washington, DC

A sweaty Pyotr Malkin entered the Russian embassy with a bellyache. *Will I ever stop feeling this way every time I come here?* His family had escaped to America from the Soviet Union when he was a teenager, and he could never shake the feeling he was going to be arrested and sent back to Russia. His bosses at the State Department sent him to the embassy today because neither the Soviet ambassador nor the next tier of diplomats below him were willing to talk to anyone from State. Malkin's lower rank matched the consulate officer he was going to meet.

Malkin's mission was clear: find out what had happened to the astronauts who were aboard *Buran* when the shuttle rescue mission failed and, most importantly, get them under US control. *NASA is apoplectic about their missing crew, and I don't blame them,* thought Malkin, *but the Russians don't do well when the borscht hits the fan.*

He was ushered into a dark-paneled room and the consul behind a large desk said, "Please have a seat, Mr. Malkin. Tell me, do you miss your homeland?"

"I see you know my history, sir. No, I'm thoroughly American now, and my joy comes from serving my adopted country. I hope you're enjoying your assignment in the US." Malkin smiled and focused on relaxing the white-knuckle death grip he had on his armrests.

"I like living in America well enough. The toilet paper is much better here, eh?"

Not that old joke again, please, thought Malkin. Most of the embassy staff who weren't spies would be happy to spend their entire career in America if they could bring their families over. The two made small talk for a few minutes until Malkin said, "Sir, I've been sent to get an update on the status of the three astronauts who were aboard *Buran* and the body of their dead comrade. We know there was an emergency return from orbit, but we are totally in the dark about our people's welfare. You can understand NASA's distress. They're imagining the worst."

Leaning back in his chair, the consul tented his fingers and said, "Your NASA has been notified through proper channels that your astronauts are doing well and recuperating at Khorol, one of our eastern landing sites. I am sorry that your crippled vehicle caused a death and an aborted rescue while leaving two of your crew to perish. That is tragic, but we did save two of them. And of course, the woman astronaut who launched from Baikonur is with them."

Malkin didn't know if this were true or not, but it didn't matter. His experience kept him on track. "Be that as it may, sir, we need you to transport our surviving and deceased crew members back to us immediately. They are our responsibility." He gazed steadily into the impassive face of the diplomat across the desk from him. *Nothing to read there.*

"Mr. Malkin." The consul sighed and put his finger to his lips. He rolled his eyes upwards, and briefly gestured to the ceiling. "I truly am sorry this has played out so badly for NASA and your country."

Even this level bureaucrat is wary of being recorded saying something improper, thought Malkin.

"We Soviets feel space should be a place for peace and cooperation. Sometimes, on the ground, this is more difficult, you know?"

"I would regret if President Bush had to call Chairman Gorbachev and escalate the issue to that drastic level. All we want is our people back. What's the problem?"

"Let us say, the chairman has been personally involved since he initiated this rescue plan with your president. He is very . . . upset and concerned about this situation. He wants all personnel to remain together until an investigation of this tragedy is complete."

Something screwed up the rescue, and Gorbachev is not happy. He wants to nail down a scapegoat while he still controls the scene. "And how long is that going to take? It's inhumane to hold our innocent astronauts as hostages. I am authorized to ask permission for a transport from Japan to come to your base and repatriate them."

"That will be quite impossible. You know these situations will play out as they must, Mr. Malkin." The consul reached in a desk drawer, retrieved an expensive-looking pen, and handed it to Malkin. "Here. I always give my guests a finely crafted Soviet memento. My sadness at the unfortunate events with your space program is genuine. Please come back anytime."

Malkin sighed and took several deep breaths as he reached the Georgetown sidewalk, but he didn't have much to take back to State, except the pen, which he disassembled when he got back to his car. He half-expected a surveillance bug, but instead there was a scroll of paper inside the tube. It was scrawled in Russian and not likely to be traceable. This espionage prop made his stomach pain worse, but the message was welcome:

Buran *malfunctioned. Military faction that wanted crew to disappear is overruled. 3 crew + body+ rats are on way home in next 24 h.*

As usual, any communication with the Soviets raised as many questions as it answered. *So, the big secret is they messed up, and he couldn't just tell me. Does NASA know this?* Why did he take the risk to inform us? Was he not supposed to know? *What rats—what the fuck?* Malkin's head was throbbing, but he hurried back to the State Department to spread the welcome news.

Eastern alternate aerodrome
Khorol, Primorsky Krai

None of the Americans could sleep after the cosmonauts' visit, but they felt more like human bipeds after several day's rest in one-g. With the arrival of a food cart, they dined on beans and toast; the coffee wasn't bad.

After soldiers cleared their trays, a Soviet officer and two adjutants rolled chairs into the room and placed themselves in a semicircle facing the astronauts. The officer was carrying a metal ammunition box. Terry was relieved to hear him speak proficient English.

"Good morning, spacemen comrades. I am Lt. Col. Moskalenko. My condolences on the death of your Col. Badger. I hope you are doing well this morning after your ordeal."

"Yes," Terry said, "we are grateful to be alive, but it is well past the time for us to speak with our own country's representatives. We do still have two astronauts aboard *Intrepid*. Why are we being held in isolation?"

"I will try and address these complicated issues for you, Commander. But first, I will tell you that you will all be on a plane to Moscow tomorrow to rejoin your associates from NASA."

"That is very good news," said Dom. Terry waited for the complications.

The colonel said, "As this rescue mission was only a partial success, it did not fully meet the expectations of the Central Committee of the Communist Party. There are many people, including myself, who have invested much and worked very hard on the *Buran* program, yes? They do not deserve to be seen in a bad light. It is important to cast positivity on this situation."

"Colonel," Terry said, "your cosmonauts are space heroes for what they accomplished getting us home, but you cannot deny that there was a major hardware malfunction."

"Yes, of course, but we wish to emphasize the more favorable aspects of the mission. A report has been sent to the Central Committee and Chairman Gorbachev that does precisely this. Yes, it was a heroic rescue mission. It was cut short by problems with . . . well . . . it's uncertain. Let us say there were contributing failures with your *Intrepid* spacecraft."

Sharon began to rise from her chair, but Terry pulled her back into her seat. "Colonel," she blurted, "what does that lie have to do with us, besides tarnishing our crewmates who are still onboard? You dishonor our dead friend."

"Miss Maralow, I understand your feelings. What I am telling you is, you will be taken to Moscow to meet your friends. You will not say or do anything while you are on Soviet soil to contradict the true version of events, which I have outlined for you. What you do in the US is your business, but our people and our government need to hear our version, the most reasonable version."

"And if we refuse to lie if someone asks us what happened?" Terry said.

"I do not believe this will happen, Commander, but it would certainly make you an enemy of the USSR if you choose to confuse this issue. You have my word that your return to the United States will be expedited. Of course, the remains of Col. Badger and your equipment will accompany you."

"What have you done with him? To him?" asked Terry.

"Your fallen comrade has been removed from his space suit and respectfully placed in a bag and a casket. We have been attempting to keep him cool." For the first time Moskalenko looked perturbed by the conversation.

"And his EMU, his space suit?" Terry asked pointedly.

"We have been cleaning it. It will be returned also at the proper time."

Yeah, right, Terry thought. *If we ever see his EMU again, it will be in little pieces.*

"What about Nikolai and the others?" asked Dom.

"They will be returning to Moscow training center soon. I assure you they're in agreement with our communiqué. They will be due many honors, no doubt," said Moskalenko. "One more thing. Fyodor told me you were very attached to the mice you rescued from *Intrepid.*" He showed them the ammo box, which was covered by a wire mesh on top. Inside was a mother mouse and four little babies, with bedding and a water dish. "I am sorry to report the other mice have died, but as you can see, you have more mice anyway."

Dom took the box from the colonel. "Thank you for this. I look forward to thanking Fyodor myself." He went to his reentry suit and pulled out a bag of mouse chow from the leg pocket.

"Good day. Your escort to the plane will be here very early tomorrow. Have a good night's rest and a safe journey home." The Russians took their chairs and left. The three astronauts sat on their cots, looking at each other in disbelief, and then relief as they realized they were going home.

Flight Day Twenty-Six
Intrepid

Using the bolt holes in the RCC wing patch from Chirp as a template with Cat's "magic hand" gyro technique, Hayes carefully drilled pilot holes on either side of *Intrepid*'s gaping wound straight through the upper and lower part of the wing's leading edge. Two of the smaller diameter drill bits broke off, but he had spares.

Working from both sides of the wing, he slowly enlarged the holes to permit the bolts to go through. He was paranoid about having the patch panel drift away or chip at the edges, and he constantly checked that it remained in the bag tethered to his waist.

"Your EVA elapsed time is six and a half hours," Cat said from the RMS station. "Lookin' good, my man, but no way you can finish today."

"Are you ordering me to ingress, my captain? I concur," Hayes said. "I want to bring parts of the hardware inside, cut pieces of insulation for shimming and stuffing, and wrap this baby up tomorrow."

"You're very agreeable today."

"For once, everything went as planned. So far. Take me back to the bay, and I'll get the rest of the parts. You're my *deus ex machina*."

"That would be *dea ex machina* in my case. I am a space *goddess*," Cat said.

"Ooo, I forgot you are a Catholic Latin scholar."

When Hayes was back inside, Cat helped him out of his suit. She noticed that the back of his "Snoopy" communications cap was wet. "What happened here?" she asked. "Did your drinking bag leak?"

"I felt the damp, but I thought it was just my head sweating. The cooling garment might protect me from heating by the sun but not from flop sweat worrying about a bad performance. It's not my drinking bag. I drank that up early on."

"Feel this. It's soaked," Cat said. Her skin prickled with foreboding. "Has this ever happened before?"

"Not to me. Let's get Snoopy dried out. I've only got to go out one more time."

His expression became more serious. "I don't know what it is, but there isn't anything to do about it now, except carefully examine the suit and get it hooked up and prepped for tomorrow."

When he was back in his shorts, Cat wrapped her arms around him. "You're my very own single point failure, Major, but I never worry about your performance."

"A man is quite honored to hear such a thing from you, ma'am."

◆

"How are we doing on gas resources?" asked Hayes while they were eating.

"The oxygen supply is getting tight. We need it for the fuel cells, and we blow out at least one hundred cubic feet of cabin atmosphere every time you go out the airlock hatch. That costs nitrogen too."

"Flushing out the cabin is a good thing. It gets rid of my farts that you complain about."

"No more onions for you, Major Flatulence, until we get back to base."

"I like onions."

"I've used three out of the four oxygen tanks that came in the Chirp, trying to conserve the onboard liquid oxygen supply."

"Tomorrow's the final push EVA," said Hayes. "I'll stay out until I'm finished, even if I need to use my emergency oxygen packs. Then we're going home."

"I considered fiddling with the cabin atmosphere and going up to a functional eight thousand feet altitude to save oxygen. I fly my Bonanza that high with no ill effects. But I didn't want to screw up your EVA prebreathe schedule. You don't need the bends, like poor Jack had."

"Doing so many EVAs in a row without a break is risky enough. This is the kind of problem Matt and the space docs would love to noodle on, but we don't have the time or bandwidth to fool with it."

"I'll lower the cabin altitude back to normal after you're done tomorrow. Aren't you glad you didn't waste any more time on the radio transverter fix?

"Yes, I am," Hayes said. "Is it possible that sometimes you might be the slightest bit sanctimonious?"

"How would you like a sanctimonious punch in the nose?" Cat raised her fist, but Hayes wrapped his own hand around it and pulled her toward him.

"I'd much rather have a kiss on the lips."

Cat gave him a peck on the cheek. "By the way," she said, "you left the toilet seat up."

Hayes was confused and then laughed. "That's not possible with the waste collection system."

"I was speaking figuratively. You left your personal urine funnel on the end of the vacuum tube. Gross!"

"Oops. I was in a hurry to get my suit on. I'll never do that on Earth, I promise," Hayes said, with a smirk.

"Away with you and go chase yourself! What was it you told me about men always lying?"

February 1990
JSC Auditorium
Baker Commission hearing

Terry sat at the front of the packed auditorium while the Baker Commission was on a break from hearing testimony. He had already been in the witness chair that morning and was scheduled to continue after the break. He leaned over to Dom. "They weren't interested in the slightest in the launch explosion at Slick Six or in my opinion of NASA's launch anomaly decision-making," he said.

"They are more interested in Russian bashing. Dr. Feynman seems to be the only one with a good handle on NASA screwing up foam shedding as an acceptable risk," Dom said. "The others keep changing the subject." He was next up on the witness list. "Sharon was loaded for bear to give them an earful about NASA's handling of 'out-of-family' launch problems yesterday, but they cut her off. I'm surprised they didn't save her for last."

"Maybe that saved her career. Whatever career we have left, that is," Terry said.

Nearly all of Terry's questions from the commission had been about the events before and after his transfer to *Buran*. Chairman Baker particularly was interested in Terry's professional impression of the Soviet vehicle and its crew and the role he played as a crew member during the emergency deorbit and landing. Terry had gotten a laugh with a remark about entering an alternate universe, as in a *Star Trek* episode. There wasn't much for him to say about the *Buran* ride back to Earth. He helped set up the seats and, thereafter, was along for the ride.

He didn't tell the commission how awkward and frustrating it had been for him to be a passive passenger at such a critical time, unable to do anything to save his crew. He was accustomed to being the one responsible for everyone. And this wasn't the venue to convey his sadness at the loss of Jack Badger and leaving two crewmembers behind in the doomed *Intrepid*.

Dom said, "They also weren't interested in hearing what an amazing job Commander Kondakova and his crew did to get us back safely. I plan to slip that into the record if you don't get a chance. The Russians deserve that. We have no idea if the *Buran* crew are now heroes of the Soviet Union or disgraced scapegoats."

"I know what they're going to ask you," Terry said.

"Yeah, I do too. I'll be in the paper tomorrow, not you."

Excerpts from Baker Commission Hearing Transcript

Chairman Baker: Commander Rogers, can you take us through what happened after you were released from the Khorol air base where *Buran* had landed?

Terence Rogers, the Witness: After our meeting with Lt. Col. Moskalenko, we were loaded on a Soviet transport jet the next day for the long flight from the far eastern edge of the USSR to Moscow. Colonel Moskalenko and a few troops came with us, but they stayed in the front of the plane. We sat in the back, with John Badger's casket. We were also accompanied by a crate containing EMU components and any other US parts the Russians felt like giving back to us. They kept most of Colonel Badger's EMU and Sharon Maralow's MMU. They still have them, as far as I know.

We had no further substantive conversations with Colonel Moskalenko. We ate, tried to catch up on sleep, and arrived in Moscow. We were transferred to a big van and finally, finally, were taken to Star City and a reunion with Kurt Robertshaw and his team.

Chairman Baker: Have the Soviets had access to that kind of technology transfer previously, access to one of our space suits?

Terence Rogers, the Witness: Not according to Kurt Robertshaw, who was very involved during the Apollo-Soyuz Test Project in 1975. That was the last time the Soviets had any direct dealings with NASA hardware.

Chairman Baker: The people who had remained at Baikonur Cosmodrome were brought to Star City also?

Terence Rogers, the Witness: Yes, our crew surgeon, Dr. Wallace; the MMU team; and the photographer all arrived in Moscow before we did. It was a bittersweet reunion, given the death of Jack Badger and the status of Bartlett and Riley onboard *Intrepid*. Doctors Wallace and Patel checked us over and certified us as fit to go home. By that point, we were getting what my father would have called "the bum's rush" from the Russians. They flew us to the closest exit, which was Schönefeld Airport in East Berlin, and trucked us over to Checkpoint Charlie. We immediately flew in a US Air Force transport back to Houston from Tempelhof Airport. We had no contact with the Russian or German public during the whole episode. We didn't see any of the demonstrations that were going on, which led up to the fall of the Berlin Wall last year.

Chairman Baker: That was fortunate, wasn't it—that you were not forced to deal with anyone asking you about the Soviet propaganda version of the rescue?

Terence Rogers, the Witness: Yes, Mr. Chairman, it was.

* * *

Dr. Sally Ride: Since that concludes everyone else's list of questions for you, I have one more. Do you have any comments on the murine experiments you oversaw during your mission?

Dominick Petrocelli, the Witness: (laughing) I was hoping to escape this drama, but I know it has captured the media's interest. The murine gestation/memory experiment was onboard after it won a nationwide competition among elementary schools for inclusion on the STS-92A manifest. It had two objectives—one was to look for any effects on baby mice who had gestated for what was supposed to be a week in space, and the other was to observe whether a trip on *Intrepid* altered the long-term maze-running memory of mice who had been previously trained. A control group of mice remained behind in Omaha where the school is located. I was their in-flight guardian, so to speak, on the crew activity plan.

Dr. Sally Ride: You were a good guardian, Dom. You kept them alive and took them over to *Buran* with you. Your crewmates were not as enthused about your rodent solicitations, were they?

Dominick Petrocelli, the Witness: We were all very stressed, but I can state categorically that my care of the mice, or taking them with me, had no impacts on our mission. I was separated from them after our landing and detention at Khorol, and when they were returned to me one female had given birth. The males and other female had died in unknown circumstances. The babies were later humanely euthanized here in the US, but I don't know the experiment's conclusions. The mommy space mouse died a natural death, I heard.

Dr. Sally Ride: There have been reports in the press that you may have had extra motivation to take care of the mice, beyond dedication to the hard work of the Nebraska schoolchildren. Would you like to set the record straight on this matter?

Dominick Petrocelli, the Witness: The press has deeply investigated my life story because of this tragedy. That's the price of temporary celebrity. In the interest of clearing up any distortions, I'll give the commission a little of my background that would not otherwise be pertinent to its work.

I come from a large Italian family that lived in Paterson, New Jersey—lots of aunts, uncles, and cousins. I shared a bedroom with my older brother, Vinnie, who had pet mice. I asked my mother for my own pet mice, but she said I couldn't have any until Vinnie got tired of his. One night, when I was six, our home caught on fire. Vinnie carried me downstairs to my mother, and she and I escaped to safety. She didn't notice when my brother went back for his mice. Unfortunately, he perished in the fire. For some, that helps explain my emotional attachment to our rodent passengers, but I maintain I was only doing my job under difficult circumstances.

Dr. Sally Ride: Dom, thank you for your candor. I hope that will put to rest speculation about the schoolchildren's space mice. I know speaking about this painful memory was not easy.

Dominick Petrocelli, the Witness: Thanks, Sally. I understand the commission is going to award you an honorary psychology degree at the end of today's session. [laughter]

* * *

Chairman Baker: You notified the chair you wanted to make a brief closing statement for the record, Dr. Feynman. You will have an opportunity to include written comments for the final report, but you may have a few moments now to outline your position.

• *D. K. Broadwell* •

Professor Feynman: Thank you, Chairman Baker. I wanted to focus a moment on the root cause of how *Intrepid* came to be marooned in orbit, a topic the board has spent less time on than I think is appropriate. After the testimony of NASA management, we have found that certification criteria used in flight readiness reviews often develop a gradually decreasing strictness. The argument that the same risk was flown before without failure is often accepted as an argument for the safety of accepting it again. Because of this, obvious weaknesses are accepted again and again, sometimes without a sufficiently serious attempt to remedy them or to delay a flight because of their continued presence. The foam shedding is certainly in this category.

Chairman Baker: Please wrap this up, Professor.

Professor Feynman: My summary is this, Mr. Chairman. For a successful technology, reality must take precedence over public relations, for nature cannot be fooled.

Chairman Baker: Thank you, Professor. Meeting adjourned.

Flight Day Twenty-Six
Intrepid

CAPCOM: "Now that you have the wing patch under control, let's address reentry and landing. You both have reviewed the reentry checklists? Any questions?"

"Cat graciously says I can have the left seat. We've found all the switches and understand how to deorbit. We obviously need Houston's help to time the OMS burns so that we land at Edwards."

"GUIDANCE is working up every deorbit option for the next few days," CAPCOM said. "We are optimistic that *Intrepid* can lock onto both the TACAN and microwave landing navigational aids when you get to the autoland segment. I think you would agree this is a time to let the digital autopilot take *Intrepid* all the way to touchdown."

"You left out that autoland to touchdown has never been tested. However, I agree with you. I will be happy to merely extend the landing gear."

"LOS soon. Good luck with bolting that panel on tomorrow, Hayes. Houston out."

♦

"Why didn't NASA ever fully test the autoland system?" asked Cat.

"They were going to test it on STS-5, but NASA chickened out. STS-3 took it down to one hundred feet or so, but the autoland program wasn't even finished yet. Let's face it, commanders want to land the shuttle by hand—even if it's only the last three thousand feet. 'Gimme the stick' has been an astronaut mantra since Project Mercury. A full stop on autoland makes you and me both NASA test pilots."

"That's not very daunting, given the considerable groundbreaking human research we've done on this flight," Cat said, smiling. "Not that I plan to publish any of it." She held his face softly between her hands. "I'm an optimist, too, like mission control, but I wonder what Houston really thinks of our chances."

"NASA's modeling says the RCC patch will work. Says so right here in the instructions. And I'm not going to worry about the landing," Hayes said. He went back to studying the wing repair procedures.

Flight Day Twenty-Seven
Intrepid

She couldn't pace in microgravity, so Cat slowly bounced herself between the aft flight deck's "ceiling" and its "floor." She never took her eyes off the Canadarm camera monitors. Outside, Hayes was wrapping up the starboard wing repair. He hadn't required any repositioning in a while, nor had he said anything.

"EV1, *Intrepid*. What's new, pussycat?"

"I'm still here. But the back of my head is getting soaked. Something's not right, but aborting this EVA is not an option. Another half hour and I should have the nuts on the bottom of the wing torqued onto the bolts and the recessed safety cotter pins from the kit locked down on the nuts."

"I'm worried about your suit, Hayes. You're all alone out there. What happens if you skip the cotter pin and come on in?"

"We need the pins; I'd like to be able crank these nuts on supertight, but the torque limit per the checklist is too low. I don't want to overstress the panel, and I don't want the nuts to back off. I'm staying on it."

◆

Forty minutes later, he was done. Hayes asked Cat to retract him to a position where he could see more of the top of the wing. He didn't hear an acknowledgment, but she pulled him farther away from the wing. "That's good, Cat. Stop there."

As his movement stopped, inertia caused the accumulated water in the back of Hayes's helmet to migrate around toward his face. It sloshed and suddenly his head was in a bucket of water. At the same time, he saw a crack in the patch panel's upper side, radiating a few millimeters from the bolt head in its recessed hole. Before he could investigate further, the ever-increasing water in his helmet began to glob by surface tension over his forehead. He had done all he could do outside.

"Cat, Cat, bring me in. The water is creeping around my face." Nothing. He realized the water must have shorted out the ear speakers in his Snoopy cap. He felt himself moving away from the wing. *Good, my mike is still working.* "I can't hear you, Cat. My ears are shorted."

The water continued to spread from the top of his helmet. All at once, surface tension effects pulled it over his eyes and then his nostrils. He was blinded. He took a deep breath through his mouth and snorted out his nose. The water flowed right back. There was no way to move it.

"Cat, I can't see. You need to take me to the airlock." *Can she still hear me? Is my mike shorted, too?* There was no EVA hand signal for "Can't see," so he improvised by placing his gloves over his helmet visor and holding them there. He tried to drink any water that came close to his mouth, his only access to air. He could not afford to choke or cough or to break up the water globs any more than they already were. He resisted the urge to shake his head inside the helmet. *All this effort only to drown in the void of space? Fuck that!*

Hayes began to take slow, deep breaths and exhale slowly to keep the area around his mouth clear. He began to wave his hands like a blind man feeling his way. There was no emergency tether to grab; there had not been one long enough to reach all the way to the wing. He knew the extension on the RMS was making it hard for Cat to move it quickly. *Exhale, slowly . . .*

His gloved hand felt something, and then his helmet tapped something. He felt around. *A rim—a hole—it's round. Must be the airlock hatch.* He was moving again. He could now feel the airlock walls with outstretched arms. *Good girl.* His head was in the airlock. He held on and twisted out of his foot restraints.

Hayes's exertions and more water were making it harder to get clear breaths. He pulled himself into the airlock. By feel, he rotated the outer hatch "up" from the airlock deck, pushed it outward to close it, and cranked the rotating latch handle counterclockwise until it would go no farther. A large globule of water went down his windpipe, and he began coughing convulsively and gasping. *I'm drowning . . . can't pass out . . . won't . . .*

♦

As soon as Cat saw the airlock hatch closing on her RMS monitor, she plunged into the middeck. She had already set the shuttle environmental control to increase the cabin air pressure back to normal as quickly as possible. When she reached the inner airlock hatch, she peered through the tiny window. *Jesus, Mary, and Joseph! St. Jude! Please don't let him die! Let me help him! Hatch is sealed! Go!*

Cat turned both the hatch pressure vents to "EMERG" to repressurize the airlock as quickly as possible. Air flowed from the orbiter cabin back into the airlock. It took under a minute for the airlock pressure to equalize; it seemed like an hour to Cat. Hayes's helmet was bobbing. It did not look purposeful.

When the pressures finally equalized, Cat cranked the inner latch handle frantically and opened the hatch. She pulled Hayes into the middeck by his shoulders. *His helmet looks like a dirty fishbowl.* She simultaneously pressed the purge button on the control unit of his suit and the emergency purge valve on the side of his helmet. She was horrified to see water spurt out the helmet valve and across the middeck.

When the suit pressure showed under a half pound per square inch, she unlatched and removed his helmet. Hayes gasped and coughed up a glob of water. He blinked his eyes. Only then did Cat begin to cry.

Cradling his head, she placed an oxygen mask on him. His breathing slowly became more regular. "You bastard," she said, sobbing. "You promised not to leave me alone!" She couldn't stop crying.

A few minutes later Hayes pulled off the mask and croaked, "I didn't leave you, because you saved my sorry ass." He struggled to speak. "Space is not going to stop trying to kill us, though. Let's go home."

◆

While Hayes recovered, Cat chased around the middeck to soak up all the wayward water that had leaked from his suit. She estimated there was a least two liters of it, including what was left in the helmet. What went so wrong with Hayes's EMU? *The crew systems people have a near-fatal puzzle to solve if—when we get home.*

After a few hours of rest, Hayes joined Cat on the flight deck, where she was methodically familiarizing herself with the right seat cockpit and its hundreds of switches and controls. If any of *Intrepid*'s myriad systems developed a problem during their reentry, they would barely know where the correct systems switch was, much less what to do with it. Shuttle commanders and pilots spent years in the simulator training for complicated failures.

"How are you feeling, babe?" asked Cat.

"Like a man who nearly drowned," answered Hayes in a hoarse voice. His eyes were bloodshot, but he had stopped coughing. "I've felt better, but when Houston gives us the preliminary deorbit burn data on our next comm pass, I'll be ready. If we're pressed for time on the prep checklist, I give us permission to skip nonsafety items, like securing the WCS."

"Your ongoing lack of concern about toilets is duly noted. Pray the critical parts of deorbit prep go correctly, like the payload bay doors latching. That rescue pole did whack one of them, and now there's no way you could do an EVA to fix them."

"I also have some bad news about the fix. The moment before I went swimming inside my suit, I saw a few millimeters of crack radiating from under the outboard bolt of the patch panel. I am sure I did not overtorque anything. I don't know that it matters—it is what it is."

"I'll take it as a good omen that you finished before your suit cratered on you," Cat said. "I said we are going to be fine, remember?"

"Do we have any questions for Houston?"

"I hate to admit it, but I don't even know the important things I don't know."

"Then I'll say back at you, you're going to be fine, Cat. The almighty digital autopilot knows all."

Flight Day Twenty-Six
Near Johnson Space Center

When Matt arrived late for dinner at the Oasis restaurant, Lisa was already sitting at a table gazing out at Clear Lake. A few sailboats were plying its not-so-clear waters after spending the day out on Galveston Bay. Matt kissed her on the top of the head, saying, "I'm so sorry, Lisa, for being tardy. I finally got to speak to *Intrepid*. I came here directly from the MCC."

"That's okay. I've been enjoying the aroma of the lemons in my vodka tonics," Lisa said.

"Dare I ask how many?"

"You are only one point two drinks behind. How are Cat and Hayes?"

"They sound good, under the circumstances. They're plugging along on the repair kit NASA sent up and aren't having any medical issues. At least, no issues they wanted to talk about. They will be very deconditioned. Once they knew the Chirp was coming, they throttled back on their physical activity, and Cat depressurized the cabin in preparation for the EVAs. They were already stretching the LiOH canisters. A guesstimate is they can finish the wing fix in twenty-four to forty-eight hours, but that'll be near the end of their resources."

"That's the most encouraging news I've heard since *Buran* launched," said Lisa. "How's your jet lag?"

"I slept and ate almost normally the past twenty-four hours. How are things with you?"

"I'm starting to feel human again. My bosses are hammering me for losing the MMU, like I had anything to do with that."

"Blackguards."

After the waiter took his drink order, Matt said, "Lisa, I was hoping you'd have recovered enough to come stay with me. I guarantee the food is better."

"I needed some down time by myself, Matt. We've been on an emotional roller coaster. I know we need to talk about us."

"But first, I need to get to know you better. Are you a foreign film fan?" Matt said.

"Yes, Truffaut, Bergman—a lot. Buñuel, Fellini—less so. Is that a requirement for your lovers?"

"How about Lina Wertmüller? *Swept Away*?"

"Part of your charm is that half the time, people have no idea what you are talking about. Never heard of Lina, but I know I will." Lisa stirred her drink.

"I'm going somewhere with this," Matt said. "*Swept Away* is an Italian movie about a haughty rich woman on her yacht and her communist deckhand. They end up shipwrecked together on an uninhabited island and eventually have a torrid love affair. It's really about class warfare, but the point is they're very happy on the island. Then they get rescued. She goes away in a helicopter, and he goes back to being a sad and bitter deckhand. What they had only existed on the island, in isolation."

"Am I going to fly away in a jet and leave you a bitter and unhappy doctor?" Lisa said. "Is that your concern? Did the love we shared in the cold, scary, and emotionally jarring USSR go away somewhere over the Arctic Ocean?" Lisa took a sip from her drink and smiled.

The waiter arrived with Matt's bourbon and ice cube. He tasted it and said, "You understand me better than most."

Lisa reached for his hand. "The answer is, I do want to get to know you better. It's easy to figure out if a person is bang-worthy. It takes a little more work to see if we're intellectually or emotionally compatible. I got married young, and I didn't know about that part of the love equation then. My engineering analysis is there is a 75 percent probability I could fall in love with you."

Matt's heart was thumping hard in his chest. He looked into the green eyes of the redheaded woman across from him. "My mother told me never fall in love with an engineer, but I didn't listen," said Matt. "Lisa, I love you."

"My skills are not limited to engineering. I can cook. Let's have seafood at your house tomorrow."

For once, Matt was speechless. He smiled and nodded.

Final Flight Day
Intrepid

Hayes awakened before his alarm. There had been no wake-up music from Houston for weeks. He was anxious to begin deorbit preparation. *Catherine Riona.* He looked at her asleep in her restraint on the starboard middeck wall, her arms floating in front of her. It was Cat's turn to wear the headset that would wake them to any alarm that *Intrepid* might make while they were sleeping. *I want to see what she looks like when she's asleep in one-g with no Mickey Mouse ears. I want to take a shower with her, smell her hair, and wrap her in a towel.* Everything depended on the next few hours.

They'd spent most of the previous day stowing everything, cleaning up the cabin, and looking for wayward water droplets. Flying objects during reentry were not a good idea. MCC had coached them on how to configure the electrical switches for reentry with just two fuel cells. They reversed the "extended orbiter" fixes that had kept *Intrepid* and themselves alive for so long.

Soon *Intrepid* would begin its four-hour countdown to time of ignition for the OMS engines' deorbit burn. Everything was upside down compared to Hayes's first shuttle mission. There was no real-time support available from the mission control center. If they couldn't get updated deorbit data, they would be forced to use the old numbers from their last transmission.

Normally, Houston gave the "go" for TIG and kept the commander and pilot updated on every possible contingency parameter in case of an engine failure or other problem. But he and Cat were on their own. Their ability to recover from any bad situations would be next to nil.

Doug Lewis, as CAPCOM, had given him a meager two minutes of advice on how to safely lower the orbiter nose wheel after touchdown. No one knew how the autopilot would handle the delicate job of lowering the nose to the runway.

Their oxygen, carbon dioxide scrubbers, and propellant levels were all at critically low levels. No wave-off, no redo, no backup. In a way, that made decisions simple. *We'll do our best, and go for it,* thought Hayes. *Time to wake up my girl.*

Floating over to where Cat was berthed, Hayes gave her a kiss. One of her eyes fluttered open. "Are you one of those lads who makes advances on a helpless woman?" she murmured.

"A kiss is much better than my singing, Mary Sunshine. Time to go home. Let's see what this space jalopy has left in her."

Extracting herself from her sleep restraint, she gave him a hug and said, "I'm more than ready, Space Cowboy," she said. "Now, coffee."

◆

There were still many tasks to be done before *Intrepid* could point downhill toward home. From the commander's seat, Hayes loaded the deorbit programming into the four general purpose computers. "Shuttle computers are lame cutting-edge seventies tech. I trust the software, but the mass memory storage is on tape units. Because the GPCs have tiny little brains, we're always swapping programs in and out of their core memory." On the computer keyboard he entered, "OPS 302." His finger hovered over the "PRO" button. He pressed it and looked at Cat. "We're on our way now. We're loading it a little early, but I want time to troubleshoot if I screw it up."

Cat was in the pilot seat, reading from the flight data file to help him through the unfamiliar duties of a pilot. "What a pain," she said. "My Macintosh Plus at home has more memory than the GPCs, and it's got floppy discs."

"Shhh, the computers might hear you," said Hayes as they checked for confirmation of the memory load and proper configuration. "So, you're a Mac girl?"

"Yes, I find them much more intuitive than IBM PC systems."

"That's good to know. This explicit, analytical thinker will depend upon you for holistic intuition at the proper time. We're going to need our A game. What's next?"

"You mean on this schedule you drew and stuck next to me, with the little hearts on it? It says it's time to break for a chat with Houston."

♦

During their last on-orbit transmission from Houston, the MCC made sure the *Intrepid* crew had their exact position in space as recently measured by ground radar. They also got an updated TIG for the OMS burn. The forecasted weather at Edwards Air Force Base was good: dry with a few scattered clouds.

Cat made the final reports to mission control before deorbit. "We're good on our timeline. Ship status good with all landing system tests passed. Payload bay doors mercifully closed on the first try. Star tracker doors are closed, and we're about to drink up for fluid loading and change clothes. Ready for final review of switches."

"*Intrepid*, as a formality, you are go for OPS3; you are go for deorbit burn; you are go for everything. Loss of signal soon. See you back in Houston. Enjoy the light show. There are a lot of good people waiting for you at Edwards. You can do this. You have an entire planet rooting for you."

"Catch you after the blackout. *Intrepid*, out," Cat said.

♦

Cat had wanted to tell mission control about the water in Hayes's helmet and the crack in the wing repair panel, but that would be a waste of precious communication seconds. *Nothing to be done about any of that now,* she thought. *Tell 'em later.*

"Hayes, we forgot something," said Cat. "I'm going to set up the mission specialist two seat behind the commander."

"Are you expecting a guest?"

"No. The MS2 seat is what you step on to reach the window eight emergency exit, remember?" She pointed to the port overhead window aft of the commander's seat, which could be blown out in an emergency to allow escape from the flight deck.

"I forgot about that. Not that we'll need it, but by all means." Hayes was busy working through every switch to make sure they were all positioned correctly.

When he was done, he said, "It's TIG minus one hour. We should gear up and deactivate the WCS and the galley while we are on the middeck. It's time to get in our seats for the ride home."

♦

On the middeck, Cat and Hayes sealed up their notes and journals and put them in a locker. Maybe their records would survive to help a future crew if *Intrepid* were lost. As an afterthought, to make sure she took proper care of them, Cat looked in the locker holding the personal items Jack had taken to space. Her jaw dropped and she said, "Hayes, look at this."

Jack had brought a few patches, a picture of his mother, and three unexpected items—a picture of Helen Swansen, a note from her, and a diamond ring. "Hayes, this is an engagement ring." The note was short: *My heart waits for your return. Have fun! Love, Helen.* "Jack was planning to marry—Helen? Did you know anything about this?" Cat felt light-headed remembering Jack's loss and realizing what his death must mean to his lover.

Hayes shook his head. "No, he never mentioned anything like that to me. Dr. Swansen, the head of Flight Medicine? No way."

"Helen didn't tell me anything, either. Hayes, we can't let this break our prep. I'm putting Jack's treasures in my suit pocket. Poor Helen."

They changed into the light blue launch and reentry flight suits that were the public image of a shuttle crew. The STS-92A crew had been the first to wear them at Vandenberg. They also put on a life vest/egress vest. Cat winced and held her side as she was changing clothes. "Are you okay?" Hayes said.

"Just a cramp in my side. We haven't been in zero-g long enough to worry about a kidney stone. Probably a woman thing." Cat had a strong premonition about what her flank pain was, but that wasn't for Hayes to know. *Oh, Mary, I know this isn't my period! What do you have planned for me?*

♦

Seated in the cockpit, they donned helmets that sealed around the collar and connected to the shuttle's oxygen system for launch and reentry. The final hook up was an anti-g suit. The suit had air bladders that inflated to support their blood pressure and protect them from the gravitational forces their bodies had forgotten. "Be sure to check your PEAP," said Cat. The personal egress air pack connected to the side of the helmet would provide a few minutes of air during an emergency exit.

Seated in the cockpit at TIG minus twenty-five minutes, they maneuvered the vehicle to its burn attitude. Now belly up and tail first as it orbited, the rocket burn would slow the shuttle down several hundred feet per second. The orbital burn would have its maximum effect half an orbit later, lowering *Intrepid* deep into the atmosphere. The dense air of lower altitudes would claw at the shuttle until it fell out of the sky. The trick was to avoid incinerating the vehicle and to land it at the right spot on planet Earth.

As they waited the last few minutes till time of ignition, Hayes said, "Few people appreciate how complicated this vehicle is. It's the most awesomely frustrating and complex craft in the solar system. It's held up by tens of thousands of dedicated, hardworking people. All most folks know is it goes up like a rocket and comes down like a plane. You could spend a year learning any one system in a shuttle."

Cat looked up from her checklist. "James Michener called it 'preposterously complex' in his novel *Space*. Michener didn't think much of the shuttle's thermal tile design. I still wanted to ride in it, but I agree with him about the thermal protection system, given our situation." A moment later, she said, "There's an even more complicated part of the system than the shuttle itself, you know."

"And that would be?"

"You and me." Cat looked out the cockpit window. *Is this the last thing I'll ever see? No,* she decided. "Our mission would have been a back page tiny column in the paper if we hadn't been marooned." Rapping Hayes's helmet with her knuckles, she said, "But hey, you're the commander of this mighty vessel. Your pilot is here to serve."

"I would like to order a kiss, but we have helmets on. Later."

Cat held up her pinky and he curled his around it.

With five minutes to go, Hayes called for "single APU start," and Cat brought one of three auxiliary power units online. The APUs would power all the flight controls when the air became thick enough for them to work like on a regular airplane. Until then, control was by the RCS thruster jets.

At TIG minus fifteen seconds, Hayes pushed the button to initiate the burn. Cat felt a satisfying thump as the OMS engines flared on. When they quit, Hayes said, "Two minutes and forty-five seconds. Perfect start." They cycled the computer mode to the next phase, and the shuttle flipped over to put them in the correct attitude for reentry through the atmosphere.

"Check entry attitude," Cat said. As the shuttle approached an altitude of 400,000 feet, it needed to maintain a very high nose-up angle on its flight path. This angle allowed the best heat dissipation by the thermal tiles on the underside of the shuttle's wings and body. If they were going to burn up, it would be soon.

Hayes looked at the "meatball" attitude indicator on the instrument panel in front of him. "Roll zero, pitch thirty-eight degrees, yaw zero." He cycled the computers to the next phase and double-checked that all the flight surfaces of the orbiter were set for automatic control. "It's showtime, Cat. I want to—"

"No dramatic final speeches, Major Eeyore; they're bad luck. We're going to get through this fine. Sit back and enjoy."

"I forgot the Irish are superstitious. May I hold your hand?"

Cat reached to take his hand and said, "I'll hold it until you need it again." Hayes began to sing, "Will You Still Love Me Tomorrow," by the Shirelles, but Cat interrupted him. "Stop that, or I will let go of your hand."

The shuttle rudely slammed into Earth's thickening atmosphere with a kinetic energy equal to nearly a thousand tons of exploding TNT. The vehicle needed to shed all that energy before it could roll to a stop on the runway. The air molecules could not get out of the way—they were instantaneously compressed into a shockwave as hot as the sun. Electrons were stripped from their nuclei, and the air was no longer strictly a mixture of gases; it was superhot, incandescent plasma. The orbiter design was focused on keeping this shockwave from directly contacting the orbiter. They had to hit the reentry energy corridor perfectly. If the shuttle lost altitude too slowly, the heat would overcome its thermal protection tiles before it landed. If it came down too quickly, it would also get too hot and incinerate. The margin for error was slim, but the *Intrepid*'s computers knew what to do.

Inside the crew compartment, the forward windows went from gray, to red, to being blanketed by a bright orange glow that obscured everything. Looking at the overhead flight deck windows, a magical blue St. Elmo's fire danced around the windowpanes. Cat knew that, back at the tail, large orange balls of plasma were forming and popping off. "It's terrifyingly beautiful," she said.

"Reminds me of you. High voltage radiance—handle with care."

"You say the nicest things. Here goes our first S-turn."

As part of its balancing act, *Intrepid* entered the first of four steeply banked rolls, back and forth across the desired direction of flight. The vehicle stayed pitched up at a high angle without slowing its descent, a configuration that was critical for the heat protection systems to work. The S-turns provided drag, slowing the vehicle. The rudder and elevons took over the vehicle's control as it transitioned to a hypersonic glider.

"We're still here," said Hayes at landing minus twelve minutes. "We're flying! Speed brake going to 100 percent." They only had to rid themselves of the energy equivalent of two hundred tons of TNT. *Intrepid* had survived the worst of the atmospheric heating stress.

"Mach 15.5, 1.4 g's, 185,000 feet," said Cat. "I guess I'm stuck with you."

At landing minus six minutes, Cat called, "Ninety thousand feet, Mach 3.3." The earth was fast approaching.

"Deploy air data probes."

"Both probes deployed."

"*Intrepid,* NASA 909, how copy?"

Cat was startled. "Loud and clear. Is that you, Terry?"

Terry was calling on the UHF radio that was their only communications mode. "Ex-Commander Rogers, here. Good to hear you, Cat. I'm in a T-38 chase plane near Edwards. No visual on you, but MCC reports you are looking good and on track to begin terminal area energy management in about thirty seconds."

"I'd trade places with you, but I can't fly a jet either," Hayes said. "Control transferring to TAEM guidance, heading for waypoint one to enter heading alignment cone."

At around fifty thousand feet and three minutes out, the shuttle went subsonic, and the people on the ground would have heard two distinct sonic booms—one from the nose and one from the tail. The orbiter buzzed as its lashing shock waves moved past the cockpit to the front of the nose. There was only a ton of TNT energy left in the shuttle.

Intrepid had been programmed to land on Edwards's Runway 04R, paved and fifteen thousand feet long, where many prior shuttle missions had landed. On a normal mission, the commander would take manual control and guide the vehicle during the last few minutes to touchdown. In this case, the digital autopilot was in control all the way.

"*Intrepid,* 909, visual contact; looking good," reported Terry.

The autopilot began flying a left-hand spiraling turn down an imaginary upside-down cone, to lose altitude and to roll out lined up with the runway centerline. At about twenty thousand feet, *Intrepid* locked on the microwave landing system to guide it for the remainder of the flight.

As they passed 18,000 feet, Cat and Hayes felt a jolt, and *Intrepid* abruptly rolled to the right, departing the flight path. After a few seconds delay to react, Hayes instinctively grabbed the control stick and disconnected the autopilot.

"Something broke bad," Cat said. "Keep flying."

Terry's voice came over their comm. "*Intrepid*, heads up. Your patch has broken free; radar saw it go." The cracked panel patch had given up under the stresses on the orbiter wing. Now, instead of smooth air flow, the hole in the right wing had the effect of a giant pizza pan held flat into the wind. "Stay with the ship; keep flying it; keep the stick back for nose up. Rudder for yaw, keep losing altitude. Speed brake 50 percent. Try to stay over Rogers Dry Lake. You can land anywhere out there, any direction."

"Drag chute?" asked Hayes as he entered a more controlled, descending turn to the right.

"Didn't work in the simulator runs we did," Terry said. "Cat, put the body flap full up manually—that should help."

"Speed four hundred knots, altitude 10,500," called Cat. "Body flap up."

"Terry, the body flap is helping," Hayes said. "Will it roll out level for landing?"

"Don't know. The more you flare, and the slower you go, the worse the roll. At two thousand feet go to 100 percent speed brake and preflare. You'll lose some of the rudder authority. You've got miles of desert in front of you." Terry was tracking in formation, his T-38 so close Cat could see his helmet.

At two thousand feet, the shuttle had only a quarter ton of TNT energy left, still more than enough to destroy the vehicle. Hayes was almost at the limits of the control stick but was keeping the nose nearly level and only flying a little to the right.

"Just try to keep the nose out of the ground. Land run-on or try to flare, your call," Terry said. "You want to land as slow and as flat as possible, but the delta wing design of the shuttle will lose lift suddenly, dropping the nose, and you can't be high when that happens."

Cat and Hayes slammed their helmet visors down. "One thousand feet, 280 knots," Cat said. "One thousand feet per minute descent. Hayes, we might be a little slow if you flare."

Hayes closed the speed brake to correct and began to pull back on the stick to slow their descent rate for landing. He reached the back limit of the stick. He was nearly fully left, as well. As the orbiter nose struggled to rise, their descent slowed, but their turning increased. "Gear arm. Gear down," he called.

Cat said, "No."

Hayes said, again, "Gear down."

"Gear down," Cat said.

Hayes fired the drag chute a few seconds before they touched down, knowing it would take time to have a full effect. *Intrepid*'s sink rate was down to one hundred feet per minute when they touched down, moving at two hundred knots. The right main gear touched down first, but immediately snapped off due to the side loads from the persistent, shallow right turn. The tip of the broken right wing contacted next, digging a trough in the desert and slewing the craft to the right nearly 180 degrees over the next hundred meters. Along the way, the outer half of the right wing sheared off.

As the nose gear snapped, the nose dug in, crumpled, and the tail began to lift skyward. The drag chute, which had been fired level to the ground, slowed the tail enough to keep the craft from flipping or doing a cartwheel. It didn't prevent the heavy tail from slamming back down to the ground. The shuttle came to rest heavily tilted to the right. Somehow, the left main gear had remained attached.

Terry's T-38 made a low pass over the shuttle as the NASA convoy of fire and rescue vehicles screamed across the desert toward the crash site many miles away from their station.

♦

Inside the cockpit, a stunned Hayes tried to focus. *Am I hurt?* He didn't feel anything but gravity. *No fire. No smoke or fumes. Yet. Intrepid* was a wreck. He called for Cat. No answer. He unbuckled and moved to her. *My limbs are so heavy.*

Hayes lifted her visor. Cat was dazed, and moaned, "Leg." A jagged piece of orbiter metal had come up through the deck and stabbed her right leg. Her flight suit pants were soaked in blood. She was holding her right wrist.

The shuttle was tilted, and the main hatch was nearly the ceiling now. Hayes felt wobbly from weeks of zero-g living, and his muscles begged him to plop down and sit. *Every second counts.* He removed the console T-handle cover, pulling the ring to blow the overhead escape window on the aft flight deck. *Thank you, Cat, for remembering the exit seat.* He caught an acrid whiff of RCS oxidizer and shut their visors again, activating their PEAPs. *Six minutes of air. Got to get her out. She might need a tourniquet on her leg. Got to get her out. Got to.*

Hayes struggled to get Cat up to the tilted edge of the seat below the window. He extended a small fold-out climbing bar from the seat frame. He deployed the Sky Genie, the nylon rope system he would use to lower them to the ground. He stuck his head out the hatch and saw the rescue trucks in the distance, raising a huge cloud of dust. He also saw threatening orange vapors leaking from the tail of *Intrepid*. A faint breeze was drifting the toxic cloud toward them.

No time to wait. Must get her out. Tossing the end of a rope out the escape hatch, he again realized how weak he was in one-g. *I can't go down holding her. I'll have to lower her. Running out of time. Hurry up, guys!* With maximal effort, he lifted Cat's PEAP canister, trailing its hose up and out the hatch. He disconnected his own PEAP and placed another Sky Genie rope around Cat's chest and under her arms. *Sorry about your armpits, baby.* Struggling to climb out the hatch, he hauled her up and out with the rope. He could hear her moan inside her helmet. The fumes were making him gasp. He struggled to get her head out. The lines to her helmet made it a tight squeeze.

The first members of the crash, fire, and rescue team arrived, wearing hazmat suits. A rescue worker in a cherry-picker truck reached Hayes and took Cat into his bucket. He handed Hayes an emergency air tank and mask, then signaled, *Back in two.* He took the bucket down as an ambulance pulled alongside. Hayes's eyes were starting to burn and water, and he was grateful for the full-face mask and fresh breathing air. *I've got to get off this wreck.* He clipped the Sky Genie carabiner onto the ring of his vest and lowered himself to the ground before the bucket man could come back for him. Two rescuers grabbed his arms, helping him into another waiting ambulance as a fire truck positioned itself to pour water on the shuttle from a distance. Personnel wanted clear of the wreckage as quickly as possible, and the ambulance pulled away.

◆

Matt pulled off his hazmat hood as the paramedic put an oxygen mask on Hayes. "Welcome home, Major Bartlett," he said. "How much of that rank propellant did you inhale back there? Anything hurting you?"

"Dr. Matt! Imagine meeting you back here in California. Thank you, it's good to be home. I feel weak, but Cat got the worst of it. How is she?"

"Don't know yet. Dr. Patel has her; his ambulance got there first. You did a good job getting her out of the crew compartment. What about the fumes?"

"My eyes, nose, and throat are burning." He coughed. "I got a couple of good snootfuls, but I feel all right."

"That RCS propellant you sucked in can give you a delayed chemical pneumonia," Matt said. "We'll be observing you closely in the hospital. Maybe give you steroids, we'll see. Sorry your wing repair job came apart. You were doing well there until the very end. Commander material. You did forget to say 'wheels stop' when you were done."

"You're such a card, Doc. Shouldn't it be 'wheels off' in my case?" Hayes had another coughing fit. "I would have fixed the wing better, but I was drowning."

That caught Matt off-guard. "You were what?"

"You'll have to wait for the debrief, Doc. I can't explain anything until I know Cat is okay." He coughed. "My lungs have been taking a beating lately." He closed his eyes.

"We're going to start an IV to fill up your body's fluid tank again. Relax. We're going to medevac both of you to Loma Linda Medical Center in San Bernardino. You'll see Cat there." Matt nodded to the paramedic riding with them, who was setting up an intravenous fluid kit. Hayes had passed out and didn't hear him.

♦

The whirling blades of a helicopter whupped into Cat's returning consciousness. *I must have fainted from blood loss and too much gravity.*

But I'm home. I'm on Earth. She couldn't see much past her oxygen mask and tubes. *Hayes . . . Hayes pulled me out. He's alive.* She smiled under her mask. *Finally rid of him. Then why do I miss him already?* She drifted off again.

Jack Badger was standing in front of her. Not speaking, he held out his hand to offer her something. She couldn't reach for it. He smiled.

"Dr. Riley, how is your pain? You look upset." The medic was holding her uninjured hand.

"I'm feeling pretty numb," Cat said. "Okay on pain meds for now." She turned her head and started to cry. *Jack, why can't you come home, too? Goddamn fuckers killed you. What did you want to give me?*

Loma Linda University Medical Center

Hayes wheeled himself into Cat's hospital room, an IV pole and oxygen tank attached to his wheelchair and oxygen prongs in his nose. He reached out to hold her left hand. "Sure is good to see you, gal. How are you, my cher bébé?" he asked.

"Concussion, right radial fracture from bracing myself, and a repaired wound to my right hamstrings," Cat said slowly. "It's good to see you, too. How are you, lover-man?"

"Okay. A little coughing and wheezing. You look mighty fine for a woman who's been through what you have."

"You look awful, like you've been on a two-week drinking binge. You saved me from getting gassed like you were. Thanks for getting us down in one piece, Hayes." She held up her cast. "One piece, more or less."

"Thank you for all you did to get us here, too. We gave new meaning to 'coming in on a wing and a prayer.' My wing, your prayer."

"You're welcome, but I am mad at you."

"Why?" asked Hayes, coughing.

"I told you not to put the landing gear down. Every Bonanza pilot knows you leave the gear up for an off-airport landing."

Hayes shrugged. "What do I know about landing gear? I'm a helicopter pilot. If a good landing is any one you walk away from, I do admit mine was only fair. My sweet French mademoiselle isn't going to hold a grudge, are you?"

"No, but your Irish colleen might."

"I'm beginning to realize you aren't half-and-half. You are 100 percent Cajun *and* 100 percent Irish all the time. Lord, help me."

Cat tried to laugh, but sore ribs cut her short. "Now you're beginning to get the picture."

"Your witchy intuition was right," Hayes said. "We did make it. I'm glad you didn't give me the details about how the landing phase was going to shake out."

"I had a positive intuition," said Cat, "not a vision."

"What's your intuition about *us*?" Hayes asked.

"Remember the Magic 8 Ball toy we had as kids?"

"Yeah, you can still buy them."

"I just turned mine over, and it says, *Ask again later*. I have a concussion, remember? Hayes, the good news is we have all the time in the world. We did it. We made it home."

"I've gotten very accustomed to having you near me," Hayes said. "You might be thinking, 'We thought we were going to die, and we fell in love.' I don't feel that way." Hayes took off his oxygen and stood up so he could kiss Cat on her forehead. "You're going to have a hard time getting rid of me."

I find that idea comforting, Cat thought. *Can I give myself to this man?* God had given her a chance to find out. *Things may get a lot more complicated than Hayes realizes.*

Intrepid *Landing + Four Days*
Johnson Space Center
Headquarters, Bldg. 1

"Kranz, I want to know where you and Art and the rest of Mission Ops got the authorization to mount the *Intrepid* rescue pod initiative," the director of JSC said. "The NASA Administrator got a bill for 245 million dollars from the air force for their spy satellite and rocket. I told Bob weeks ago to quash whatever backroom shenanigans you were putting together. You needed to go through channels."

"You need to know Gene had very little to do with it at first." Art said. "He was busy with *Buran* logistics, and my team wasn't entirely forthcoming with him about our plans. I've worked here for fifteen years, and with the air force, going 'black' was our only choice. If we'd gone through channels, Cat and Hayes would be dead, and management would still be debating it. Let's face it, sir, NASA didn't want any publicity over another wild rescue attempt. If it had gone bad, the PR would have been worse than Jimmy Carter's botched Iranian hostage rescue. As flight director, I officially beg forgiveness."

"I'm backing up my team 100 percent for how they managed to get the Chirp into orbit," the director of Mission Ops said. "I'm proud as hell of what they accomplished by jawboning every contractor and air force person they ran into. NASA is smelling like roses, instead of taking the blame for screwing up. We're going to need good PR when the truth comes out about how much trouble NASA has had with foam shedding on other launches. We let our astronauts down."

"I'm not arguing with your results," the JSC director said. "I am telling you it's wrong to go off on your own without proper management supervision. Besides, Bob told me foam shedding was 'in family,' not considered a flight risk. Who thought foam could do this?"

"With all due respect, sir, 'in family' is a goddamn poor rationale for ignoring a problem repeatedly," the director of Mission Ops said. "The foam was knocking thermal protection tiles off nearly every flight! We hear your concern about channels. I don't like anyone going around me, either. I do expect, in this case, for everyone on this Mission Ops team to get a special commendation from HQ. They saved NASA's butt, and you know it."

"I'll put the whole team up for a special citation, *through channels.* Now, when can the program resume EVAs? Did you figure out why Bartlett's suit flooded?"

"Yes, we did. The root cause went all the way back to when that EMU was last serviced by Crew Systems. If Hayes hadn't worn the suit so many times, he might have dodged the problem. A part of the suit's ventilation system was cleaned with the wrong kind of water before reassembly. Mineral precipitates clogged and corroded the small holes in the spinning drum of the water separator and several check valves. Instead of keeping the suit's breathing circuit dry and free of humidity, the unit threw increasing amounts of water into the vent located at the upper rear of Hayes's helmet.

We know the tech who screwed up. He had already quit by the time we uncovered the instigating factor. Most importantly, we removed tap water access from the suit refurbishment lab, so it can't happen again."

"Glad that's cleared up. I do have one more question. I heard something about a videotape from on-orbit, while Cat and Hayes were marooned. I would like to see how they made out."

♦ *D. K. Broadwell* ♦

"The wreckage of *Intrepid* and all its contents are impounded in a hangar at Edwards, sir. To my knowledge, nothing like that has been released yet, not even internally. Cat told me they did keep journals, which they left on the middeck. It will take a long time to detoxify everything, much less sort it out."

Flight Medicine Clinic
JSC

"It's good to see you, Cat," Helen said as she entered the clinic exam room. "You look amazing today after all you've been through. Nurse Patty said you asked for me for your follow-up. What's up?"

"I'd rather see you any day than Matt Wallace," Cat said.

"Matt's not so bad. You and he had a rocky start."

"I'm sorry I haven't come to see you sooner. You've been welcome, sympathetic, and friendly to me since I arrived at NASA, but I didn't feel well enough to come until now."

"What do you mean? You're not here for your postflight check? You took a lot of hits."

"Helen, I have something to give you." Cat held out the engagement ring Jack had presented Helen when he proposed in California. "We found it at the last minute in Jack's things, and I brought it home in my flight suit. There are a few blood stains on the box. I tried to clean it. I'm so, so sorry, Helen. I had no idea."

Helen took the little box from Cat. She opened it and gazed at her lost future for long, silent seconds. "Thank you. I had given up any hope of ever seeing it again. I thought it was ground into the California desert when *Intrepid* crashed. Like you almost were." She snapped the box shut and put it in her clinic coat pocket. "This is a blessing for me I did not expect. It was so hard to keep our love a secret, but Jack wasn't ready to reveal it to the world until the day I visited the crew at Vandenberg. I told Matt about us, and he arranged for me to be alone with Jack that day. He proposed on Tranquillon Peak. He wanted to . . ."

Cat slid from the exam table and embraced the trembling Helen. When Helen composed herself and disengaged, Cat said, "I know what it is to lose a love at its bright beginning. I didn't think I could ever recover. Please let me stay your friend while you go through this journey of grieving."

"Thank you for that, too. I'll take you up on that offer. Now get back up on the table and let me check that arm and leg."

After the exam was done, Helen said, "You're healing quickly. You must be doing everything right. I understand you have a new man in your life, and he's not the one I would've picked for you. Is Hayes part of your rapid recovery?"

Cat looked down and said, "He's a bigger part of my biology than you might imagine. I have other news today that will surprise you."

El Lago, TX
Near JSC

"I'm going to miss your breakfasts," Lisa said, watching Matt flip an omelet. "Airline meals are such dreck. I hope your eggs can sustain me to Denver."

"I'm going to miss you, too," said Matt as he served her plate. "You're taking all of my Stevie Wonder cassettes."

"You should buy a few of his CDs. Compact discs do sound better, you know."

It was time for a "what next?" discussion, and Matt kicked it off. "It would be much easier for an accomplished engineer like yourself to get a job here in Houston, than for an eccentric flight surgeon to get a job in Denver."

"Especially if that engineer's career is in the toilet through no fault of her own," Lisa said. "I'm not ready to hang it up in Denver, but I might be convinced over the next few months."

"I plan to busy myself abusing the federal telephone system, calling you long distance every day," said Matt. "I also have vacation time due, if I can ever get finished with the interminable STS-92A mission debrief. The operations people keep going over the same ground again and again, hoping the outcome will change. Nope—still one dead, one lost orbiter, and four glorious survivors. And no one sees that NASA is so much more than the visible leadership. The smart and dedicated folks who came up with the Chirp rescue plan did so despite management."

"I'll answer the phone when you call and will come to Houston when I can. I'd like to rehabilitate myself, companywise. There are plenty of Martin Marietta people on my side, too. My team got the MMU safely to orbit on *Buran*, and Sharon did give it a good workout. The MMU acquitted itself well."

"You've reached your pinnacle; it's time to move on." Matt poured Lisa a glass of cranberry juice. "Speaking of survivors, I checked on Cat Riley yesterday. She's healing up fine. No more headaches, and her leg is much better. I was happy to tell her that *Odysseus* was sailing on toward the sun's north pole. Who knows? The sun might have a bald spot. We've never seen it."

"I'd nearly forgotten about the reason for STS-92A in the first place," Lisa said.

"Debriefing Hayes and Cat has been a hoot," Matt said. "She developed a firm conviction they would make it home safely. She says her mother was a witch, and she inherited some of her powers."

"Didn't you say she was Catholic? What's a Catholic witch?"

"A Catholic witch? Yeah, I like that," Matt said. "It's a zen koan, like the sound of one hand clapping."

"I now have something to meditate on as I fly back to Denver."

"Did you know Cat and Hayes are an item now? Amazing how adversity can forge a relationship, isn't it? What she told me was, she felt lucky God had given them a chance to see if they were good together. I feel the same way about us. All I want is that chance."

"I did hear that Cat and Hayes had gotten close. Did they, uh, actually do anything up there? Like you and I were doing in Russia?"

"Officially, no, of course not. NASA would never allow anything like that," Matt said with a smirk. "Next time I see you, we can talk more about it." He looked at his watch. "Time for the Dr. Wallace taxi shuttle to Intercontinental Airport. All aboard."

Clear Lake City, TX
near JSC
Home of Dr. Catherine R. Riley

"Your Chinese takeout is here, my sweet gal," Hayes announced, as Cat opened the door of her home. "I hope you're hungry. I brought lots."

"I'm starved. Let's eat on the patio," said Cat. She was still wearing her forearm cast but was walking almost normally, with only a slight limp.

"You know, I don't consider myself a spiritual guy," said Hayes as they were eating, "but making it back alive to Mother Earth has given me a deeper appreciation for life. I'm grateful for Chinese food, traffic lights, thunderstorms, and even other humans, in a way I never was before. I'm also thankful every second you're here with me. You look great, by the way, and I'm not just blowing smoke. No one would know by looking at your beautiful, glowing face that you recently cheated death."

"You say the nicest things, but I suspect you talk to all the girls like that. You're right, I feel damn good. I'm almost through wearing this cast. I can write nearly legibly with my left hand now."

"I think we may be at the end of the debrief cycle for STS-92A. What do you think NASA will do with us? Are we damaged goods? Don't you want any of this wine? It's not Chinese, it's Napa Valley."

"No, thanks. Since my concussion I've cut out all alcohol. Who knows what NASA is going to do? I assume you got the invitation for the meeting next week with Scott and Ron Grant. Ron was promoted to director of Flight Ops just after we crashed. Apparently, it's just you and me, without the rest of the crew."

"Yeah, the agenda is very vague," Hayes said. "Any private meeting with the head of the astronaut corps and Grant sounds momentous, if not ominous. I don't think I've ever spoken to Grant about anything serious."

"I may decide to discuss how my near-death experience has changed my view on NASA's safety system." Cat's face was serious.

As Hayes rose to clean up their dinner dishes, he said, "It looks to me like you could use a hand or at least two good arms around the house. How about I sleep over, give you a one-g back rub, and be your cleanup slave?"

"You are painfully transparent, HB. We'll see. First, we have our fortune cookies." Cat handed him a cookie.

"I bet it says, 'You are the luckiest man alive,'" Hayes said, as he opened it. He read his fortune, his mouth dropped open, and he plopped down in his chair. "But . . . but . . ."

"Read it to me. It must be a doozy."

"It says, *You are going to be a father*, but, ermmm, uh, is this real?"

"As real as it gets, Major Stud. You should have brought more condoms. I missed my period, pregnancy test is positive, and I thought I felt a twinge of implantation pain in my side as we deorbited. You know how sensitive I am. So far, this kid is tough and appears to be hanging on. Sit there a minute. Take deep breaths."

Hayes began to smile, but he was still speechless.

"I hope you don't suspect anyone else, Dad. She's most definitely yours," said Cat.

"You're carrying my baby!" Hayes said, gathering himself enough to speak. "Is he . . . is she . . . going to be all right? Radiation, reentry, crashing, I mean . . ." Worried thoughts about the first space baby's welfare careened through his head.

"I wasn't on-orbit long enough to worry much about radiation," Cat said. "Women in early pregnancy have been taking rough rides since forever—covered wagons, pushing carts. Babies usually find a way to overcome maternal adversity. Of course, I'm concerned too, like any woman at this early stage of pregnancy. The first trimester is always the riskiest."

"Have you been to the obstetrician yet? Have you been sick?" asked Hayes, sliding his chair over to put his hands on her knees.

"No morning sickness—too early. No OB yet. Only Helen Swansen in flight medicine knows about this right now, and that's the way it's going to stay. She's my friend, and she can keep a secret. No one else needs to know. I don't want my pregnancy to become a circus. Our baby isn't going to be an astrobiology poster child. She'll be born a little bit premature, officially."

"You've had time to think about this. I'm still in shock," Hayes said. "I'm also very much in love, now with both of you, and I *am* the luckiest man in the universe."

"We love you, too."

Office of the director, Flight Operations Division
Bldg. 1, JSC

"It's good to see both of you looking so well," said Ron Grant. "I see you still have your cast, Cat. Are you back to full duty, Hayes? Lungs okay?" For someone in senior management, Grant looked uncharacteristically uncomfortable. Everyone was sitting around a conference table in Grant's office.

"Yes, sir. I'm back to biking and jogging," Hayes said.

Scott Jenkins, the head of the Astronaut Office, said, "It's a miracle you two are here at all. You pulled off NASA's greatest rescue since Apollo 13."

"I don't mean to accentuate the negative, Scott," said Cat, "but it's hard to forget that we came back without Jack Badger."

"I blame the Soviets and their piece of junk *Buran* shuttle for that," said Scott. "We're lucky Terry and Dom made it back—with Sharon—in one piece."

"There's plenty of blame to go around on STS-92A," said Grant. "NASA needs to pay more attention to how we track and address flight safety problems. We owe it to Jack and all the astronaut corps to make this program as safe as possible. We also need to all pull together and keep public support for the space program and Space Station *Freedom*. Our public image for professionalism is everything when it comes to public relations." Grant looked at Scott.

Scott leaned back in his chair and said, "PR is the reason we asked you here today, besides to give you our admiration and congratulations. You two have become personally very close during this ordeal, right?"

"No secret there," Hayes said. "She's my serious girlfriend. I've had a crush on her since we met. Is that a problem after all we've been through?"

"Not exactly, no." Scott said. He was obviously choosing his words very carefully. "We're returning the journals you kept in orbit and hoped would survive you in case the worst happened. We're preserving copies, of course, for posterity. There is one video recording, however, that we are destroying. You know which one."

"The birthday party?" Hayes asked with a puzzled look.

It began to dawn on Cat what Scott meant and the true purpose of the meeting. *Sweet Baby Jesus! Somehow that video cam I unplugged must have been recording our lovemaking.*

Scott nodded his head.

A horrified Cat clenched the edge of the table. "No, Hayes, not that video. A video we didn't know we were making, just before you got the Morse code message."

Hayes looked at Cat. "You mean, when we . . ."

"Who has seen it?" Cat asked.

Grant took over. "Officially, nobody has seen it. It didn't happen. You'll never mention it to anyone—ever."

There was a profound silence. Grant said, "The tech who gathered and screened all the middeck contents—obviously he watched it, and his supervisor. They sent it directly to me, and I locked it in my desk, unseen."

"Do you really think NASA can keep a lid on something like sex in space?" Cat asked.

"Officially, yes," Scott said. "Consider the lid tightly clamped. In reality, of course not. Rumors are flying. Nobody's asked you about it?" He looked from Cat to Hayes expectantly.

"Now that you mention it, there have been a few insinuations," Hayes said. "We've been so tied up in debriefs, though, we've barely talked to anyone else. Since we didn't perish, the press lost interest quickly after the initial circus."

"If asked, your answer will be: 'Never happened. No way,'" said Scott. "Hell, tell them you can't get it up in zero-g. People will believe that."

Cat was getting steamed about the tone of the conversation and got up to leave. Hayes followed her. "Thanks for the uplifting conversation, gentlemen," she said. "Since we didn't die, I had hoped the privacy of our journals would be preserved. I see now that NASA has no concept of personal rights or boundaries. Until next time, good-bye."

Cat said, as they walked down the hall, "I almost said, 'Enjoy the tape, you creeps.'"

Outside, Hayes said, "Assuming we wanted to be assigned to another mission, I'm not sure where we stand. Heroes or naughty children?"

"Rest assured Nannies-R-Us is not going to assign us together," said Cat. "What a laugh."

"They can't because it's against NASA policy to send married couples on the same shuttle mission."

"Who says I'm marrying you?" Cat said.

"Do you want our kid to be a little bastard?" asked Hayes.

"You mean, like his father?" Cat punched Hayes in the shoulder with her good arm. He turned and took her into his arms. Cat said, "You are making a scene on a JSC sidewalk. What will people think?"

"People already know," Hayes said. "There are probably fifty copies of our video out there already. I hope it doesn't show up at Blockbuster Video for rent."

Mid-July 1990
St. Luke's Hospital, Houston

Cat Riley held her newborn baby boy so his father could see him in all his neonatal glory. Hayes was enthralled. "Will ya look at that? Ten fingers, ten toes, and check out the size of his equipment. I know for sure he's my son."

"I hate to burst your male bubble, but all baby boys are born with enlarged genitalia." Cat swaddled the infant, and he began suckling at his mother's breast. "He's certainly figured out the breastfeeding part."

"I can't believe how beautiful he is . . . how beautiful you both are. The first name needs to be a saint, right? Stephen Hayes Bartlett, Jr. would pass muster. There's a Grateful Dead song called 'St. Stephen.' We've floated other names, but he looks like a Stephen."

"Your knowledge of theology astounds me," said Cat. They spent the next few minutes adoring their new child, and then she said, "We should use the name that keeps popping up in our discussions. You know the one. Now that I see him, I know that's the right name."

Hayes pondered this for a moment, and then said, "As much as I'd like a junior, I feel the same way. S. B. B. it is. Hello, Stephen Badger Bartlett. Pleased to meet you."

As little Stephen drifted off to sleep, Cat said, "I've been thinking, Hayes. After STS-92A, any other shuttle mission would be boring. I believed proving that I was the best would bring me peace, but it turns out choosing love is a much better answer. Figuring out just the right amount of 'being excellent' is hard for me, but I'm getting there. I've been to the mountaintop, and I've plenty of challenges left in the surgical world. But I want to be a full-time mom for his first years.

"I'm going to turn my maternity leave into a one year leave of absence," she said. "There's a precedent for that—Anna Fisher had another baby after her first shuttle mission, and her leave was just approved. NASA owes me big-time. I can't imagine leaving this little guy, even for space travel, while he's a baby. I wanted to be on-orbit in zero-g during the last three months of my pregnancy, while our son was breaking my back, but now I don't have the passion to return to space yet. When he gets a little older, I can balance space work and motherhood better."

"I saw that one coming, Mommy. Your choice might seem like a cop-out to some feminists, but you've always done things your way, in your own time. Being a full-time mom is a tough and underappreciated occupation. You just delivered a baby, though, and you might want to postpone your decision."

"You are the least qualified person I know to lecture me about feminism. You think I have postpartum depression? I'm not going to change my mind," Cat said emphatically.

"You never do." Striking his forehead, he said, "What was I thinking?"

"How about *your* career? Besides your new job as a dad, will the best EVA performer and biggest stud in the corps ever fly again? Did I mention you're now also a sensitive, new age man thanks to your association with me? What is the Astronaut Office telling you?"

Hayes shrugged. "I keep asking, but the wind seems to blow from a different direction each day. Whatever their decision is, every day will be a good day because I have you and this little man. NASA will do what it's going to do, and I'll be the last to know. As the crew surgeon on my first shuttle mission used to say, 'You know what NASA stands for? Never a straight answer.'"

Cat had never been happier. Captivated, she and Hayes stared at the face of newborn life.

Glossary

CAPCOM—Capsule communicator. An astronaut who handles communications with the shuttle from the JSC Mission Control Center. The name is a throwback to Project Mercury days.

DCS—Decompression sickness. The bends can happen to space suited astronauts as well as divers.

EGIL—Electrical generation and integrated lighting systems engineer. A flight control room console position.

EI—Entry interface. The portion of a shuttle's reentry that starts at 400,000 feet and begins the most thermally taxing part of returning to earth from orbit.

EMU—Extravehicular Mobility Unit, A space suit.

EVA—Extravehicular activity. A spacewalk.

FCR—Flight control room. The room in the Mission Control Center where the flight director and systems controllers sit. Pronounced "ficker."

FMC—Flight Medicine Clinic. Astronaut medical support at Johnson Space Center.

GPC—General Purpose Computer. One of five orbiter computers that control the vehicle in flight.

INCO—Instrumentation and communications. One of the many console stations in the Mission Control Center at JSC.

JSC—Johnson Space Center, Houston, Texas.

KSC—Kennedy Space Center, Cape Canaveral, Florida.

LC—Launch Control. The room at Kennedy Space Center or Vandenberg's SLC-6 that controls the launch and first minutes of a shuttle flight.

LiOH—Lithium hydroxide. Canisters that absorb carbon dioxide expired in orbit. Pronounced "lie-oh."

LOS—Loss of signal. The point when the shuttle moves out of range and loses communications with the ground.

MAG—Maximum absorbency garment. A space diaper worn in an EMU to handle human waste products.

MCC—Mission Control Center at JSC.

NASA—The National Aeronautics and Space Administration.

OKPD—Control center for *Buran* at the Baikonur Cosmodrome, where *Buran* launches and lands.

OMS—Orbital Maneuvering System, the on-orbit engines of the shuttle.

PEAP—Personal egress air pack. Provides six minutes of unpressurized breathing air to escape shuttle in an emergency.

PMC—Private medical conference. A consultation between NASA flight surgeons and a shuttle crew member done over a confidential communications channel.

RCC—Reinforced carbon-carbon. A very heat resistant material. Panels of RCC make up the shuttle wing's leading edge.

RCS—Reaction Control System. The forty-four-jet system used for fine maneuvering of the shuttle on-orbit.

RMS—Remote Manipulator System. The Canadarm robotic arm of the shuttle. Controlled from inside the shuttle.

Sim Sup—Simulation Supervisor. The person responsible for managing ground-based simulator training for shuttle crews. Pronounced "sim soup."

SLC-6—Space Launch Complex 6, the shuttle launch site at Vandenberg Air Force Base in California. Known as "Slick Six."

SRB—Solid rocket booster. One of two boosters strapped onto the orbiter and external fuel tank that provides 85 percent of the shuttle's thrust at lift-off.

STS—Space Transportation System. The official name for the shuttle program. It includes the orbiter, two solid rocket boosters, and the external tank.

TsUP—Russian Mission Control Center in Kaliningrad near Moscow.

V-bar—Velocity vector orbital rendezvous. An approach where the "chaser" vehicle comes from behind or ahead in the same direction as the orbital motion of the "target." A parallel approach with both vehicles at the same orbital altitude (in the same orbital plane).

WCS—Waste Control System. The shuttle's "space toilet."

WETF—Weightless Environment Training Facility. A giant swimming pool at JSC for practicing EVAs.

Acknowledgements

I would like to express my thanks to my beloved and patient wife, Christine, for putting up with me. I thank my son Gregory for inspiration for the book cover design and my daughter Whitney for her help navigating the 21st century online world. My copy editor Robert Kenney did a remarkable job. My beta readers, especially Jeff, Staples, Genie, SL, Dave, and Paul deserve sympathy and kudos. My old boss, Dr. Jim L., gave me "Never A Straight Answer." And thanks to you for reading this book.

Author Bio

D.K. (Kim) Broadwell is a physician and specialist in aerospace medicine. This is his debut novel. He was a flight surgeon at NASA's Johnson Space Center during the space shuttle era. He is a pilot and operated a charter aircraft company for many years. He performed many hours of medical experiments in NASA's zero-gravity KC-135 aircraft and would have been an astronaut if his eyes weren't too weak. He's sticking by this story despite the facts.